JOEY FLY 2
PRIVATE EYE
IN
BIG HAIRY DRAMA

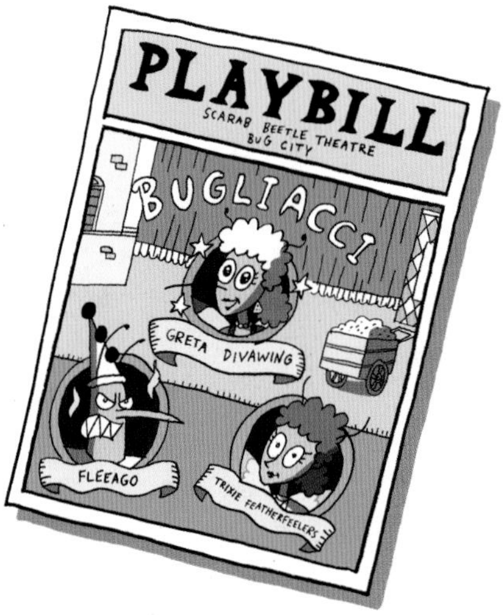
PLAYBILL
SCARAB BEETLE THEATRE
BUG CITY
BUGLIACCI
GRETA DIVAWING
FLEEAGO
TRIXIE FEATHERFEELERS

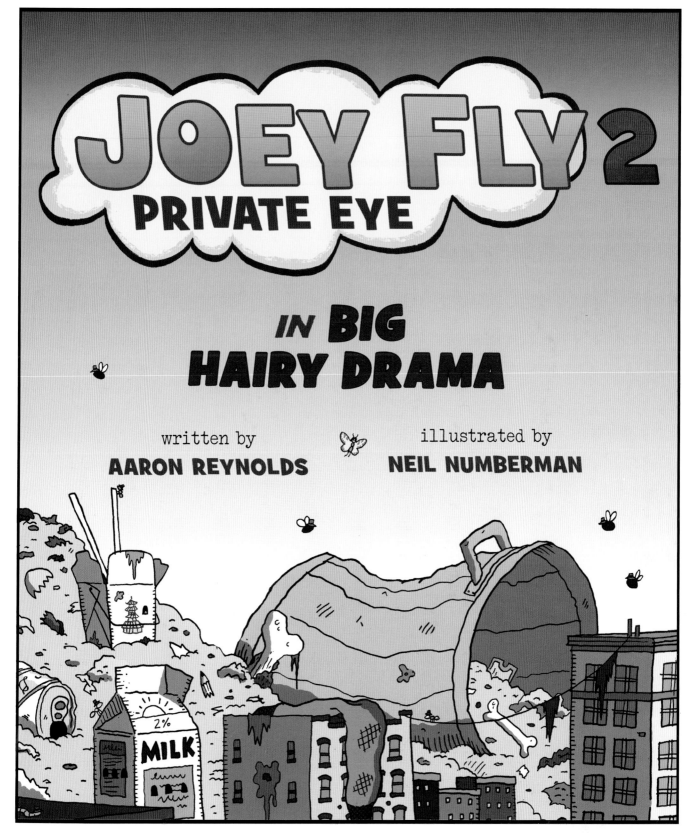

JOEY FLY 2
PRIVATE EYE

IN BIG HAIRY DRAMA

written by
AARON REYNOLDS

illustrated by
NEIL NUMBERMAN

HENRY HOLT AND COMPANY

NEW YORK

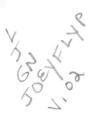

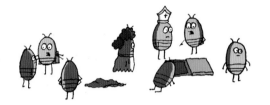

Henry Holt and Company, LLC
Publishers since 1866
175 Fifth Avenue
New York, New York 10010
www.HenryHoltKids.com

Distributed in Canada by H. B. Fenn and Company Ltd.

Library of Congress Cataloging-in-Publication Data
Reynolds, Aaron.
Joey Fly, private eye in Big hairy drama / by Aaron Reynolds ; illustrations by Neil Numberman. — 1st ed.
p. cm. — (Joey Fly, private eye)
Summary: When Greta Divawing, butterfly star of the Scarab Beetle Theatre, goes missing a week before the opening performance of "Bugliacci," Joey Fly is called in to investigate her puzzling disappearance.
ISBN 978-0-8050-8243-2 (hardcover)
1 3 5 7 9 10 8 6 4 2
ISBN 978-0-8050-9110-6 (paperback)
1 3 5 7 9 10 8 6 4 2
1. Graphic novels. [1. Graphic novels. 2. Flies—Fiction. 3. Insects—Fiction. 4. Theater—Fiction. 5. Mystery and detective stories. 6. Humorous stories.] I. Numberman, Neil, ill. II. Title. III. Title: Big hairy drama.
PZ7.7.R45Jo 2010 741.5'973—dc22 2009027416

First Edition—2010
Printed in August 2010 in China by South China Printing Company Ltd., Dongguan City, Guangdong Province, on acid-free paper. ∞

Answer key for page 128: Squish Wilson: 28; Buzzie Fly: 123; Creepy Nelson: 16; Eddie Bugsworth: 119; Frosty the Snowbeetle: 8; "Baby" Lice Johnson: 36; Johnny Onewing: 120; Darryl the Flea: 27; Slug Masterson: 126; Cutter Macintosh: 119; Michael Fivelegs: 14; Split Inchworm: 123.

To Mark Greenberg, my high school drama director,
who, despite not being an enormous spider,
inspired me in enormous ways

—A. R.

To my sisters, for taking good care
of their bratty little brother

—N. N.

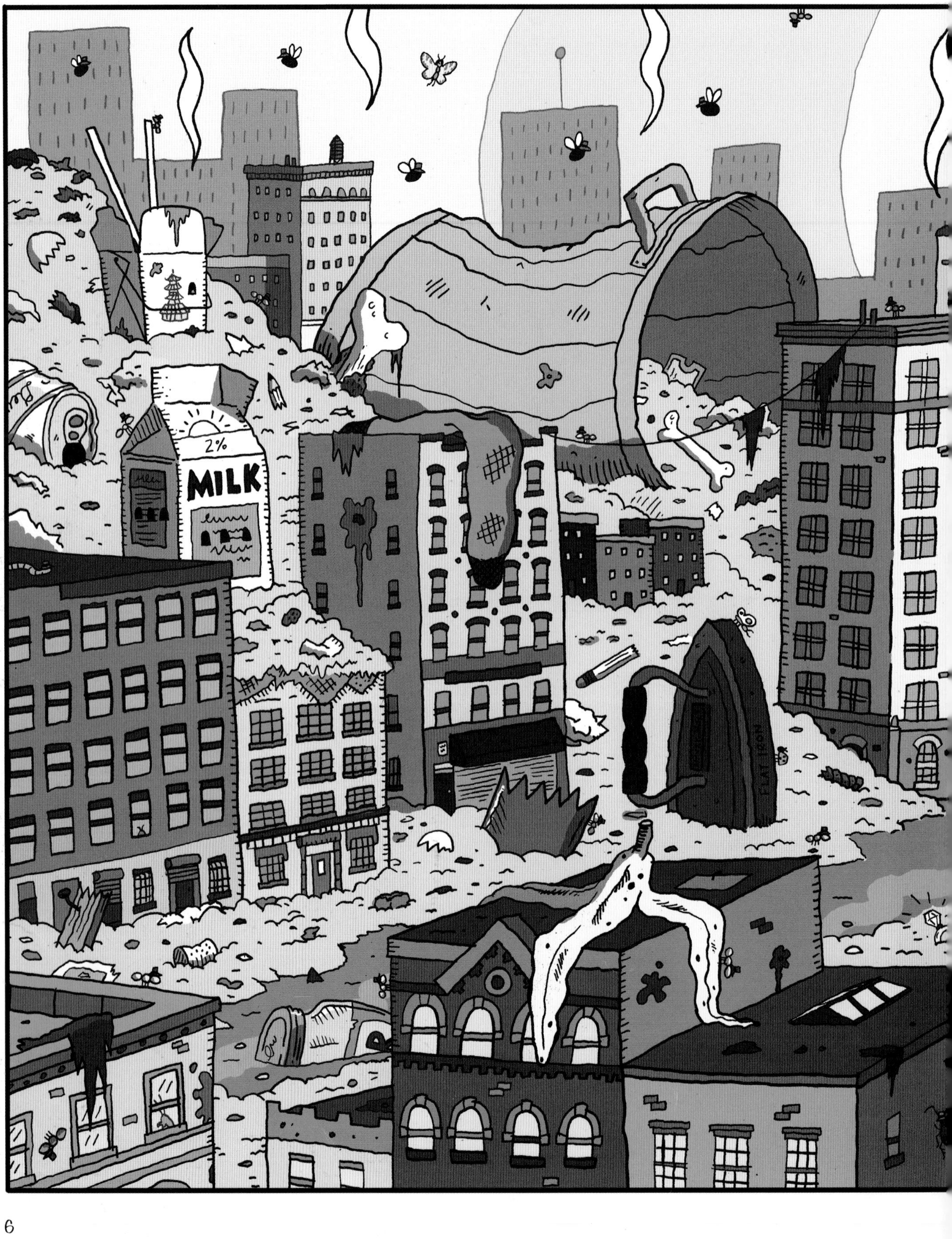
2%
MILK
FLAT IRON

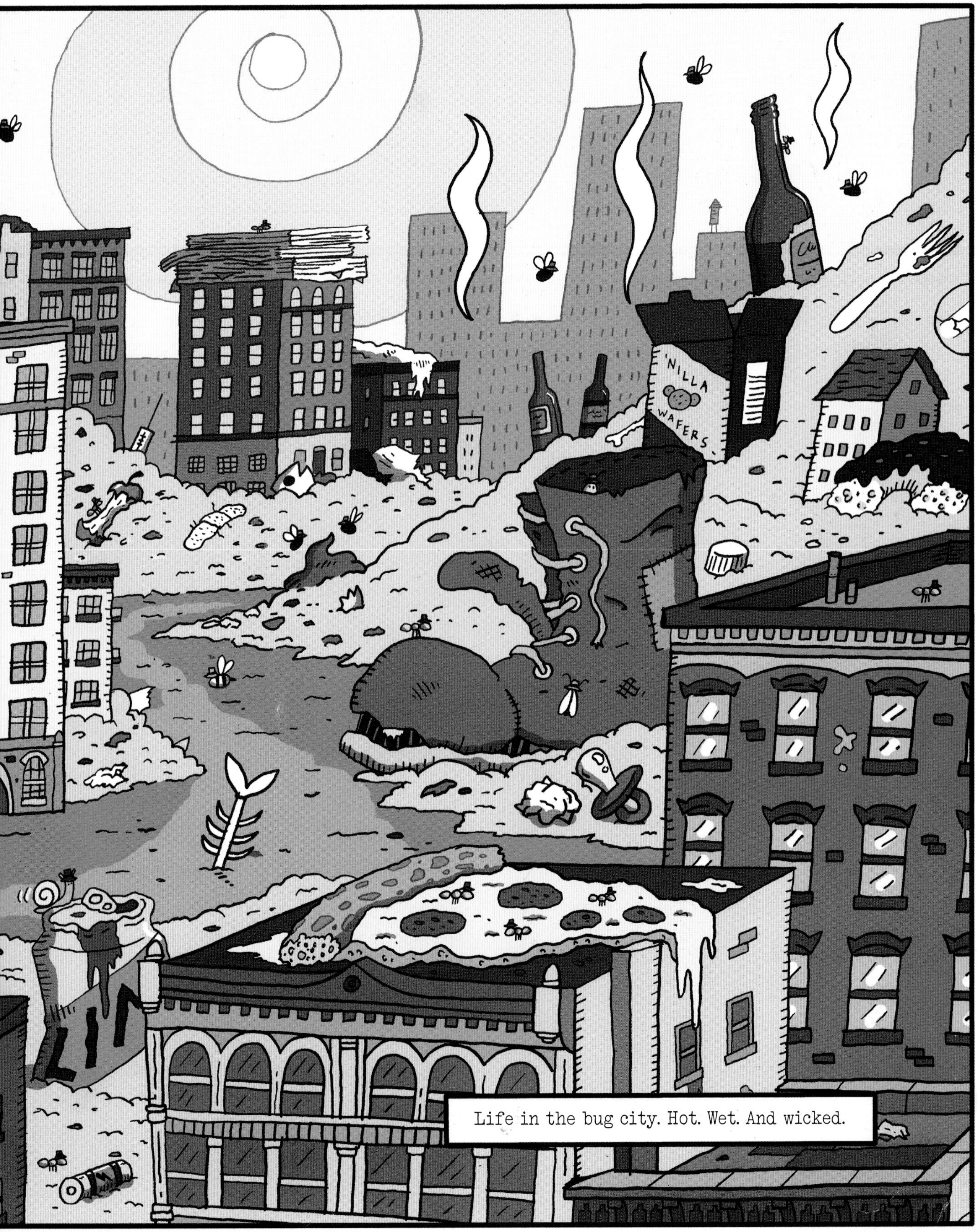
'NILLA WAFERS
Life in the bug city. Hot. Wet. And wicked.

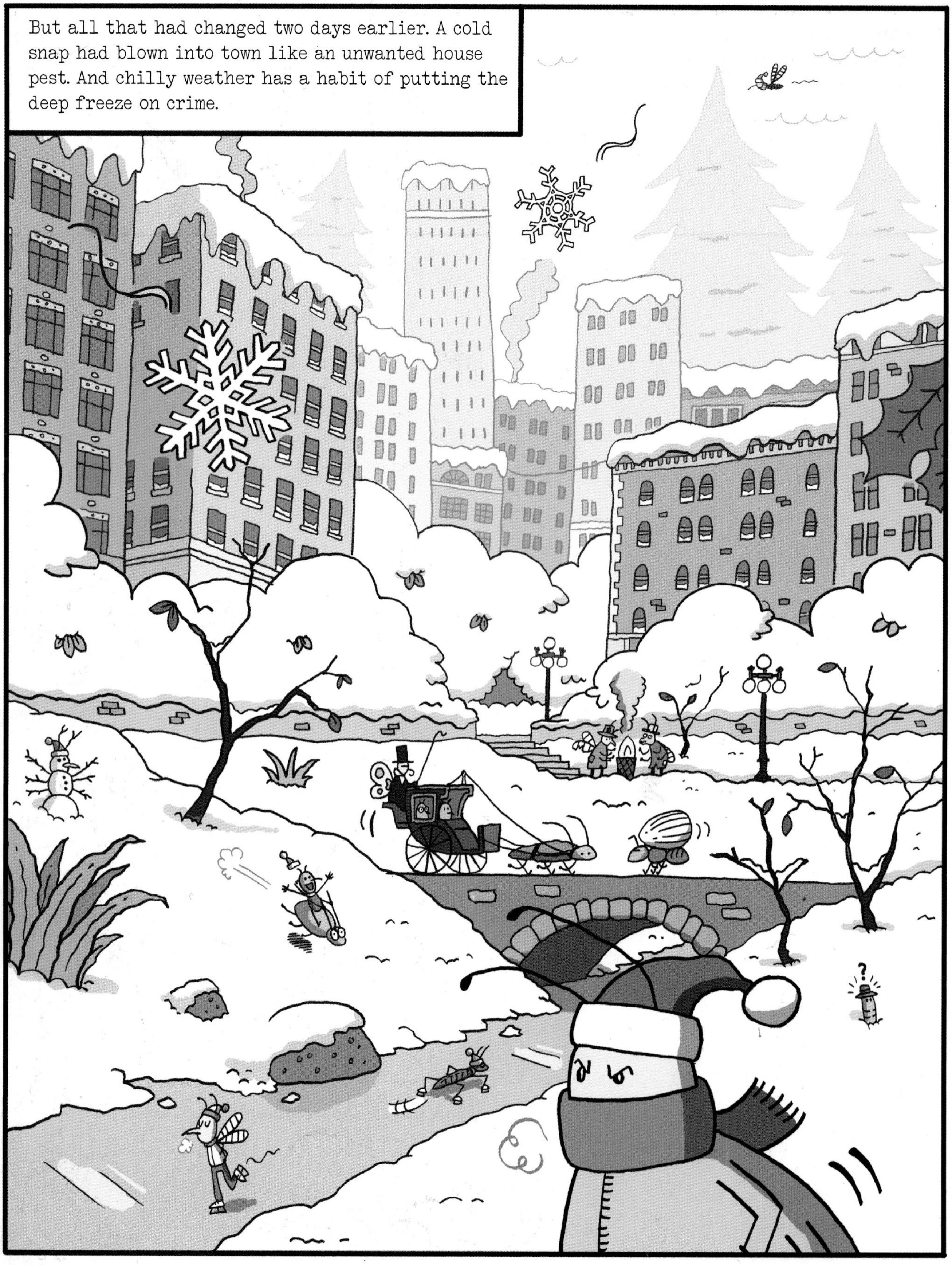
But all that had changed two days earlier. A cold snap had blown into town like an unwanted house pest. And chilly weather has a habit of putting the deep freeze on crime.

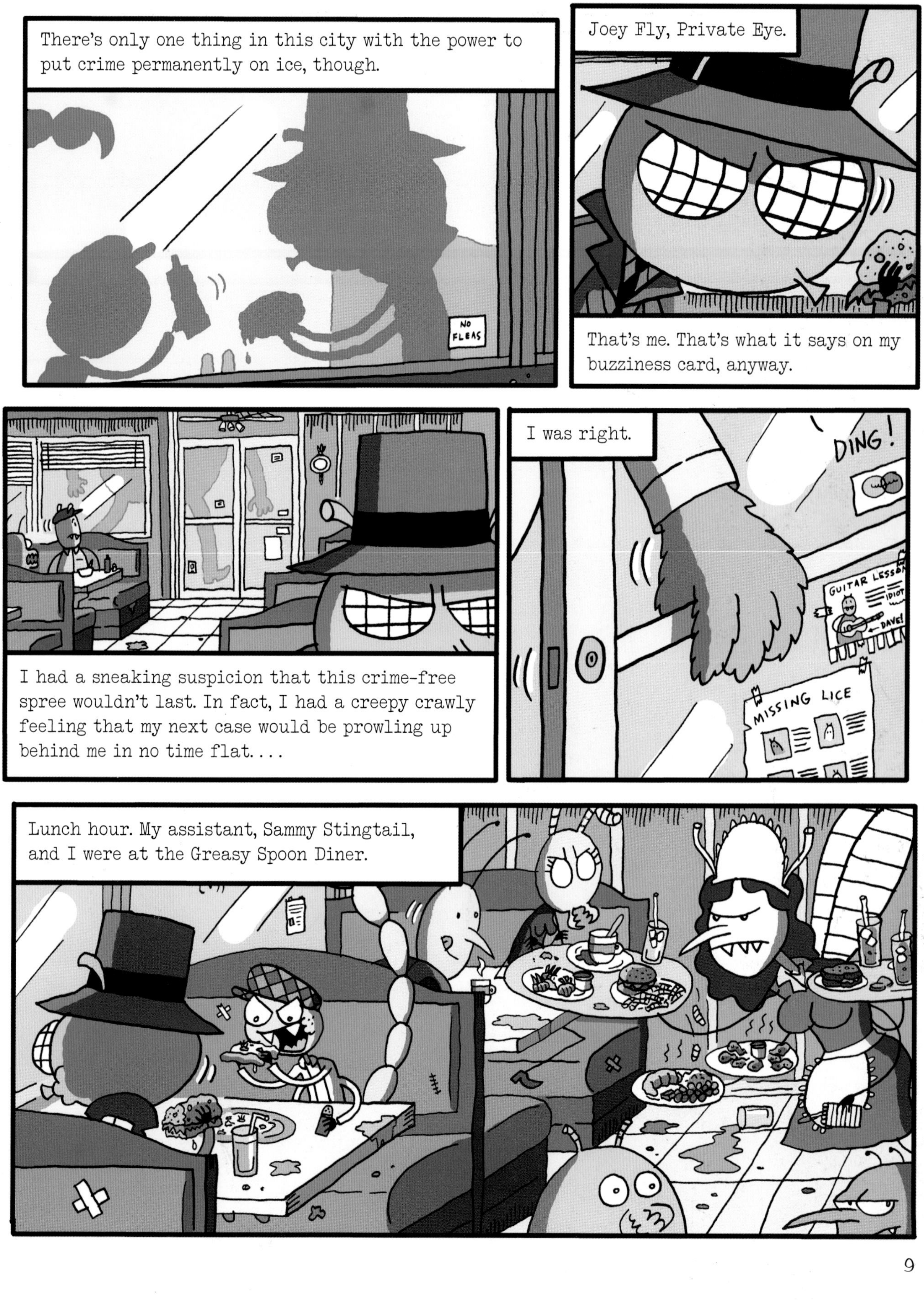
There's only one thing in this city with the power to put crime permanently on ice, though.
NO FLEAS
Joey Fly, Private Eye.
That's me. That's what it says on my buzziness card, anyway.
I had a sneaking suspicion that this crime-free spree wouldn't last. In fact, I had a creepy crawly feeling that my next case would be prowling up behind me in no time flat. . . .
I was right.
DING!
GUITAR LESSON
IDIOT
DAVE!
MISSING LICE
Lunch hour. My assistant, Sammy Stingtail, and I were at the Greasy Spoon Diner.

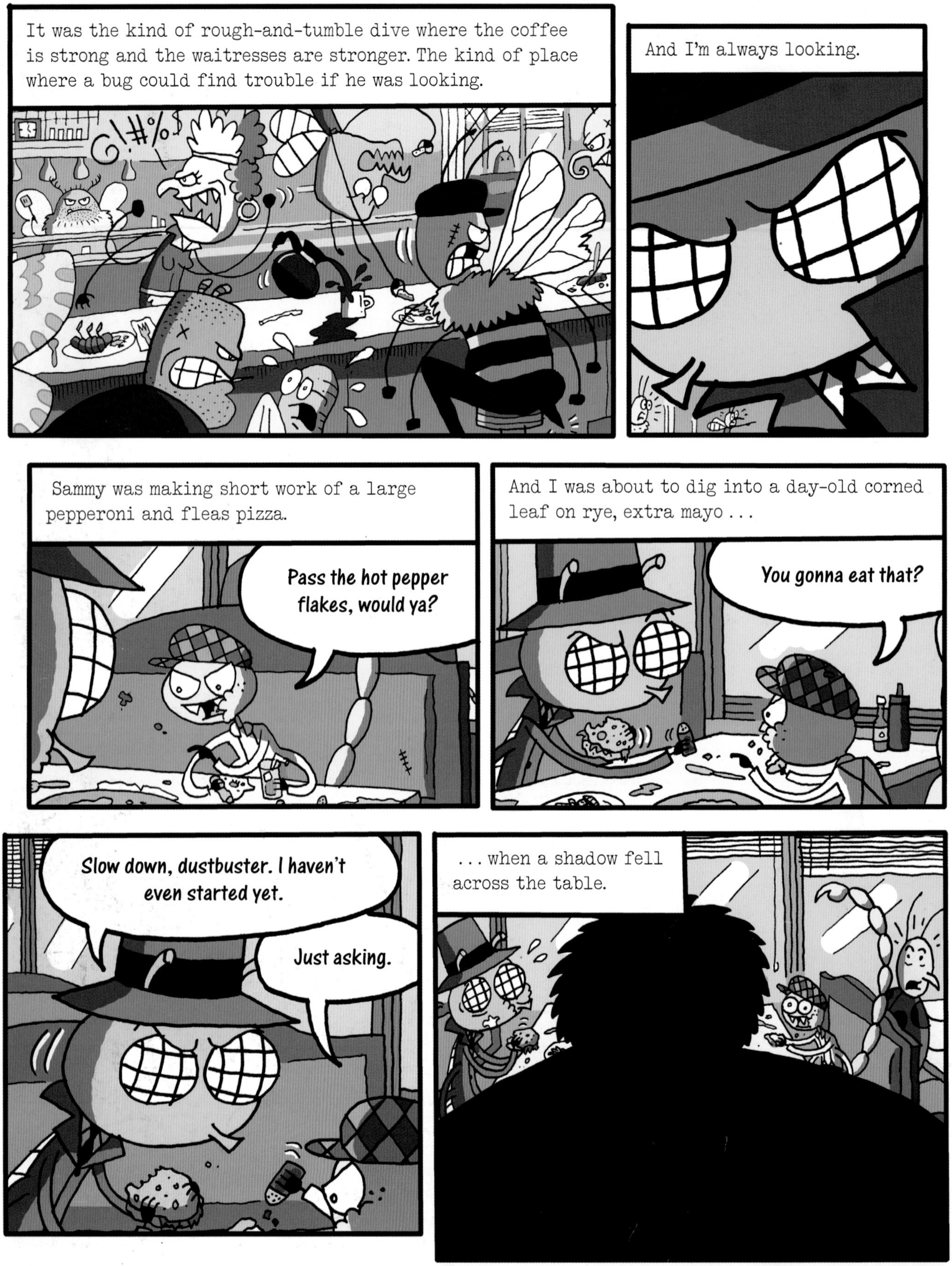

It was the kind of rough-and-tumble dive where the coffee is strong and the waitresses are stronger. The kind of place where a bug could find trouble if he was looking.
G!#%$
And I'm always looking.
Sammy was making short work of a large pepperoni and fleas pizza.
Pass the hot pepper flakes, would ya?
And I was about to dig into a day-old corned leaf on rye, extra mayo . . .
You gonna eat that?
Slow down, dustbuster. I haven't even started yet.
Just asking.
. . . when a shadow fell across the table.

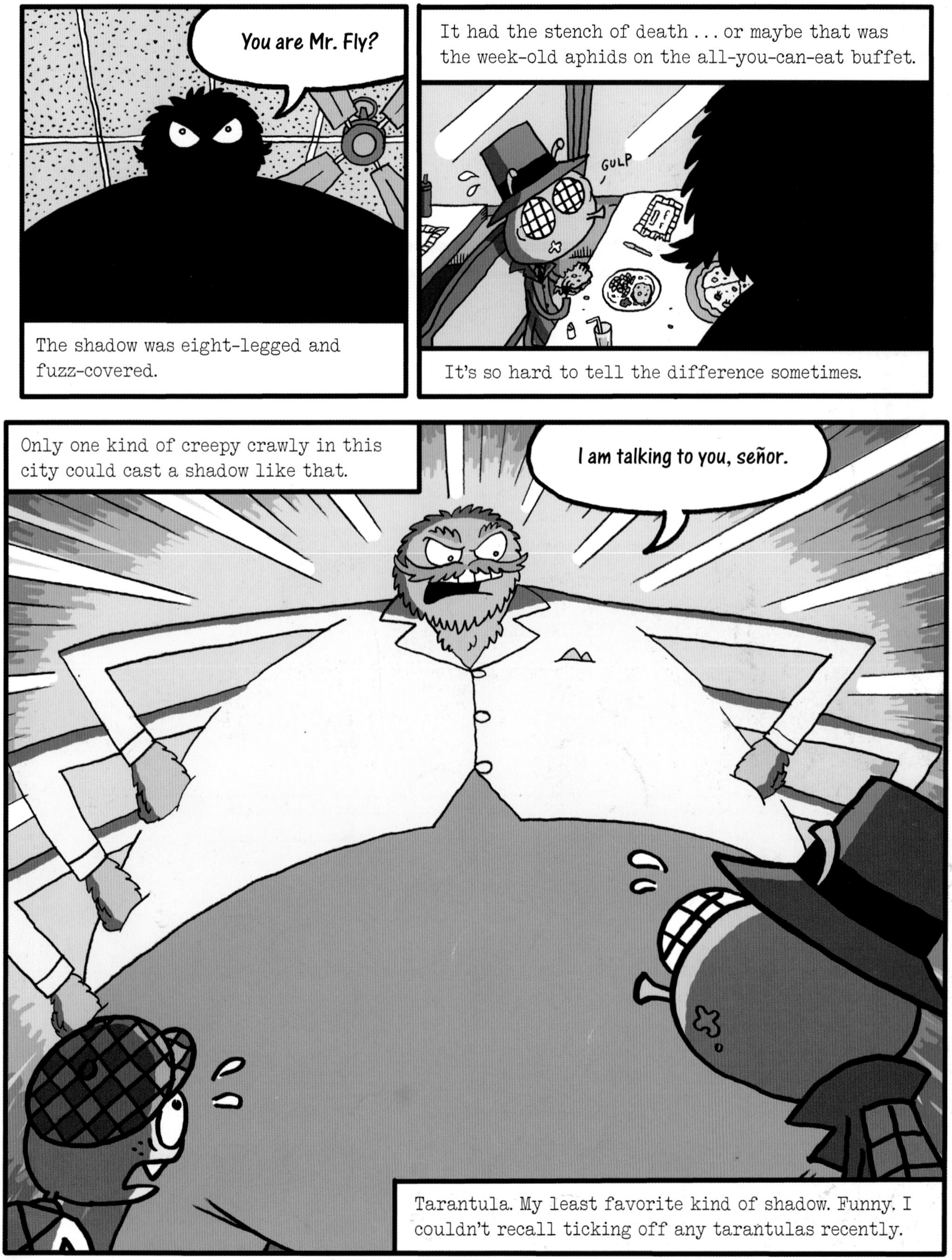
You are Mr. Fly?
The shadow was eight-legged and fuzz-covered.
It had the stench of death . . . or maybe that was the week-old aphids on the all-you-can-eat buffet.
GULP
It's so hard to tell the difference sometimes.
Only one kind of creepy crawly in this city could cast a shadow like that.
I am talking to you, señor.
Tarantula. My least favorite kind of shadow. Funny. I couldn't recall ticking off any tarantulas recently.

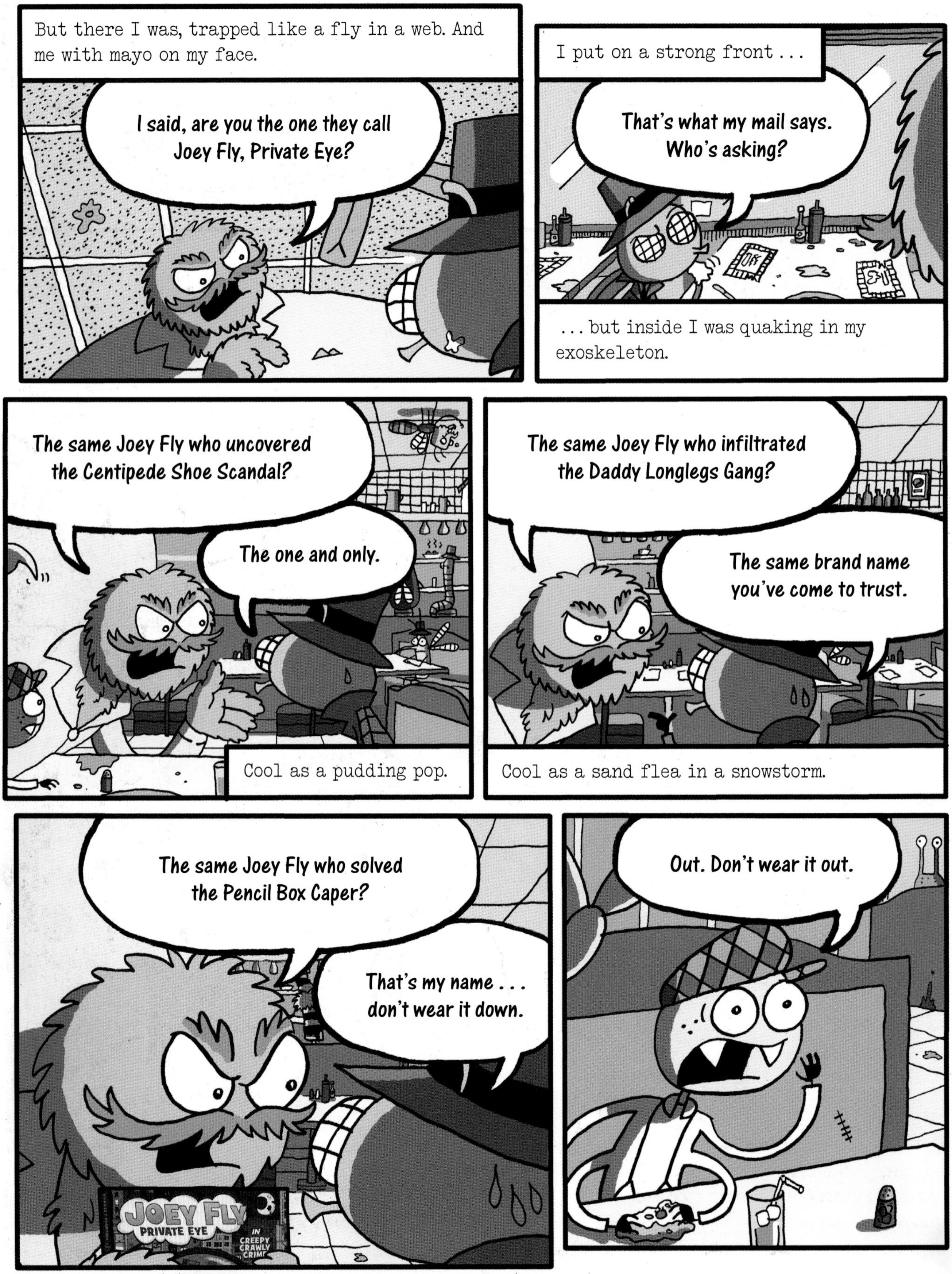

But there I was, trapped like a fly in a web. And me with mayo on my face.
I said, are you the one they call Joey Fly, Private Eye?
I put on a strong front . . .
That's what my mail says. Who's asking?
. . . but inside I was quaking in my exoskeleton.
The same Joey Fly who uncovered the Centipede Shoe Scandal?
The one and only.
Cool as a pudding pop.
The same Joey Fly who infiltrated the Daddy Longlegs Gang?
The same brand name you've come to trust.
Cool as a sand flea in a snowstorm.
The same Joey Fly who solved the Pencil Box Caper?
That's my name . . . don't wear it down.
JOEY FLY
PRIVATE EYE
IN CREEPY CRAWLY CRIME
Out. Don't wear it out.

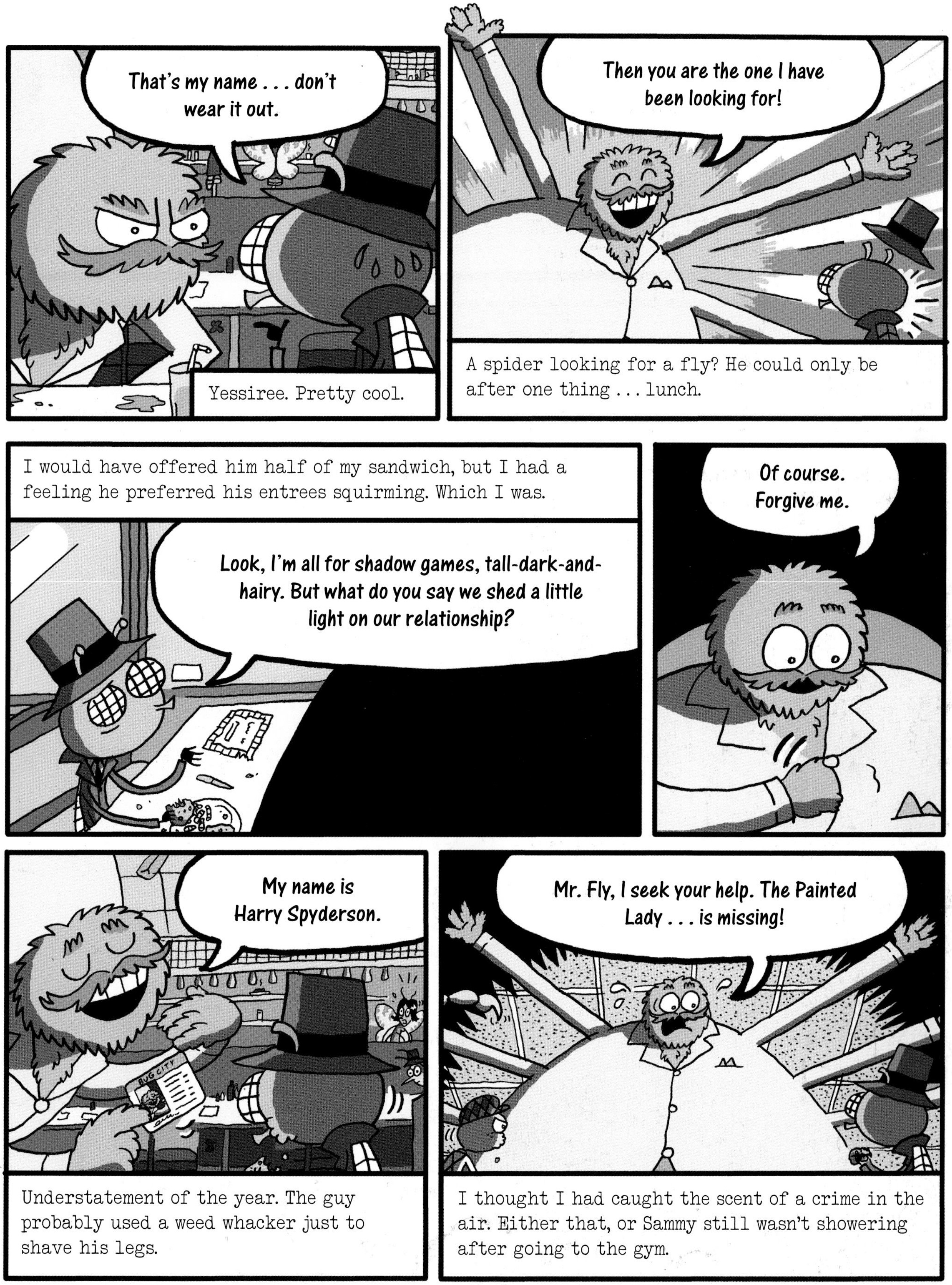
That's my name . . . don't wear it out.
Yessiree. Pretty cool.
Then you are the one I have been looking for!
A spider looking for a fly? He could only be after one thing . . . lunch.
I would have offered him half of my sandwich, but I had a feeling he preferred his entrees squirming. Which I was.
Look, I'm all for shadow games, tall-dark-and-hairy. But what do you say we shed a little light on our relationship?
Of course. Forgive me.
My name is Harry Spyderson.
Understatement of the year. The guy probably used a weed whacker just to shave his legs.
Mr. Fly, I seek your help. The Painted Lady . . . is missing!
I thought I had caught the scent of a crime in the air. Either that, or Sammy still wasn't showering after going to the gym.

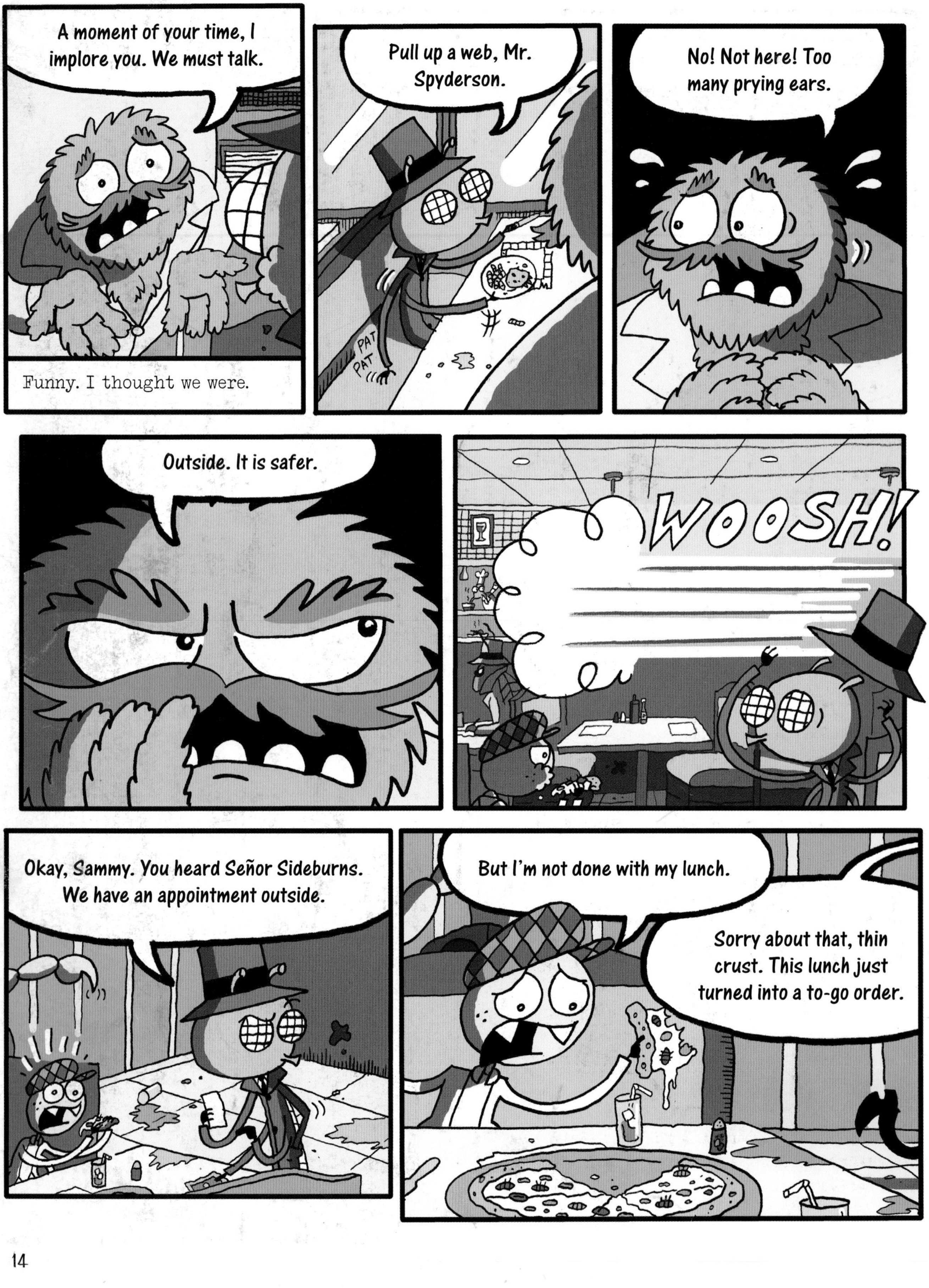
A moment of your time, I implore you. We must talk.
Funny. I thought we were.
Pull up a web, Mr. Spyderson.
PAT PAT
No! Not here! Too many prying ears.
Outside. It is safer.
WOOSH!
Okay, Sammy. You heard Señor Sideburns. We have an appointment outside.
But I'm not done with my lunch.
Sorry about that, thin crust. This lunch just turned into a to-go order.

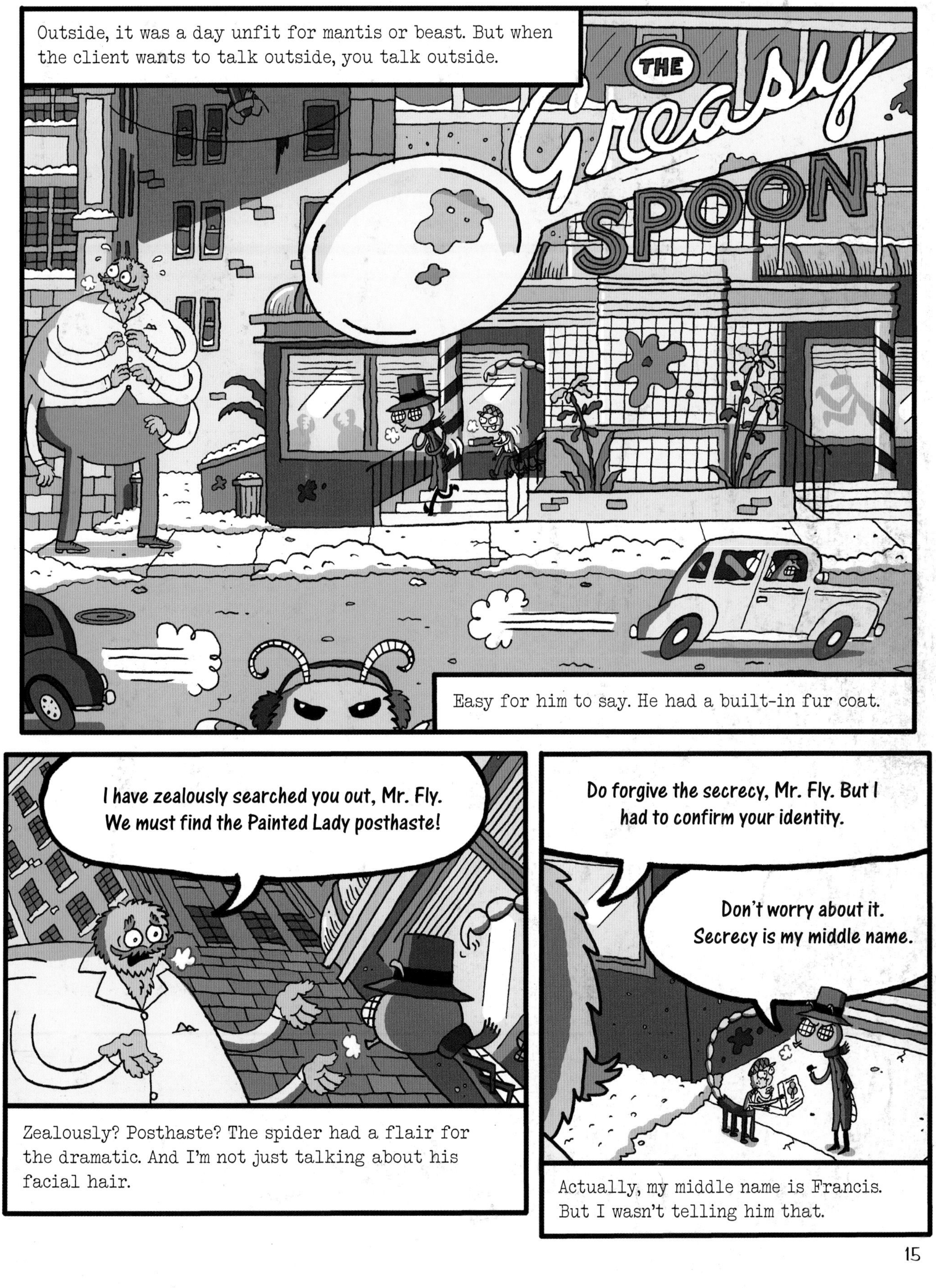

Outside, it was a day unfit for mantis or beast. But when the client wants to talk outside, you talk outside.
THE Greasy SPOON
Easy for him to say. He had a built-in fur coat.
I have zealously searched you out, Mr. Fly. We must find the Painted Lady posthaste!
Zealously? Posthaste? The spider had a flair for the dramatic. And I'm not just talking about his facial hair.
Do forgive the secrecy, Mr. Fly. But I had to confirm your identity.
Don't worry about it. Secrecy is my middle name.
Actually, my middle name is Francis. But I wasn't telling him that.

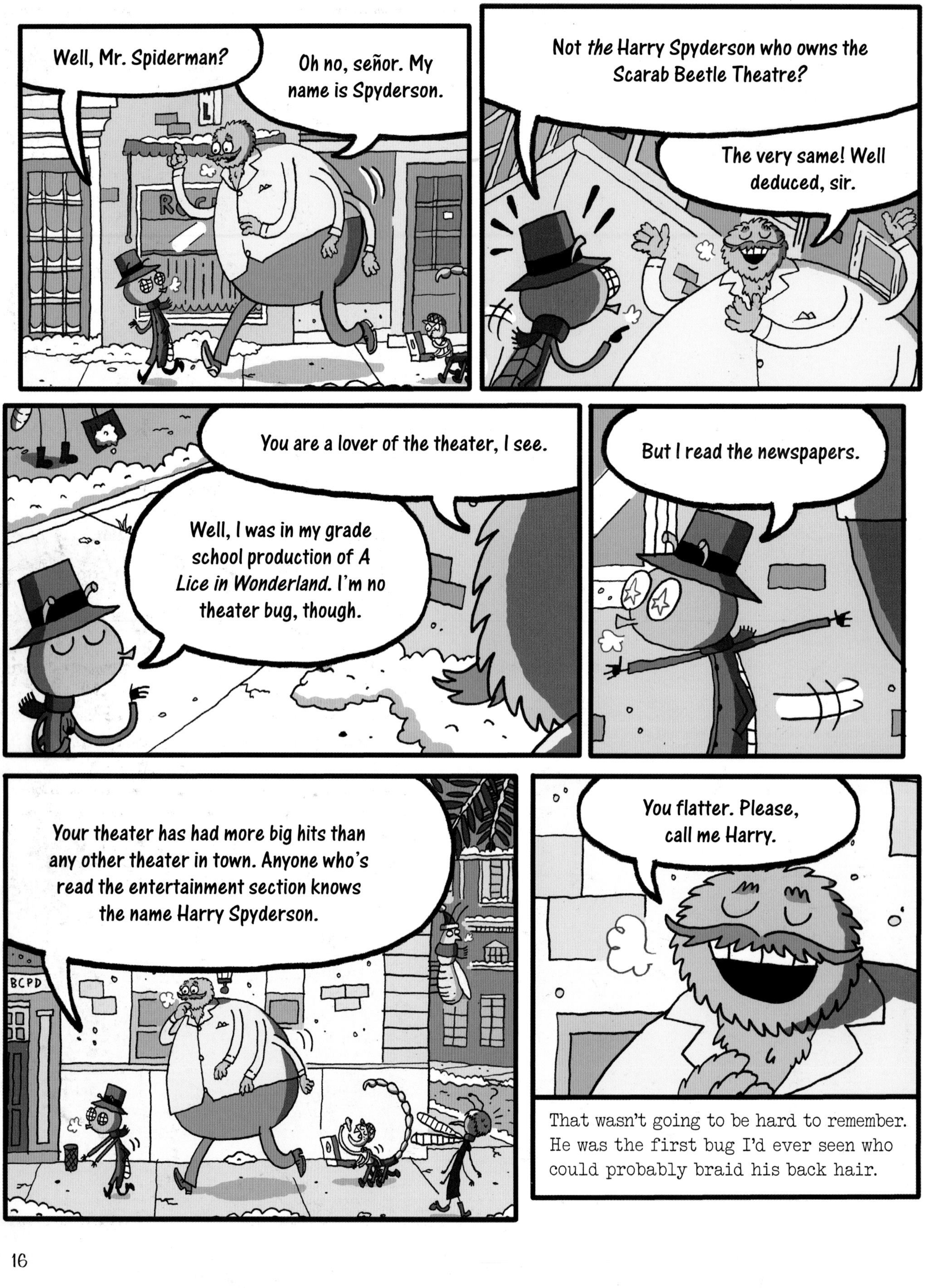
Well, Mr. Spiderman?
Oh no, señor. My name is Spyderson.
Not *the* Harry Spyderson who owns the Scarab Beetle Theatre?
The very same! Well deduced, sir.
You are a lover of the theater, I see.
Well, I was in my grade school production of *A Lice in Wonderland.* I'm no theater bug, though.
But I read the newspapers.
Your theater has had more big hits than any other theater in town. Anyone who's read the entertainment section knows the name Harry Spyderson.
BCPD
You flatter. Please, call me Harry.
That wasn't going to be hard to remember. He was the first bug I'd ever seen who could probably braid his back hair.

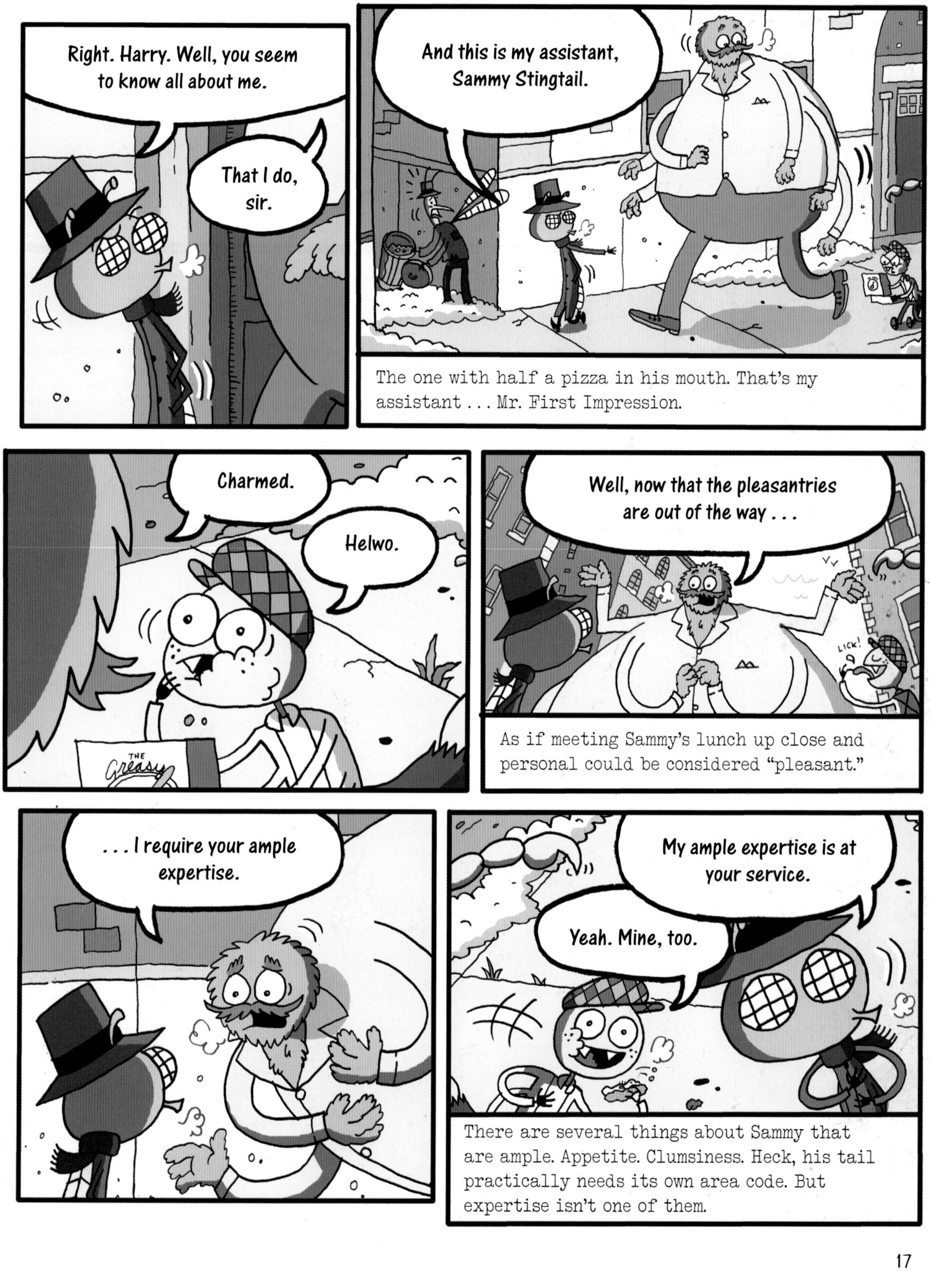
Right. Harry. Well, you seem to know all about me.
That I do, sir.
And this is my assistant, Sammy Stingtail.
The one with half a pizza in his mouth. That's my assistant . . . Mr. First Impression.
Charmed.
Helwo.
THE Greasy
Well, now that the pleasantries are out of the way . . .
LICK!
As if meeting Sammy's lunch up close and personal could be considered "pleasant."
. . . I require your ample expertise.
My ample expertise is at your service.
Yeah. Mine, too.
There are several things about Sammy that are ample. Appetite. Clumsiness. Heck, his tail practically needs its own area code. But expertise isn't one of them.

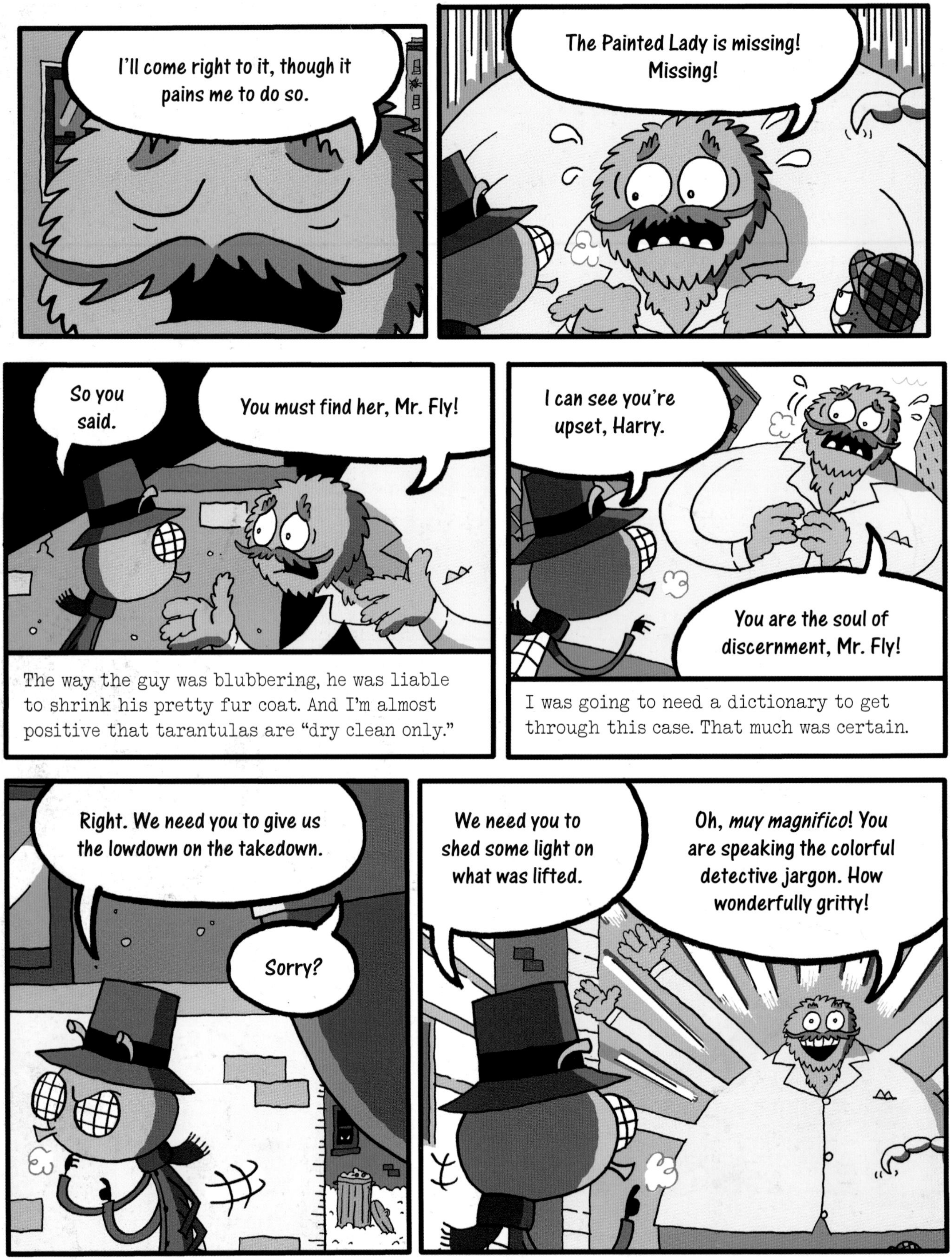

I'll come right to it, though it pains me to do so.
The Painted Lady is missing! Missing!
So you said.
You must find her, Mr. Fly!
The way the guy was blubbering, he was liable to shrink his pretty fur coat. And I'm almost positive that tarantulas are "dry clean only."
I can see you're upset, Harry.
You are the soul of discernment, Mr. Fly!
I was going to need a dictionary to get through this case. That much was certain.
Right. We need you to give us the lowdown on the takedown.
Sorry?
We need you to shed some light on what was lifted.
Oh, *muy magnifico*! You are speaking the colorful detective jargon. How wonderfully gritty!

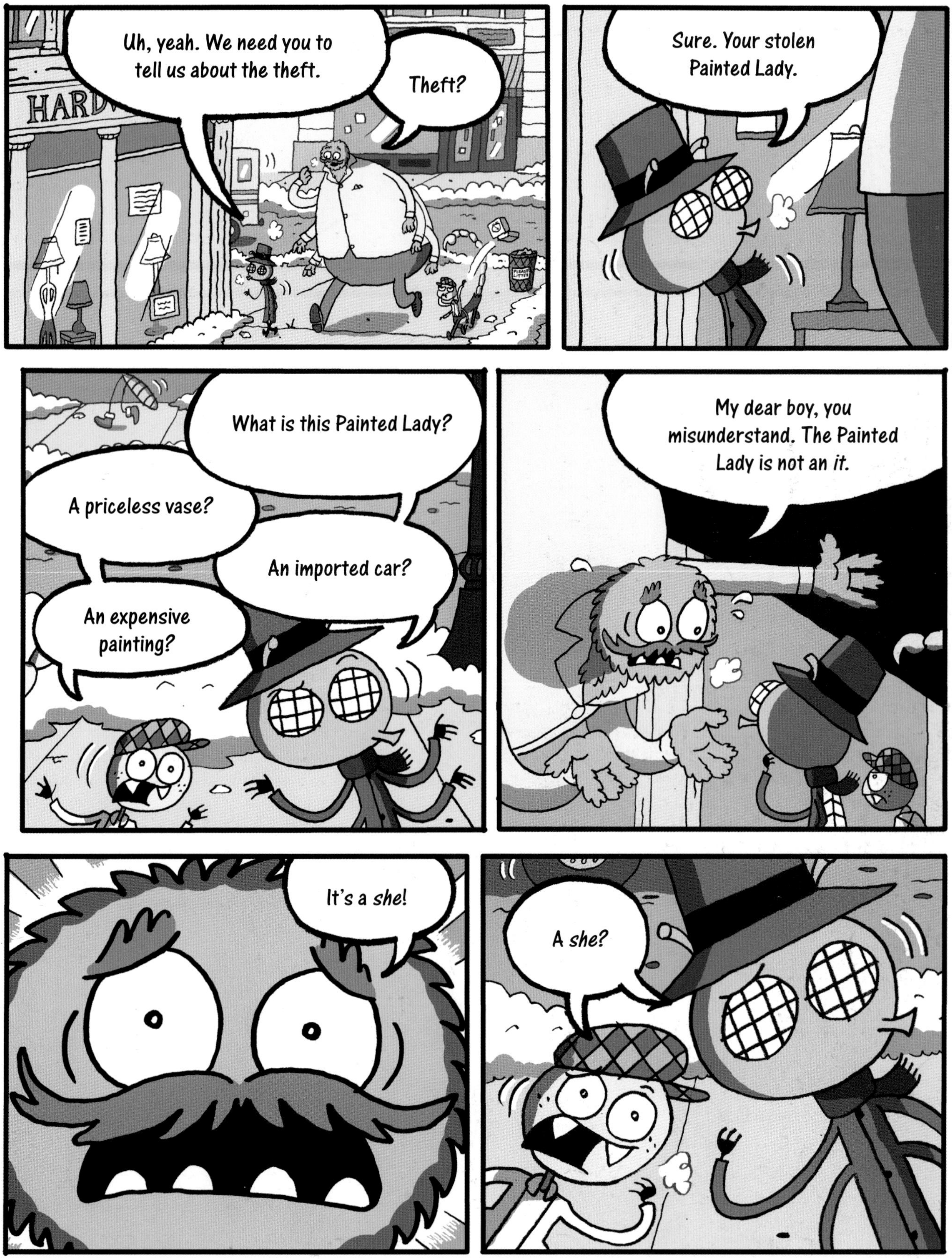
Uh, yeah. We need you to tell us about the theft.
Theft?
HARD
PLEASE LITTER
Sure. Your stolen Painted Lady.
What is this Painted Lady?
A priceless vase?
An imported car?
An expensive painting?
My dear boy, you misunderstand. The Painted Lady is not an *it*.
It's a *she*!
A *she*?

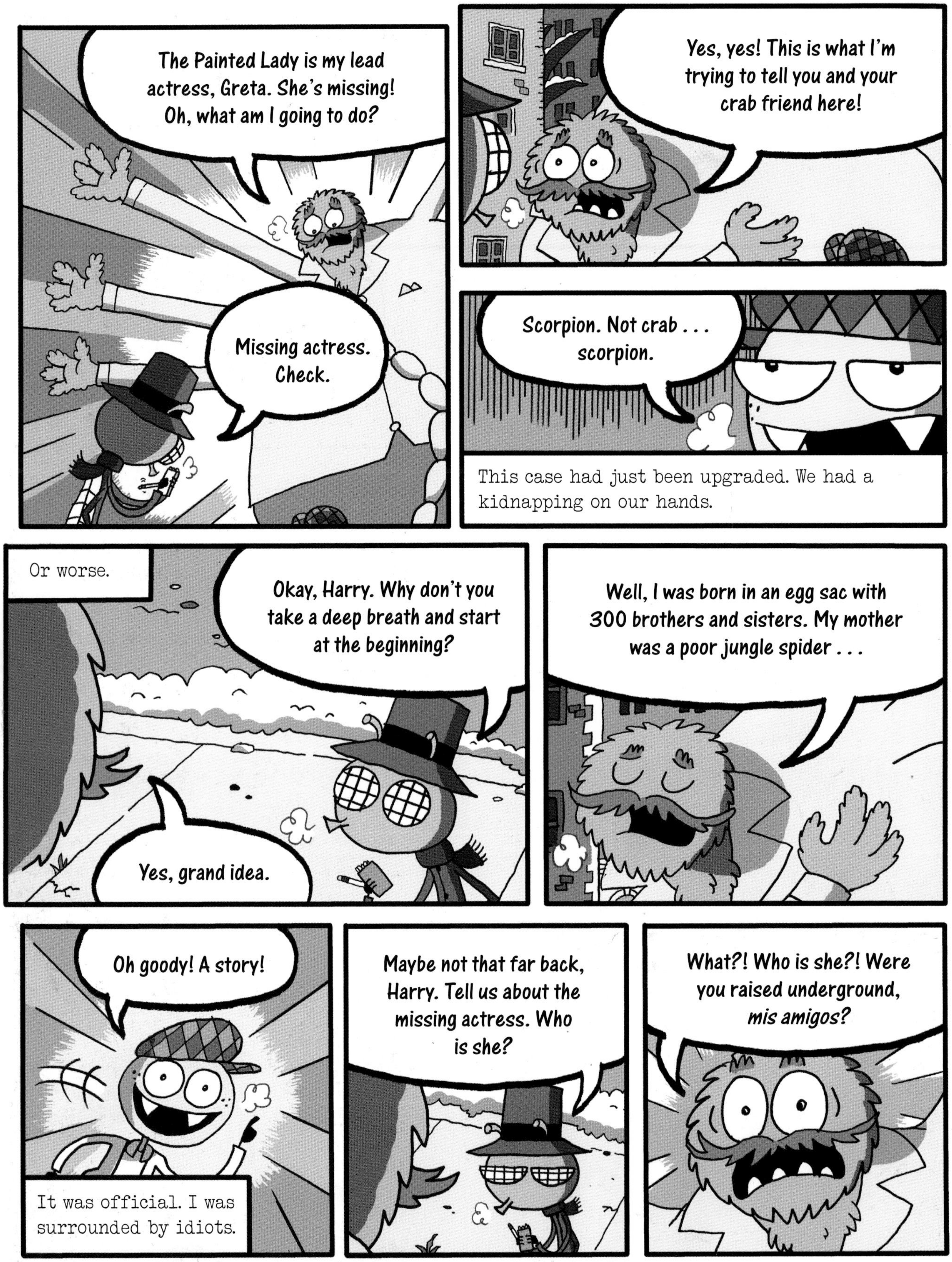

The Painted Lady is my lead actress, Greta. She's missing! Oh, what am I going to do?
Missing actress. Check.
Yes, yes! This is what I'm trying to tell you and your crab friend here!
Scorpion. Not crab . . . scorpion.
This case had just been upgraded. We had a kidnapping on our hands.
Or worse.
Okay, Harry. Why don't you take a deep breath and start at the beginning?
Yes, grand idea.
Well, I was born in an egg sac with 300 brothers and sisters. My mother was a poor jungle spider . . .
Oh goody! A story!
It was official. I was surrounded by idiots.
Maybe not that far back, Harry. Tell us about the missing actress. Who is she?
What?! Who is she?! Were you raised underground, *mis amigos?*

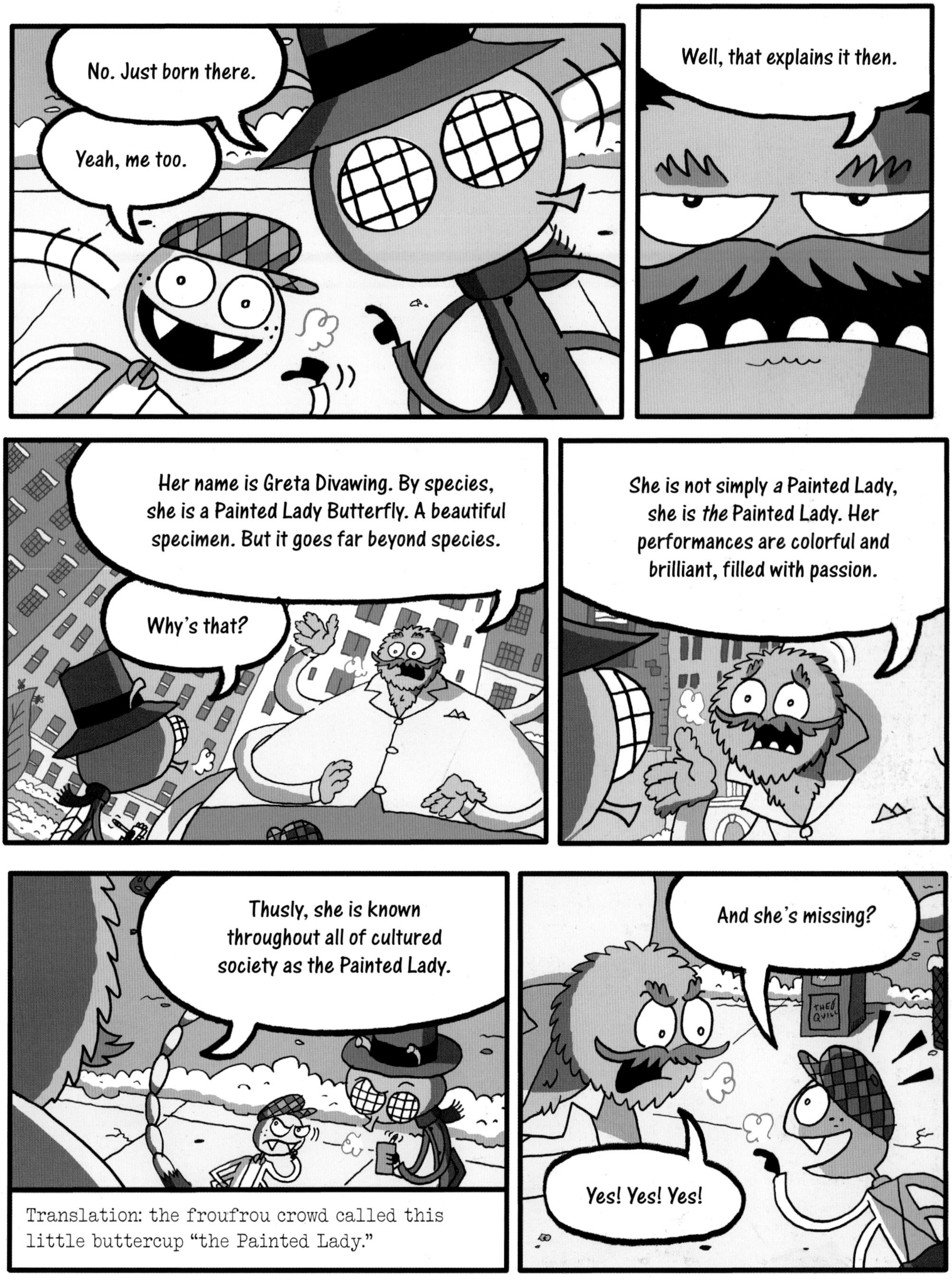
No. Just born there.
Yeah, me too.
Well, that explains it then.
Her name is Greta Divawing. By species, she is a Painted Lady Butterfly. A beautiful specimen. But it goes far beyond species.
Why's that?
She is not simply *a* Painted Lady, she is *the* Painted Lady. Her performances are colorful and brilliant, filled with passion.
Thusly, she is known throughout all of cultured society as the Painted Lady.
Translation: the froufrou crowd called this little buttercup "the Painted Lady."
And she's missing?
Yes! Yes! Yes!

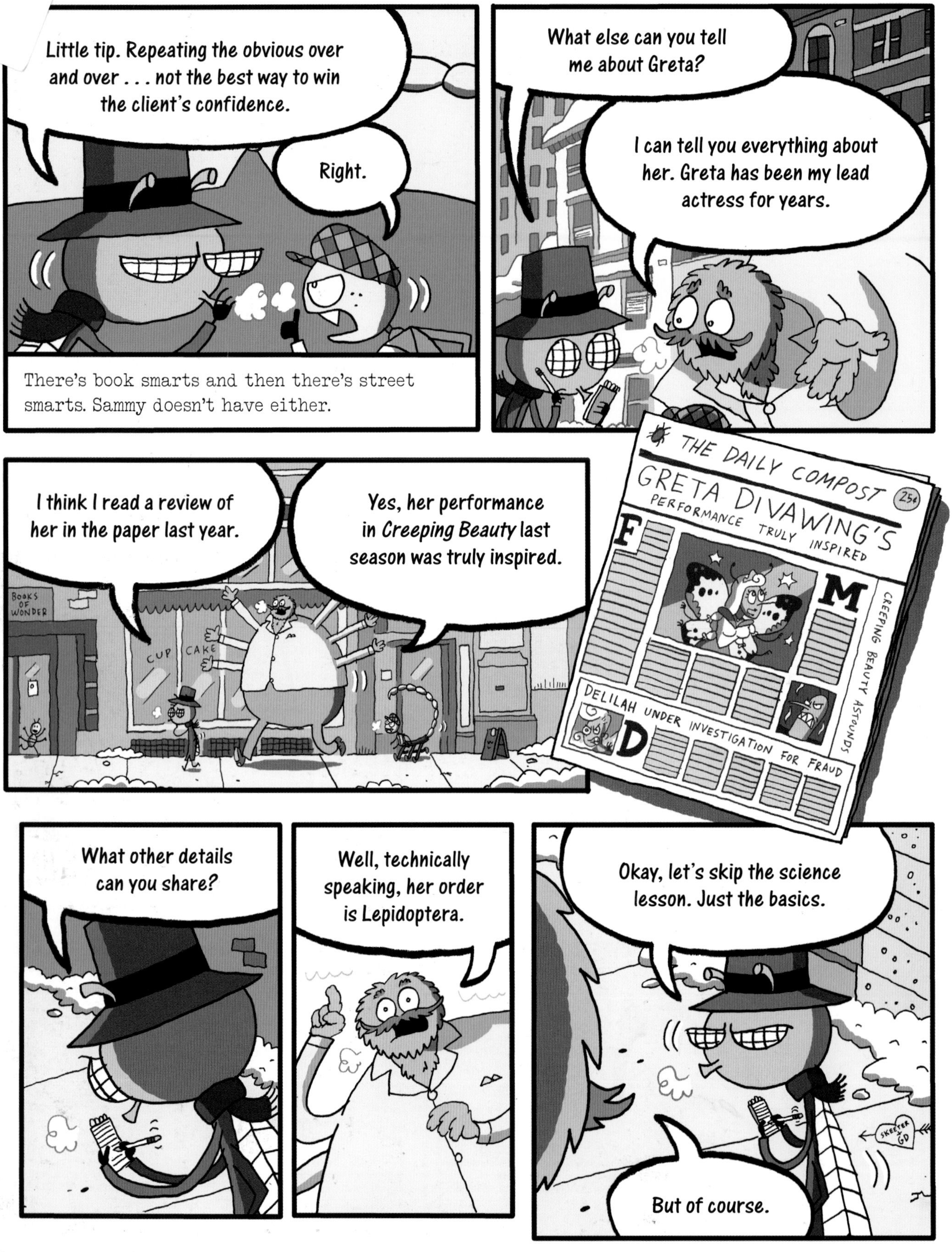

Little tip. Repeating the obvious over and over . . . not the best way to win the client's confidence.
Right.
There's book smarts and then there's street smarts. Sammy doesn't have either.
What else can you tell me about Greta?
I can tell you everything about her. Greta has been my lead actress for years.
I think I read a review of her in the paper last year.
Yes, her performance in *Creeping Beauty* last season was truly inspired.
BOOKS OF WONDER
CUP CAKE
THE DAILY COMPOST
25¢
GRETA DIVAWING'S PERFORMANCE TRULY INSPIRED
CREEPING BEAUTY ASTOUNDS
DELILAH UNDER INVESTIGATION FOR FRAUD
What other details can you share?
Well, technically speaking, her order is Lepidoptera.
Okay, let's skip the science lesson. Just the basics.
But of course.
SKEETER + GD

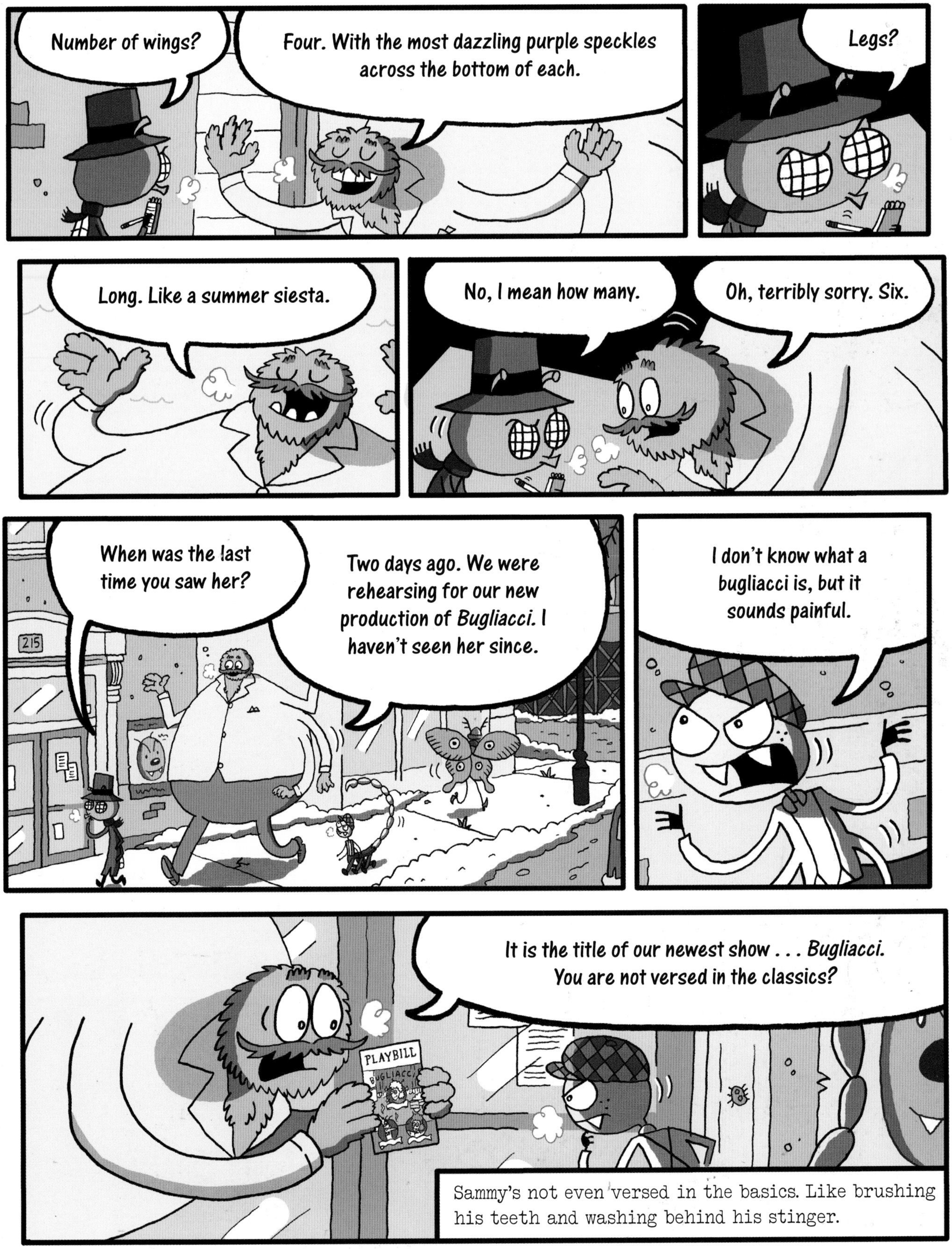
Number of wings?
Four. With the most dazzling purple speckles across the bottom of each.
Legs?
Long. Like a summer siesta.
No, I mean how many.
Oh, terribly sorry. Six.
When was the last time you saw her?
Two days ago. We were rehearsing for our new production of *Bugliacci*. I haven't seen her since.
215
I don't know what a bugliacci is, but it sounds painful.
It is the title of our newest show . . . *Bugliacci*. You are not versed in the classics?
PLAYBILL
BUGLIACCI
Sammy's not even versed in the basics. Like brushing his teeth and washing behind his stinger.

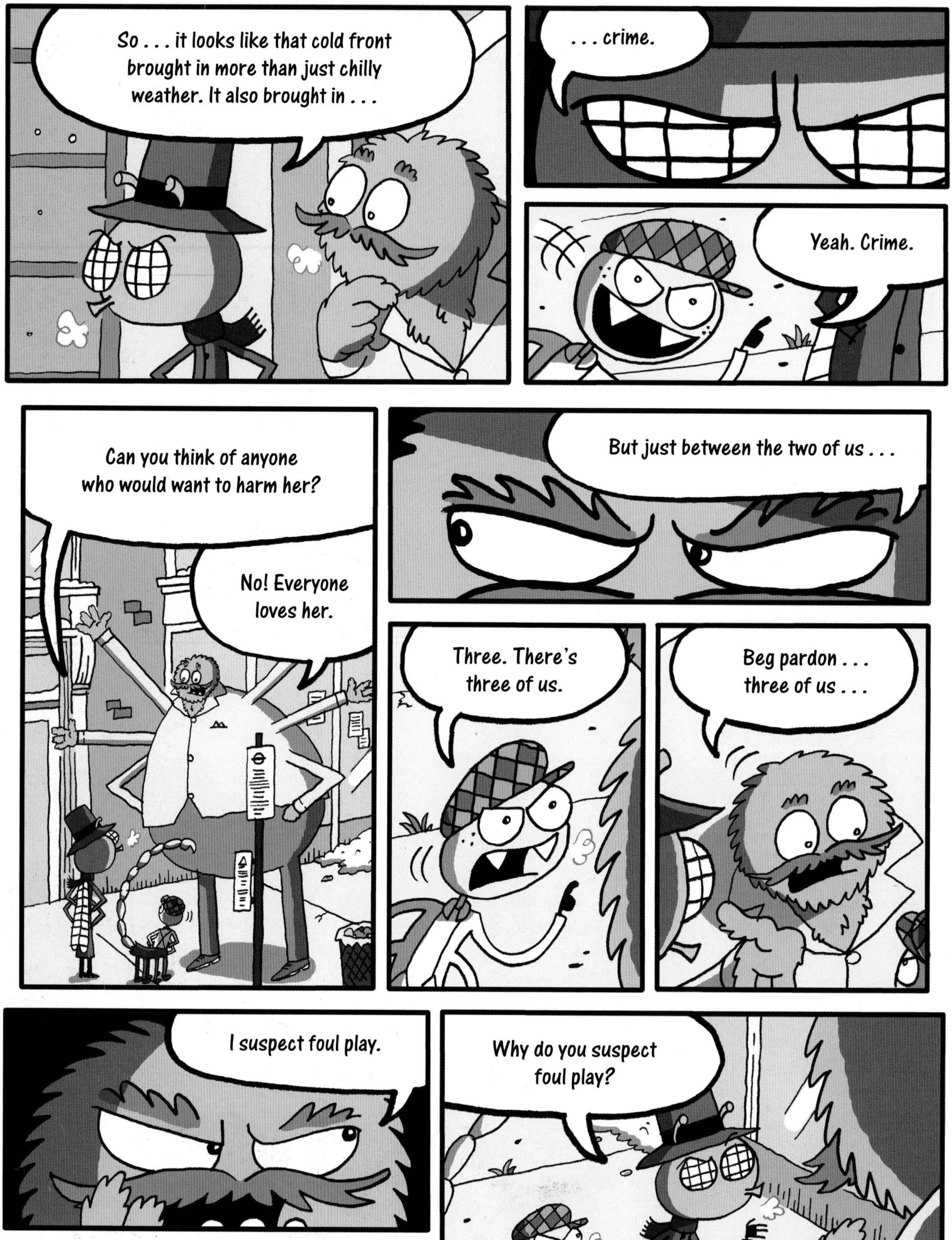
So . . . it looks like that cold front brought in more than just chilly weather. It also brought in . . .
. . . crime.
Yeah. Crime.
Can you think of anyone who would want to harm her?
No! Everyone loves her.
But just between the two of us . . .
Three. There's three of us.
Beg pardon . . . three of us . . .
I suspect foul play.
Why do you suspect foul play?

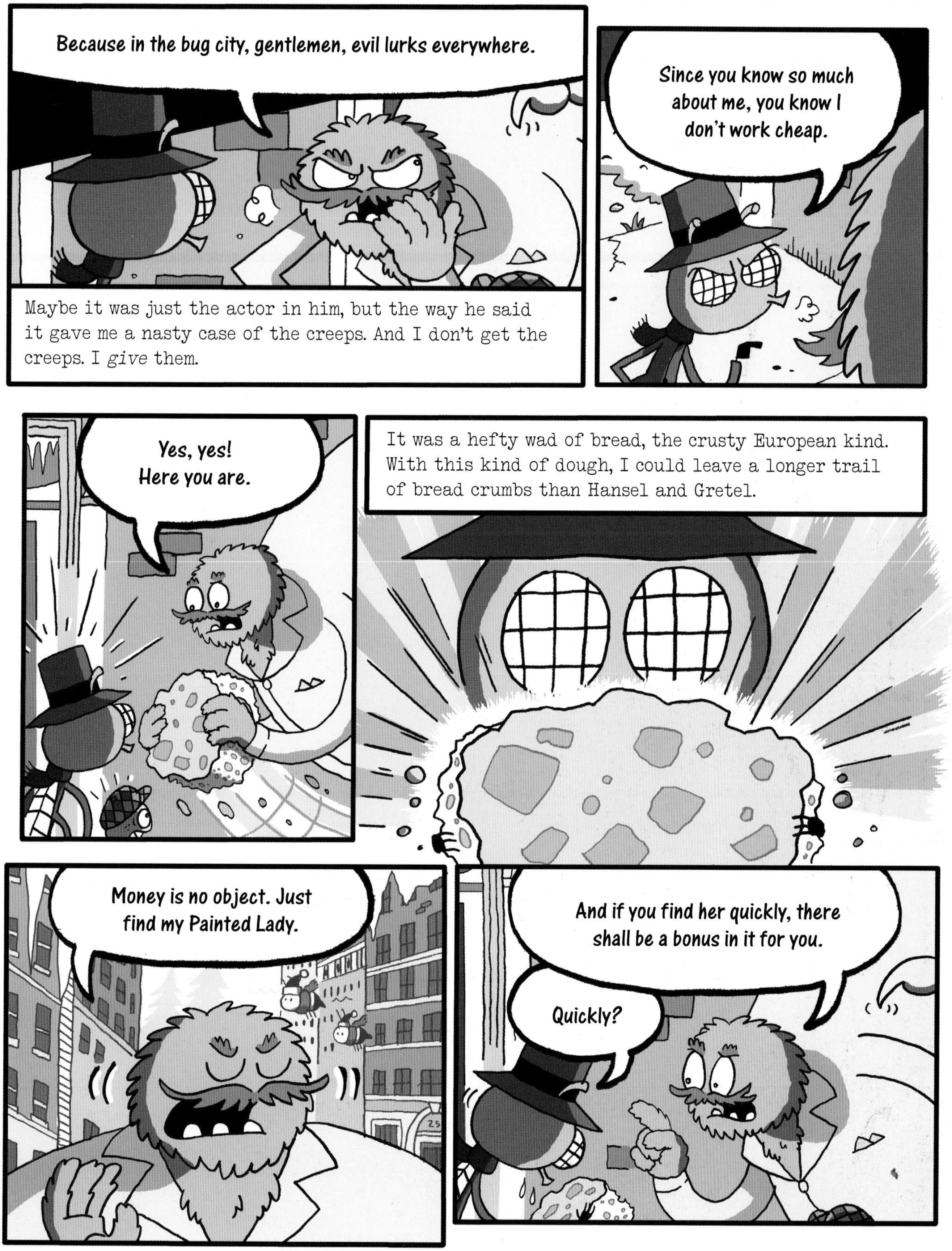
Because in the bug city, gentlemen, evil lurks everywhere.
Maybe it was just the actor in him, but the way he said it gave me a nasty case of the creeps. And I don't get the creeps. I *give* them.
Since you know so much about me, you know I don't work cheap.
Yes, yes! Here you are.
It was a hefty wad of bread, the crusty European kind. With this kind of dough, I could leave a longer trail of bread crumbs than Hansel and Gretel.
Money is no object. Just find my Painted Lady.
And if you find her quickly, there shall be a bonus in it for you.
Quickly?

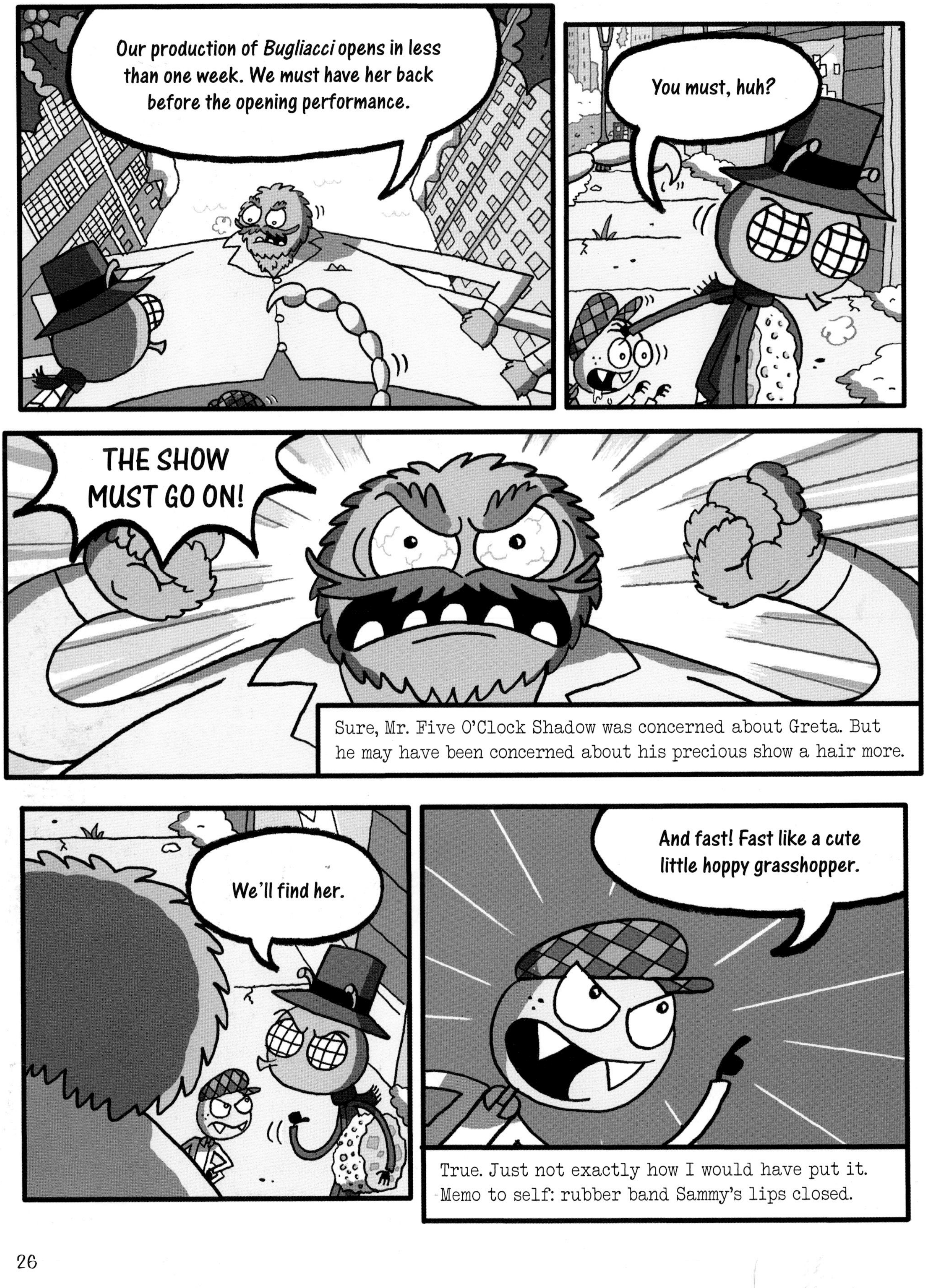
Our production of *Bugliacci* opens in less than one week. We must have her back before the opening performance.
You must, huh?
THE SHOW MUST GO ON!
Sure, Mr. Five O'Clock Shadow was concerned about Greta. But he may have been concerned about his precious show a hair more.
We'll find her.
And fast! Fast like a cute little hoppy grasshopper.
True. Just not exactly how I would have put it. Memo to self: rubber band Sammy's lips closed.

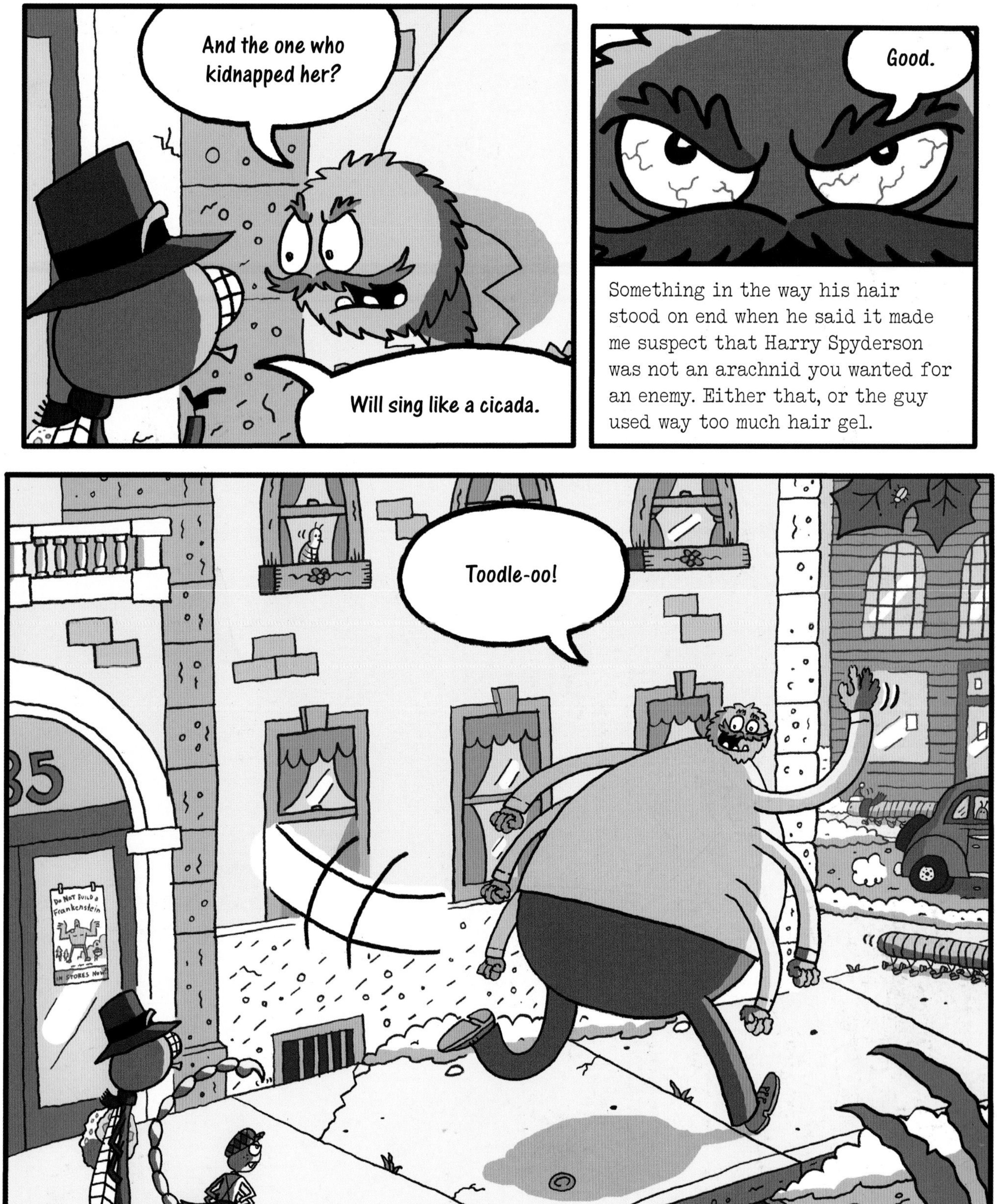
And the one who kidnapped her?
Will sing like a cicada.
Good.
Something in the way his hair stood on end when he said it made me suspect that Harry Spyderson was not an arachnid you wanted for an enemy. Either that, or the guy used way too much hair gel.
Toodle-oo!
Do NOT BUILD a Frankenstein
IN STORES NOW!
Then again, maybe I was just being dramatic. Or a little afraid of spiders. Or both.

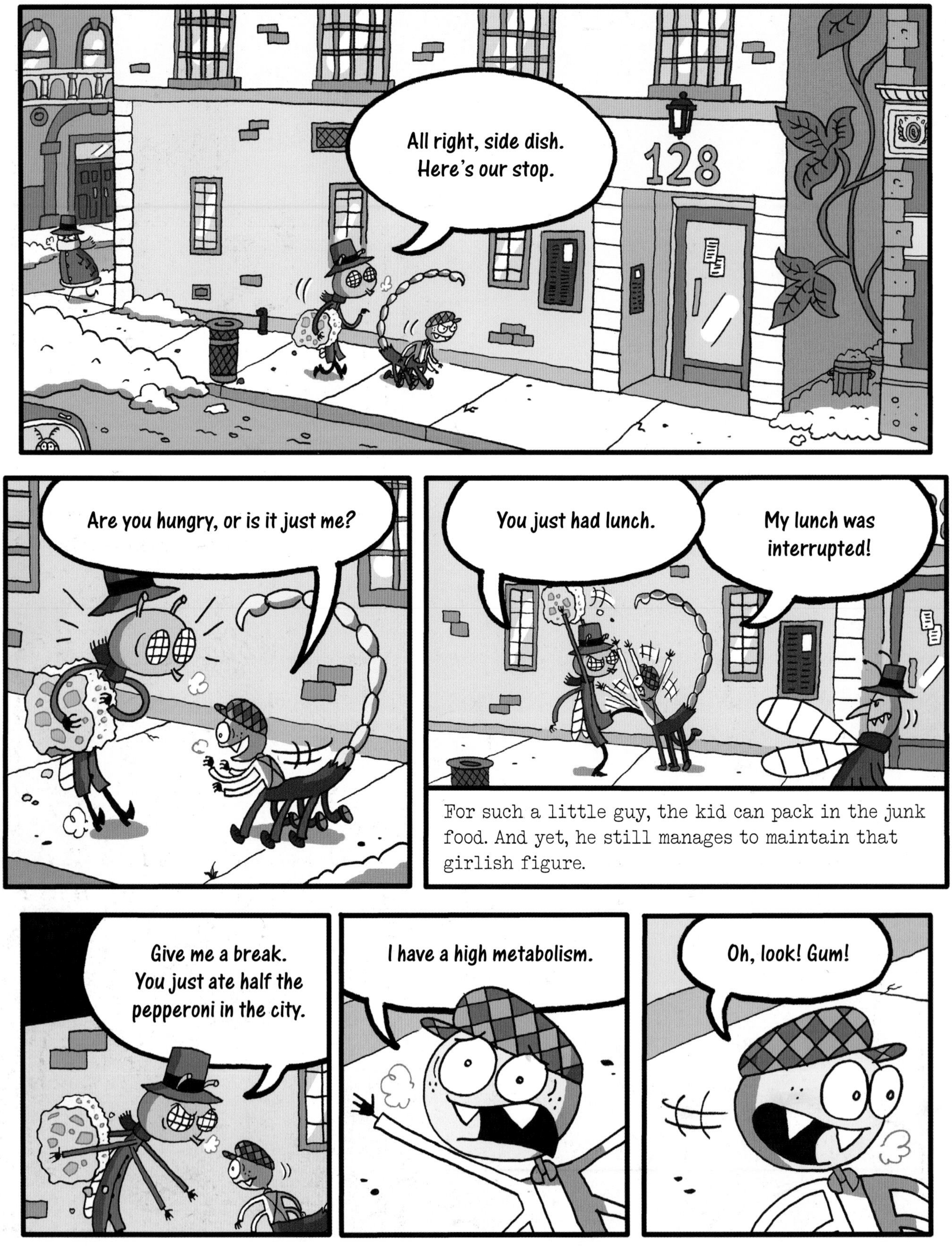
All right, side dish. Here's our stop.
128
Are you hungry, or is it just me?
You just had lunch.
My lunch was interrupted!
For such a little guy, the kid can pack in the junk food. And yet, he still manages to maintain that girlish figure.
Give me a break. You just ate half the pepperoni in the city.
I have a high metabolism.
Oh, look! Gum!

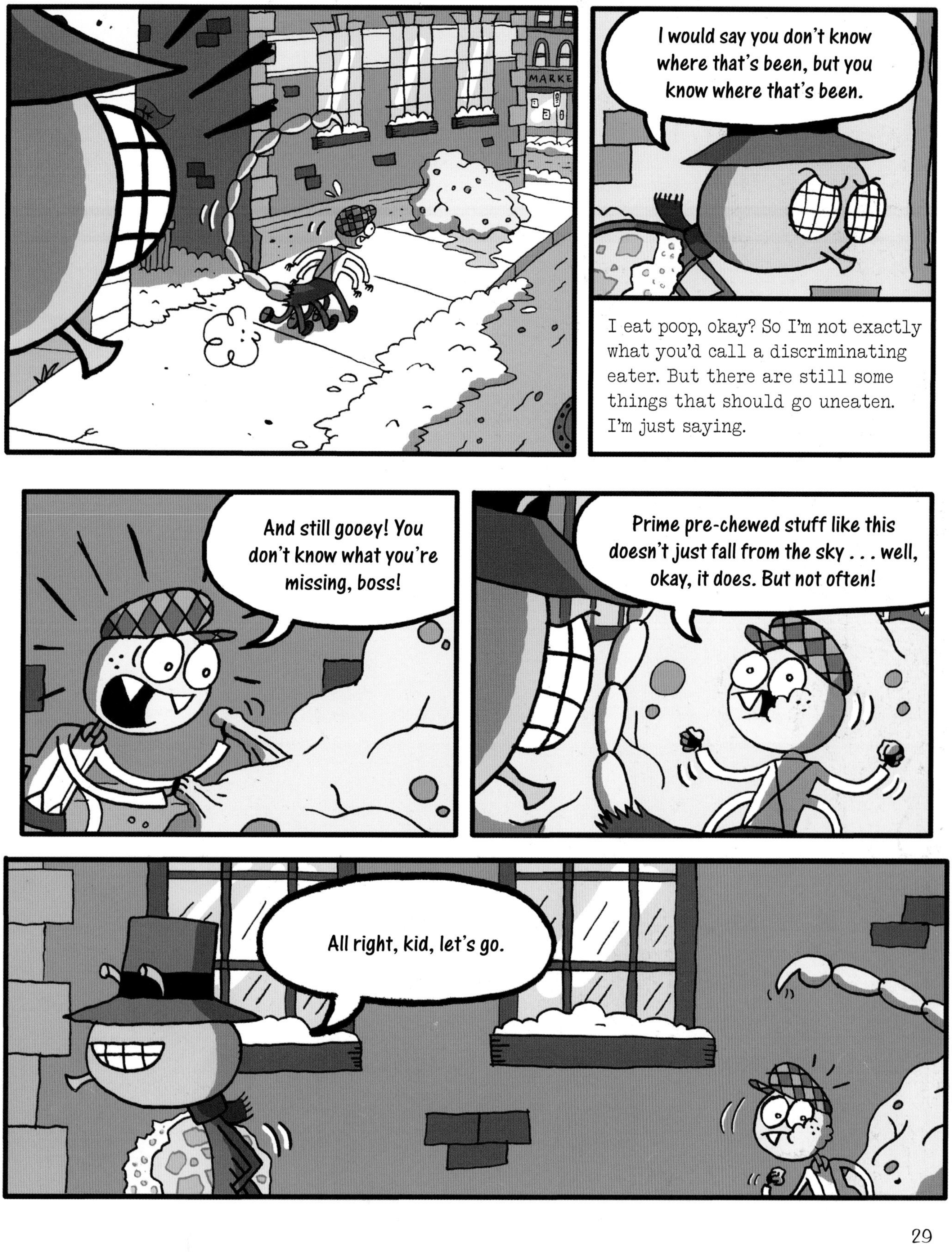
I would say you don't know where that's been, but you know where that's been.
I eat poop, okay? So I'm not exactly what you'd call a discriminating eater. But there are still some things that should go uneaten. I'm just saying.
And still gooey! You don't know what you're missing, boss!
Prime pre-chewed stuff like this doesn't just fall from the sky . . . well, okay, it does. But not often!
All right, kid, let's go.

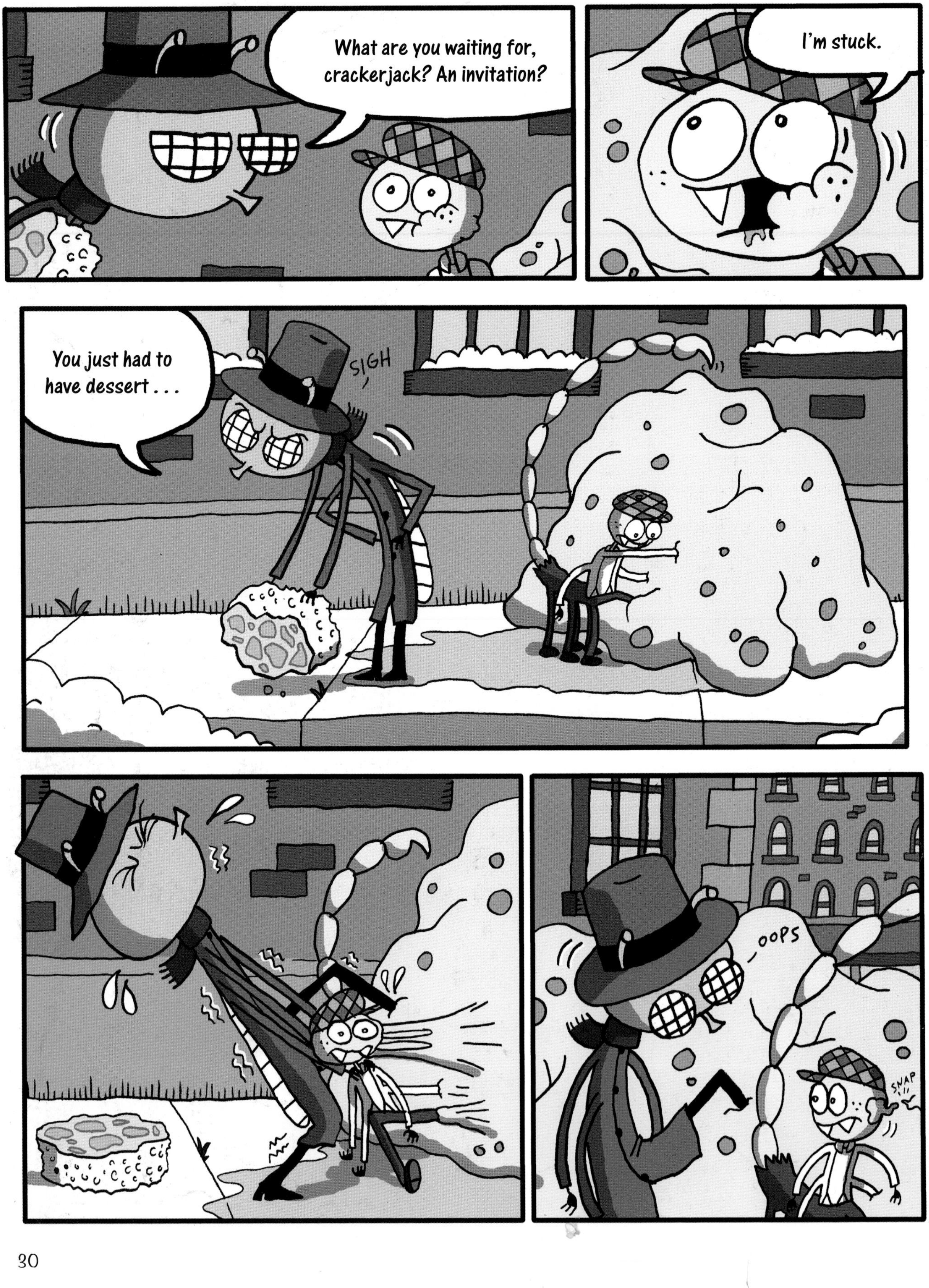
What are you waiting for, crackerjack? An invitation?
I'm stuck.
You just had to have dessert . . .
SIGH
OOPS
SNAP

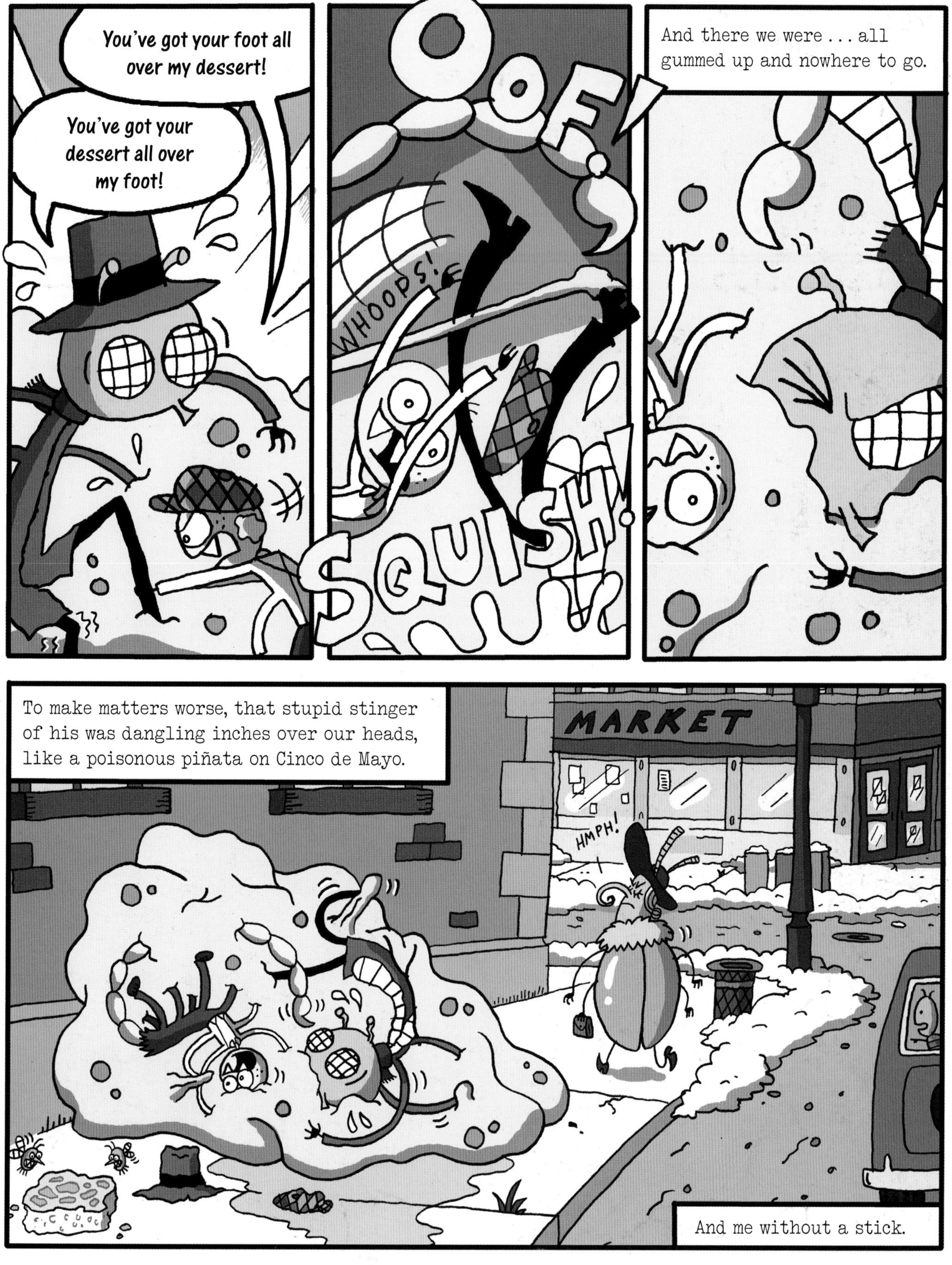

You've got your foot all over my dessert!
You've got your dessert all over my foot!
OOF!
WHOOPS!
SQUISH!
And there we were . . . all gummed up and nowhere to go.
To make matters worse, that stupid stinger of his was dangling inches over our heads, like a poisonous piñata on Cinco de Mayo.
MARKET
HMPH!
And me without a stick.

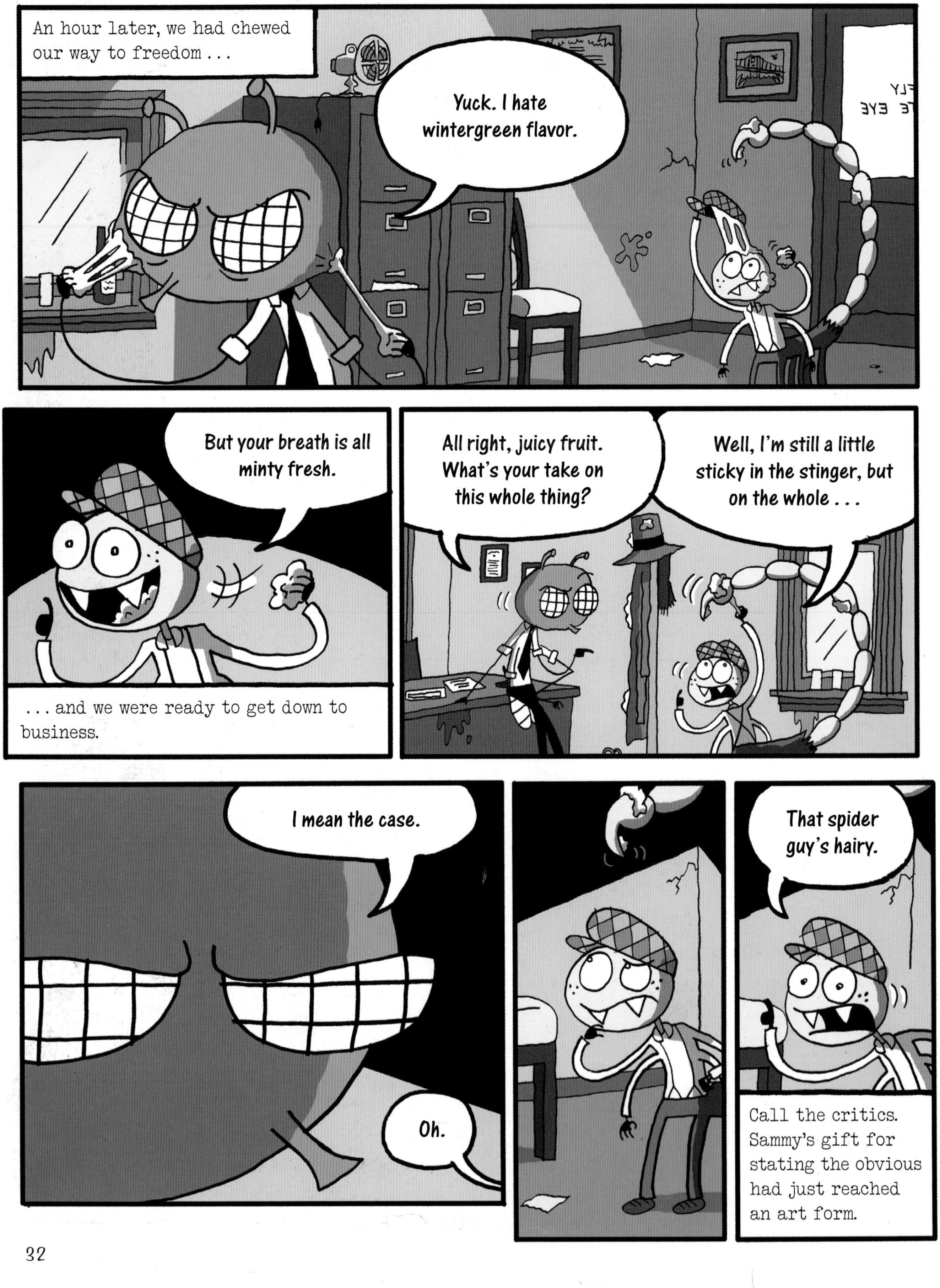
An hour later, we had chewed our way to freedom . . .
Yuck. I hate wintergreen flavor.
But your breath is all minty fresh.
. . . and we were ready to get down to business.
All right, juicy fruit. What's your take on this whole thing?
Well, I'm still a little sticky in the stinger, but on the whole . . .
I mean the case.
Oh.
That spider guy's hairy.
Call the critics. Sammy's gift for stating the obvious had just reached an art form.

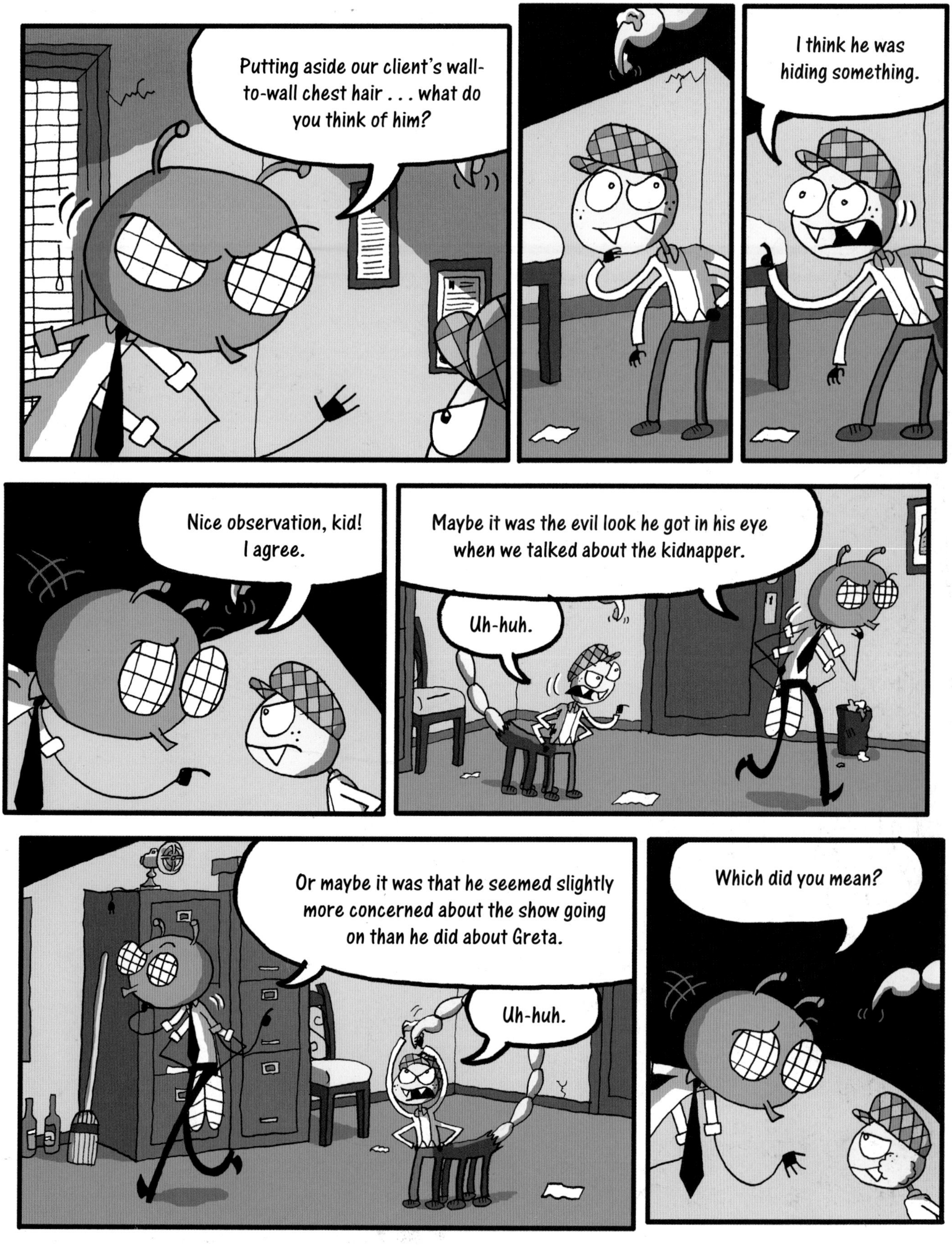
Putting aside our client's wall-to-wall chest hair . . . what do you think of him?
I think he was hiding something.
Nice observation, kid! I agree.
Maybe it was the evil look he got in his eye when we talked about the kidnapper.
Uh-huh.
Or maybe it was that he seemed slightly more concerned about the show going on than he did about Greta.
Uh-huh.
Which did you mean?

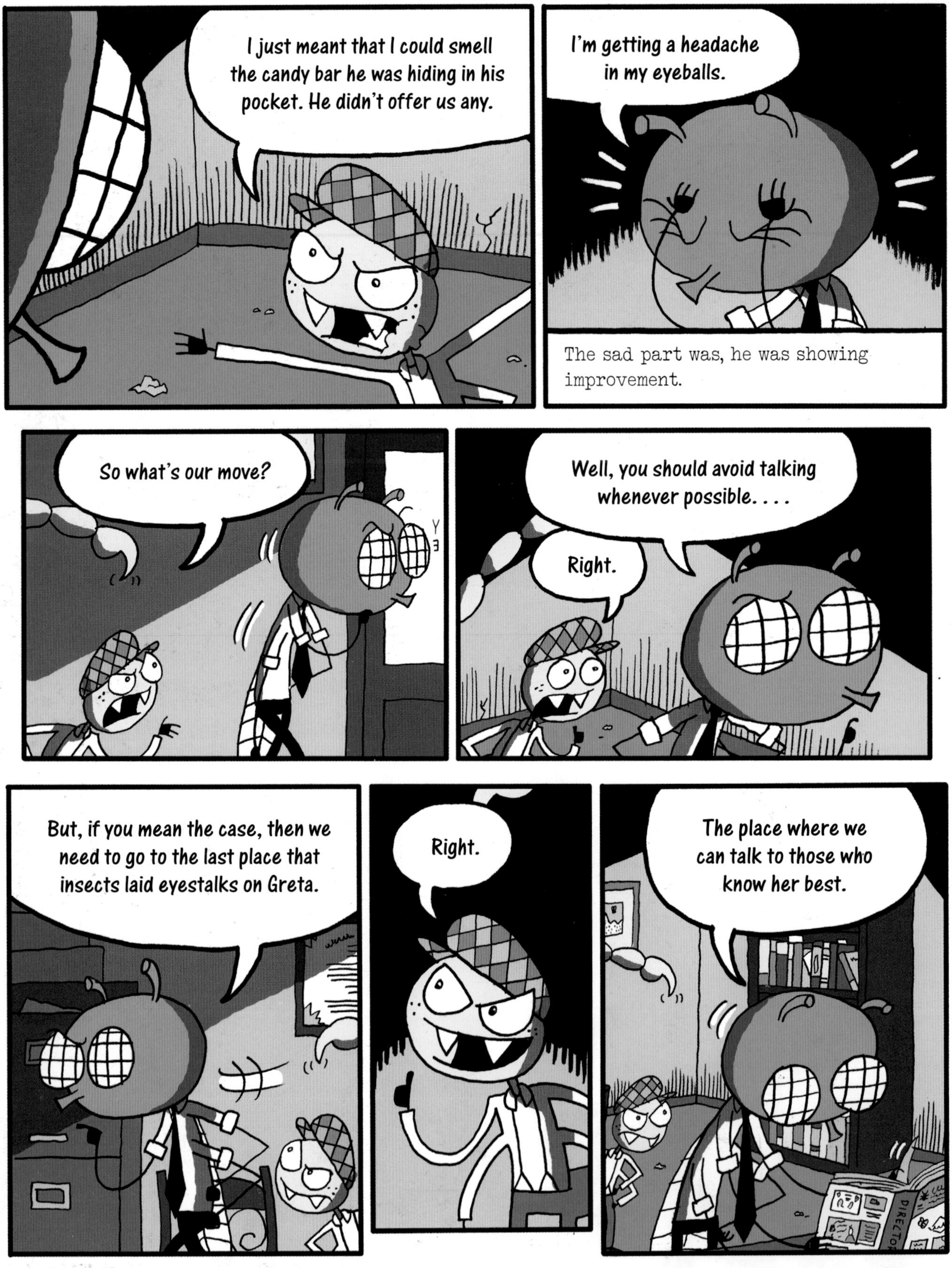
I just meant that I could smell the candy bar he was hiding in his pocket. He didn't offer us any.
I'm getting a headache in my eyeballs.
The sad part was, he was showing improvement.
So what's our move?
Well, you should avoid talking whenever possible. . . .
Right.
But, if you mean the case, then we need to go to the last place that insects laid eyestalks on Greta.
Right.
The place where we can talk to those who know her best.

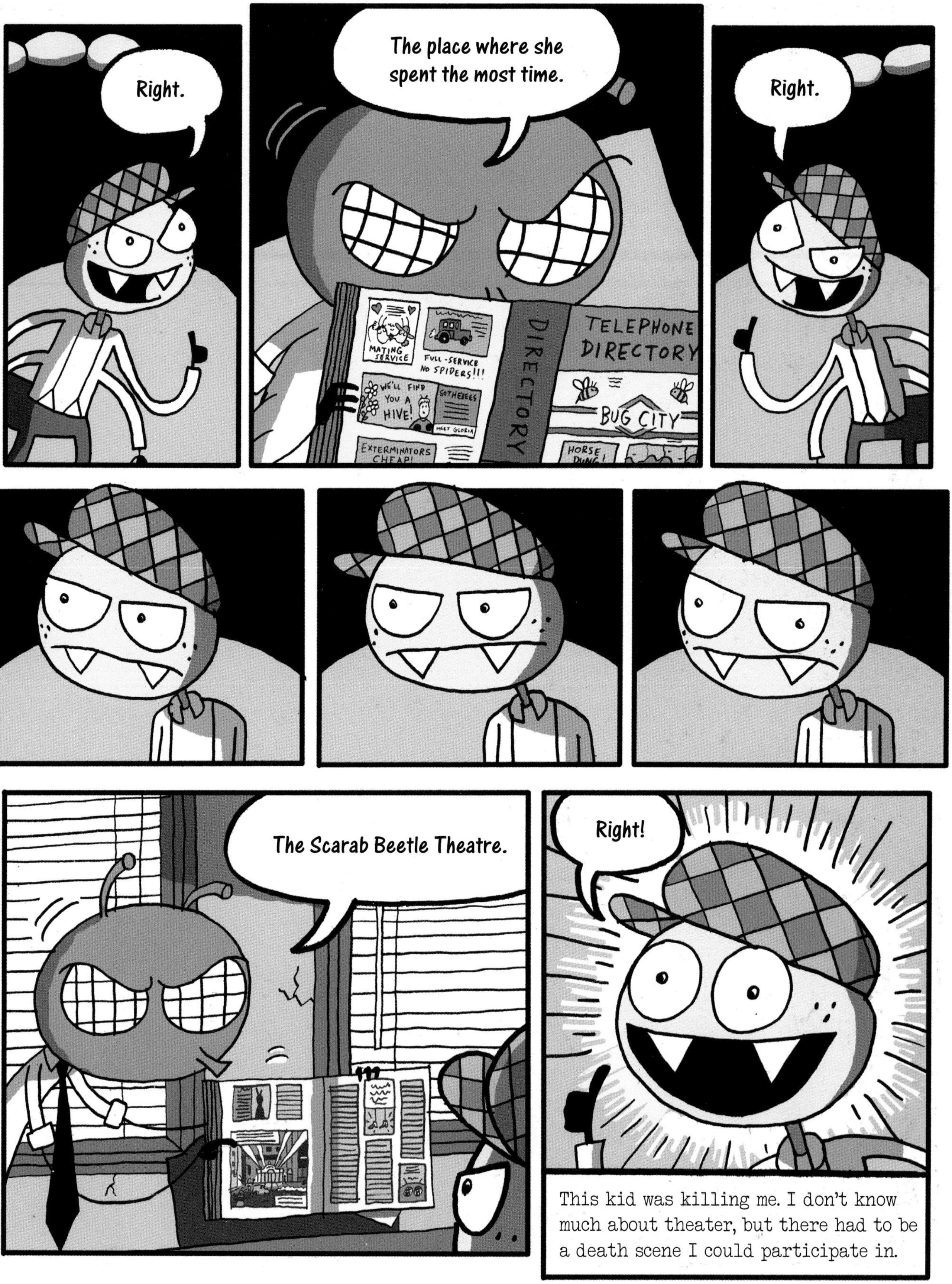
Right.
The place where she spent the most time.
TELEPHONE DIRECTORY
DIRECTORY
MATING SERVICE
FULL-SERVICE NO SPIDERS!!!
WE'LL FIND YOU A HIVE!
SOTHEBEES
MEET GLORIA
BUG CITY
Right.
The Scarab Beetle Theatre.
Right!
This kid was killing me. I don't know much about theater, but there had to be a death scene I could participate in.

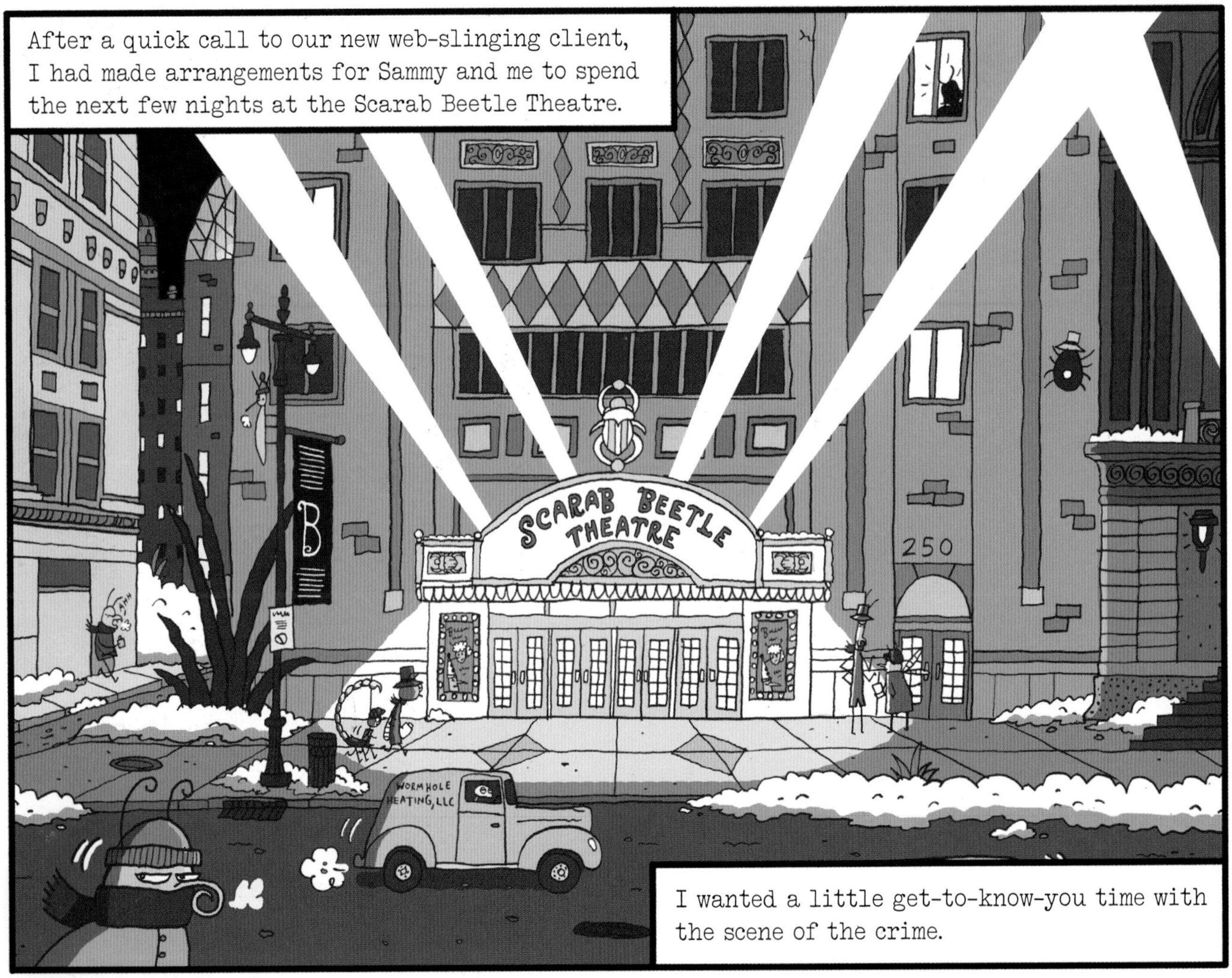
After a quick call to our new web-slinging client, I had made arrangements for Sammy and me to spend the next few nights at the Scarab Beetle Theatre.
SCARAB BEETLE THEATRE
250
WORMHOLE HEATING, LLC
B
I wanted a little get-to-know-you time with the scene of the crime.

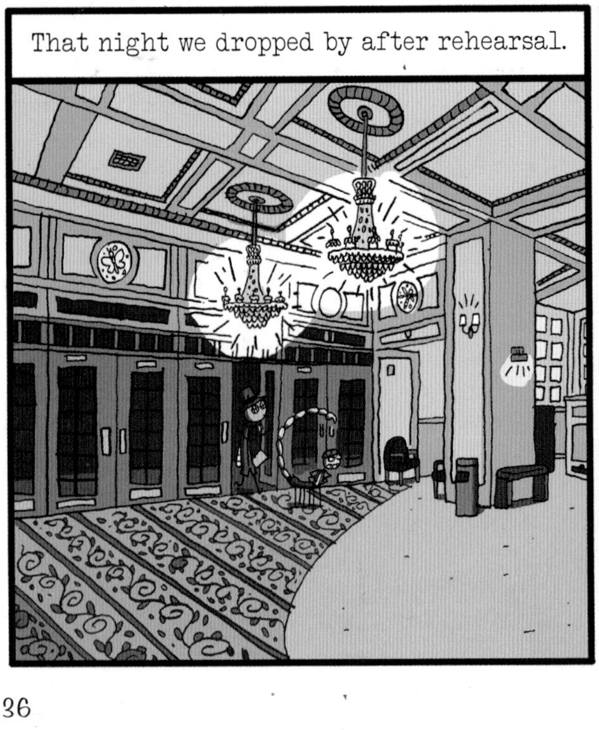
That night we dropped by after rehearsal.

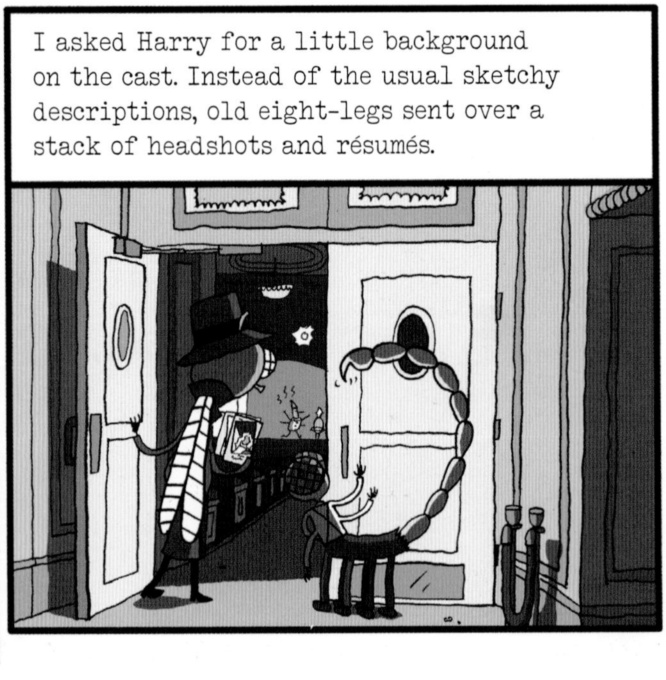
I asked Harry for a little background on the cast. Instead of the usual sketchy descriptions, old eight-legs sent over a stack of headshots and résumés.

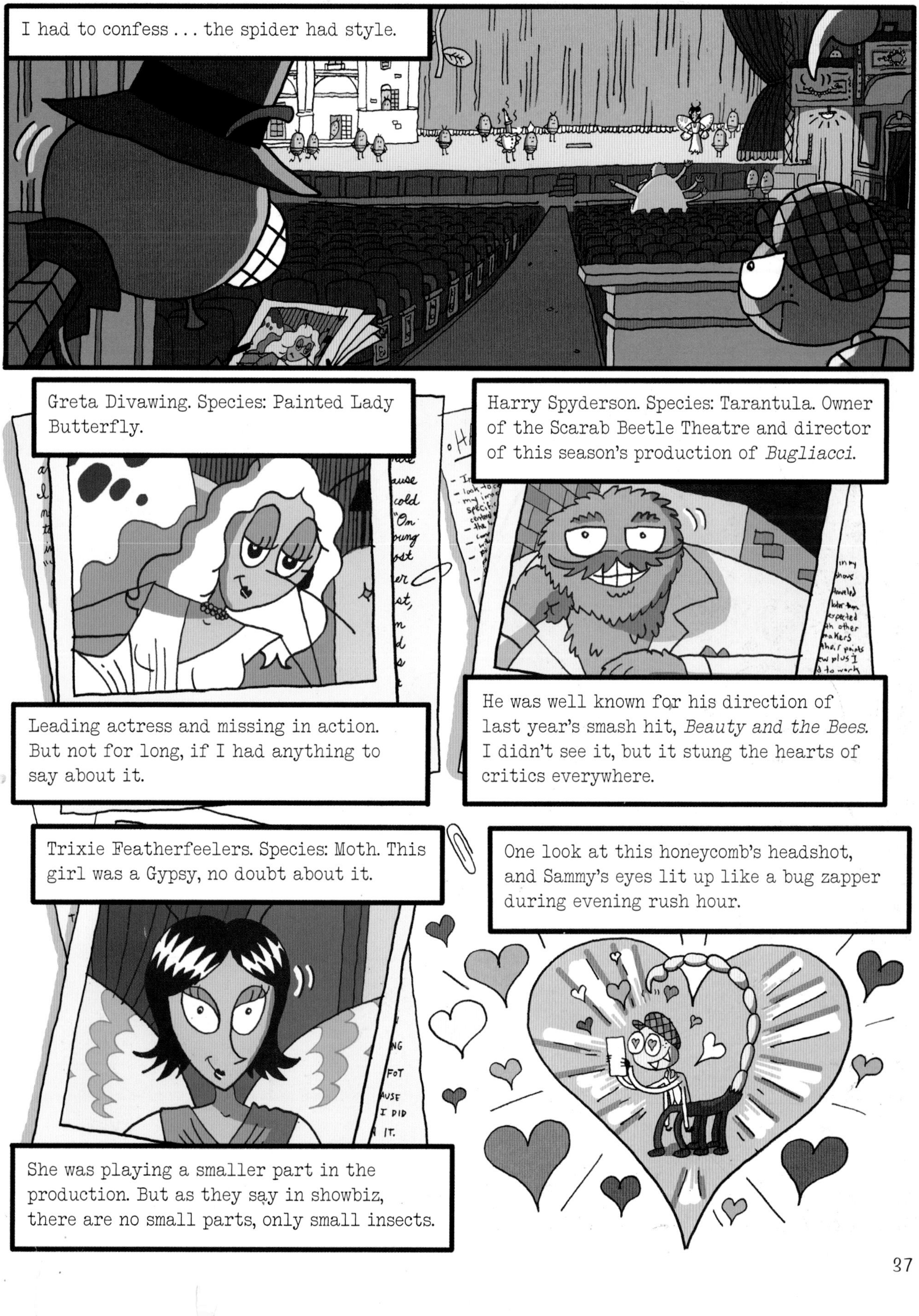
I had to confess . . . the spider had style.
Greta Divawing. Species: Painted Lady Butterfly.
Leading actress and missing in action. But not for long, if I had anything to say about it.
Harry Spyderson. Species: Tarantula. Owner of the Scarab Beetle Theatre and director of this season's production of *Bugliacci*.
He was well known for his direction of last year's smash hit, *Beauty and the Bees.* I didn't see it, but it stung the hearts of critics everywhere.
Trixie Featherfeelers. Species: Moth. This girl was a Gypsy, no doubt about it.
She was playing a smaller part in the production. But as they say in showbiz, there are no small parts, only small insects.
One look at this honeycomb's headshot, and Sammy's eyes lit up like a bug zapper during evening rush hour.

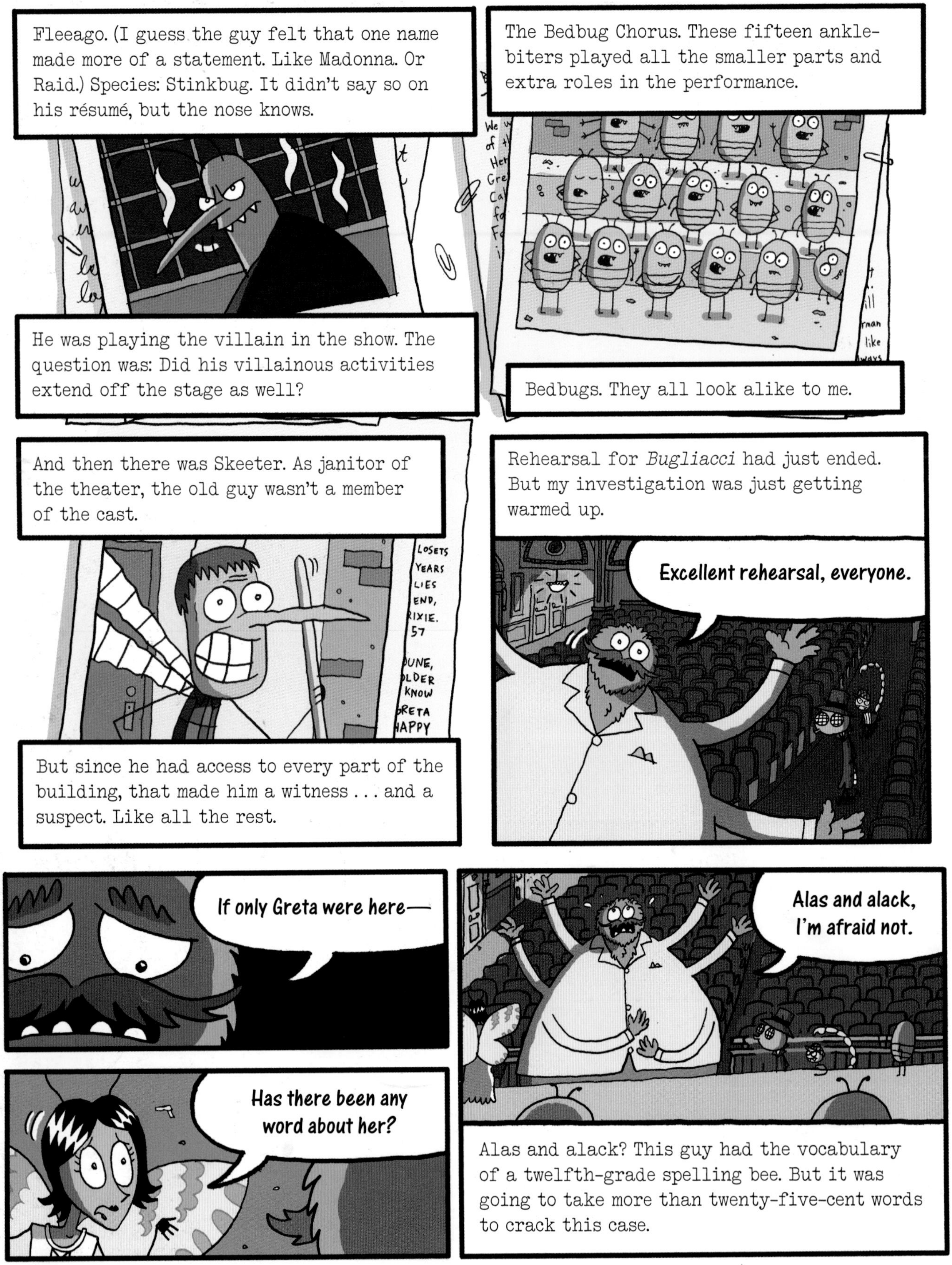

Fleeago. (I guess the guy felt that one name made more of a statement. Like Madonna. Or Raid.) Species: Stinkbug. It didn't say so on his résumé, but the nose knows.
He was playing the villain in the show. The question was: Did his villainous activities extend off the stage as well?
The Bedbug Chorus. These fifteen ankle-biters played all the smaller parts and extra roles in the performance.
Bedbugs. They all look alike to me.
And then there was Skeeter. As janitor of the theater, the old guy wasn't a member of the cast.
But since he had access to every part of the building, that made him a witness . . . and a suspect. Like all the rest.
Rehearsal for *Bugliacci* had just ended. But my investigation was just getting warmed up.
Excellent rehearsal, everyone.
If only Greta were here—
Has there been any word about her?
Alas and alack, I'm afraid not.
Alas and alack? This guy had the vocabulary of a twelfth-grade spelling bee. But it was going to take more than twenty-five-cent words to crack this case.

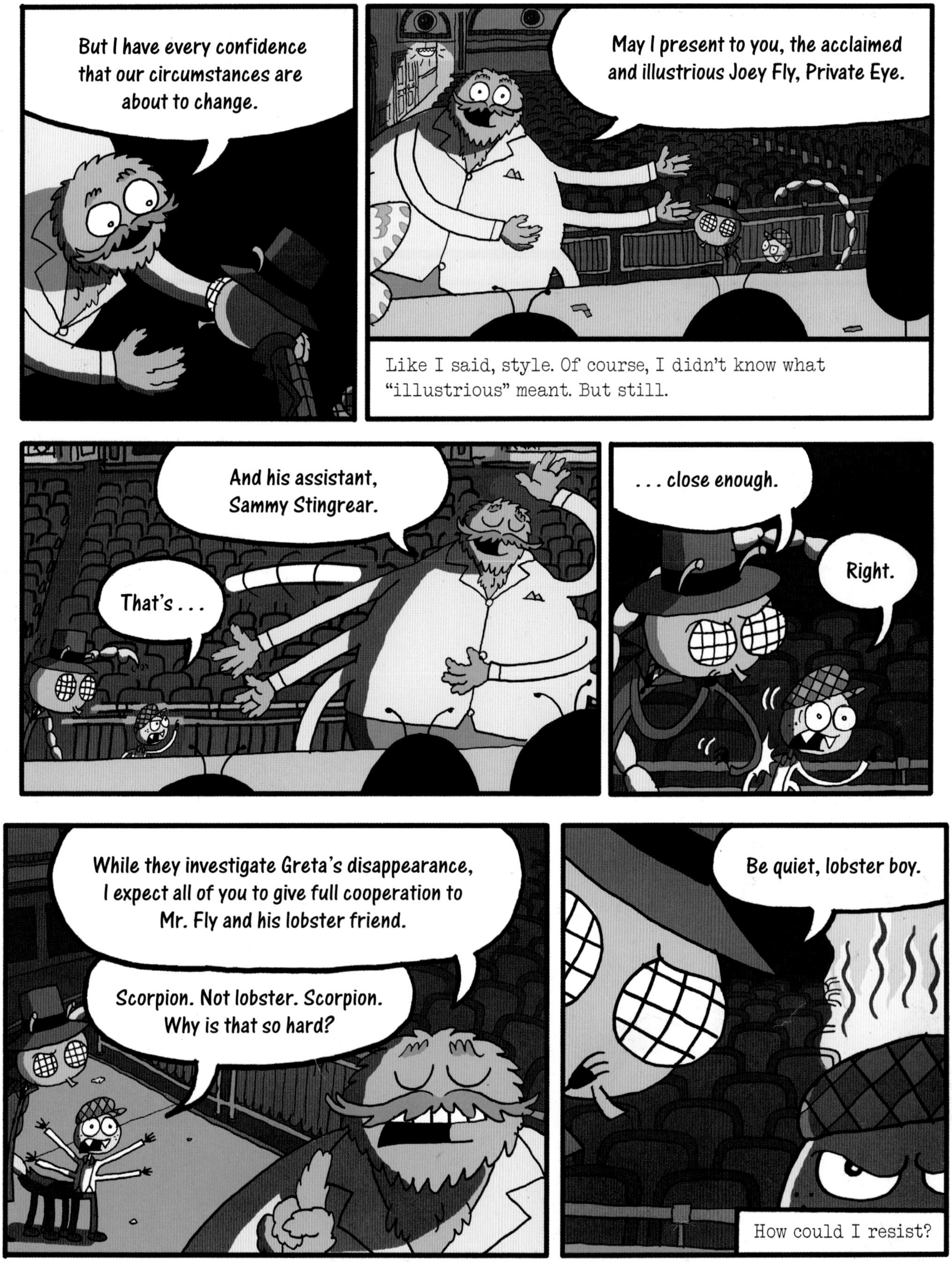

But I have every confidence that our circumstances are about to change.
May I present to you, the acclaimed and illustrious Joey Fly, Private Eye.
Like I said, style. Of course, I didn't know what "illustrious" meant. But still.
And his assistant, Sammy Stingrear.
That's . . .
. . . close enough.
Right.
While they investigate Greta's disappearance, I expect all of you to give full cooperation to Mr. Fly and his lobster friend.
Scorpion. Not lobster. Scorpion. Why is that so hard?
Be quiet, lobster boy.
How could I resist?

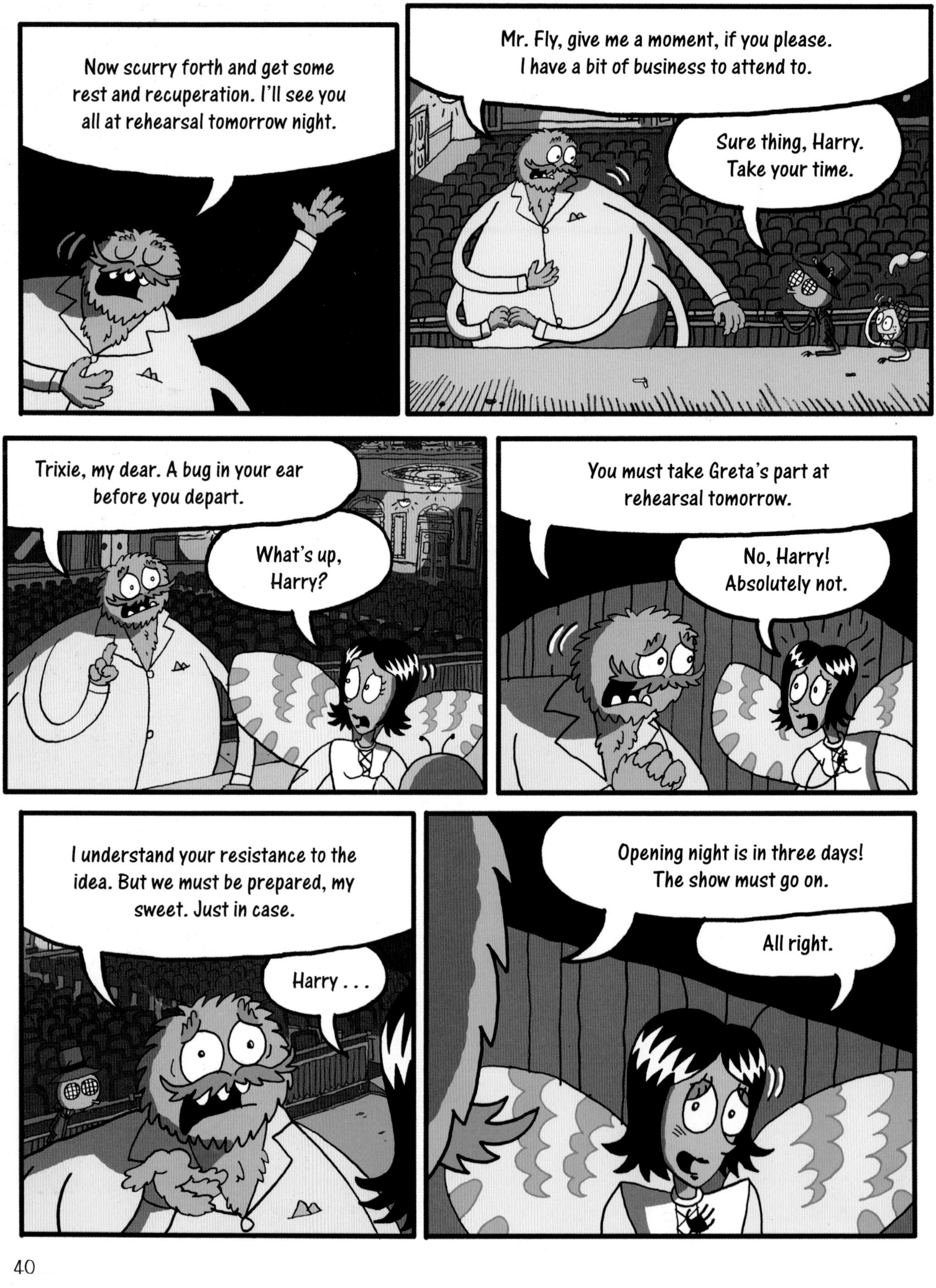
Now scurry forth and get some rest and recuperation. I'll see you all at rehearsal tomorrow night.
Mr. Fly, give me a moment, if you please. I have a bit of business to attend to.
Sure thing, Harry. Take your time.
Trixie, my dear. A bug in your ear before you depart.
What's up, Harry?
You must take Greta's part at rehearsal tomorrow.
No, Harry! Absolutely not.
I understand your resistance to the idea. But we must be prepared, my sweet. Just in case.
Harry . . .
Opening night is in three days! The show must go on.
All right.

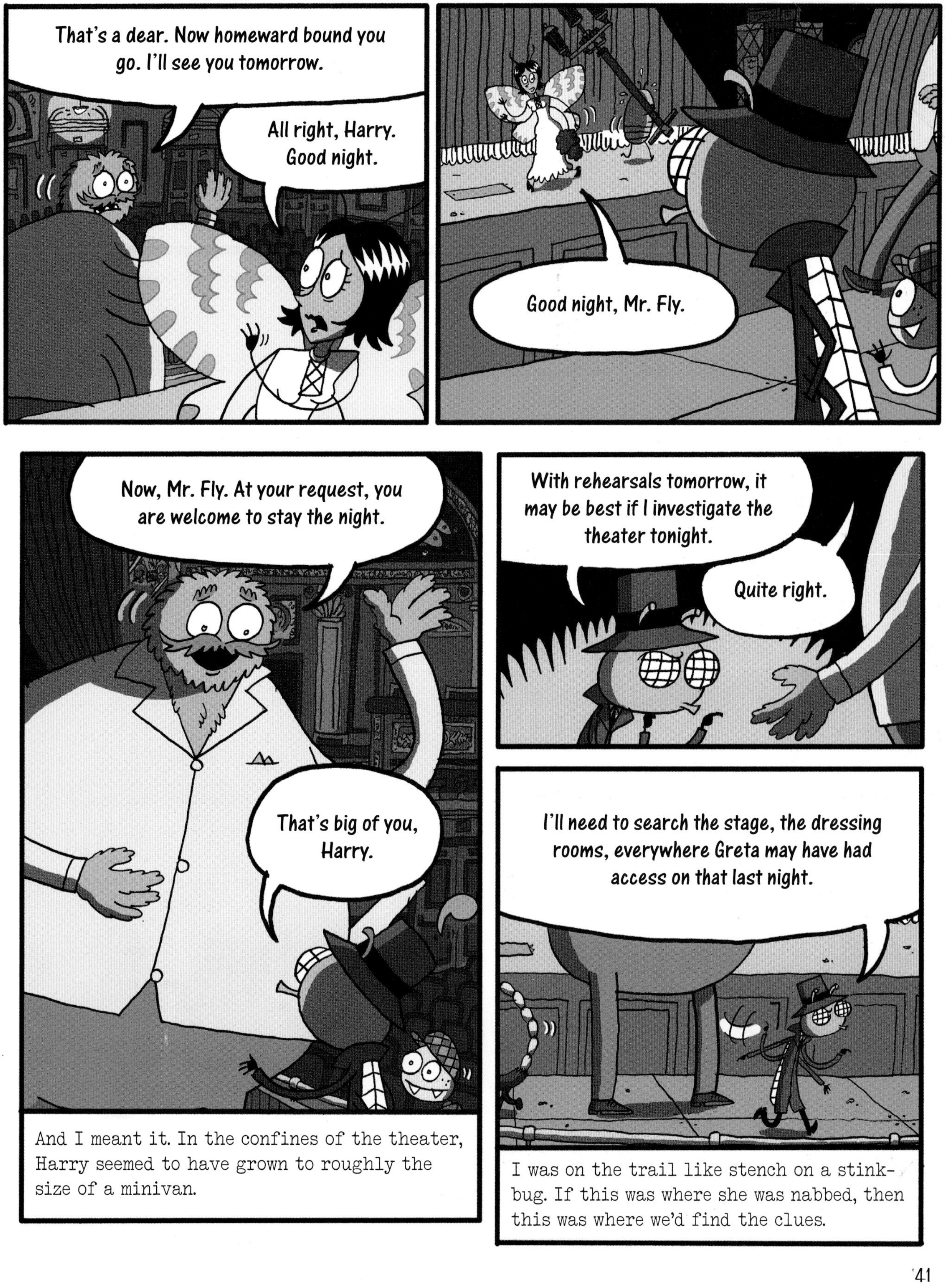
That's a dear. Now homeward bound you go. I'll see you tomorrow.
All right, Harry. Good night.
Good night, Mr. Fly.
Now, Mr. Fly. At your request, you are welcome to stay the night.
That's big of you, Harry.
And I meant it. In the confines of the theater, Harry seemed to have grown to roughly the size of a minivan.
With rehearsals tomorrow, it may be best if I investigate the theater tonight.
Quite right.
I'll need to search the stage, the dressing rooms, everywhere Greta may have had access on that last night.
I was on the trail like stench on a stink-bug. If this was where she was nabbed, then this was where we'd find the clues.

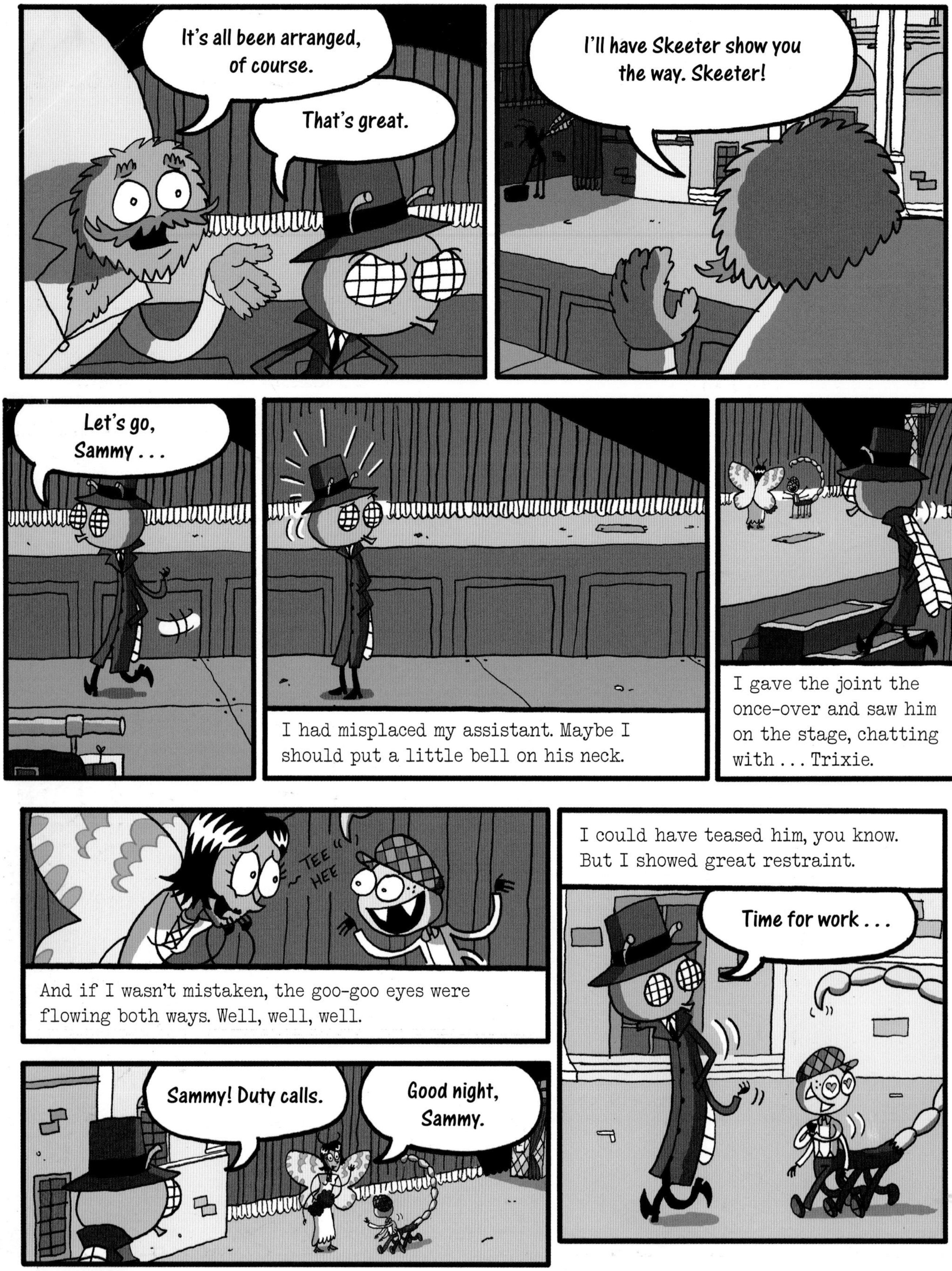
It's all been arranged, of course.
That's great.
I'll have Skeeter show you the way. Skeeter!
Let's go, Sammy . . .
I had misplaced my assistant. Maybe I should put a little bell on his neck.
I gave the joint the once-over and saw him on the stage, chatting with . . . Trixie.
TEE HEE
And if I wasn't mistaken, the goo-goo eyes were flowing both ways. Well, well, well.
I could have teased him, you know. But I showed great restraint.
Time for work . . .
Sammy! Duty calls.
Good night, Sammy.

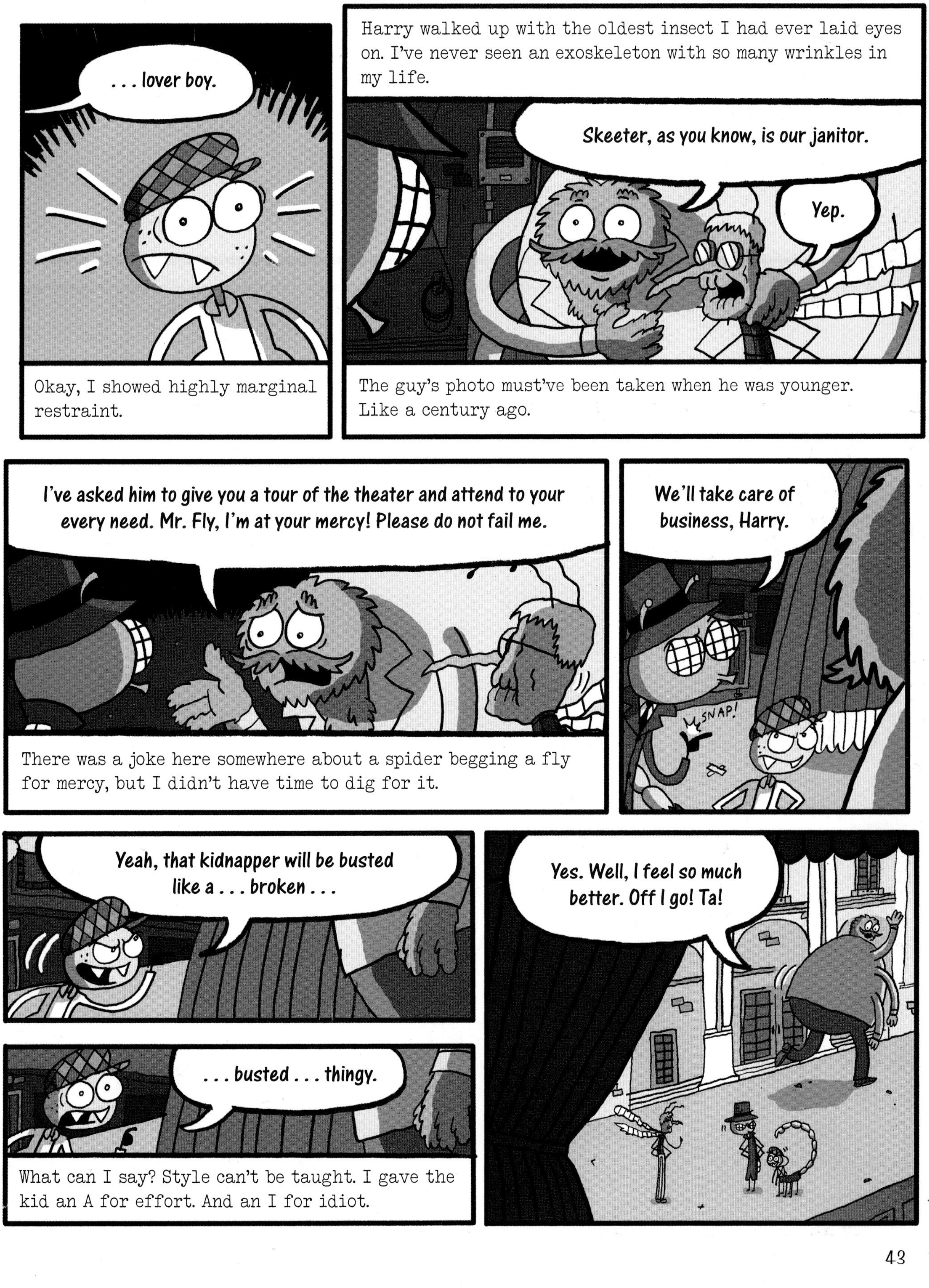
... lover boy.
Okay, I showed highly marginal restraint.
Harry walked up with the oldest insect I had ever laid eyes on. I've never seen an exoskeleton with so many wrinkles in my life.
Skeeter, as you know, is our janitor.
Yep.
The guy's photo must've been taken when he was younger. Like a century ago.
I've asked him to give you a tour of the theater and attend to your every need. Mr. Fly, I'm at your mercy! Please do not fail me.
There was a joke here somewhere about a spider begging a fly for mercy, but I didn't have time to dig for it.
We'll take care of business, Harry.
SNAP!
Yeah, that kidnapper will be busted like a . . . broken . . .
. . . busted . . . thingy.
What can I say? Style can't be taught. I gave the kid an A for effort. And an I for idiot.
Yes. Well, I feel so much better. Off I go! Ta!

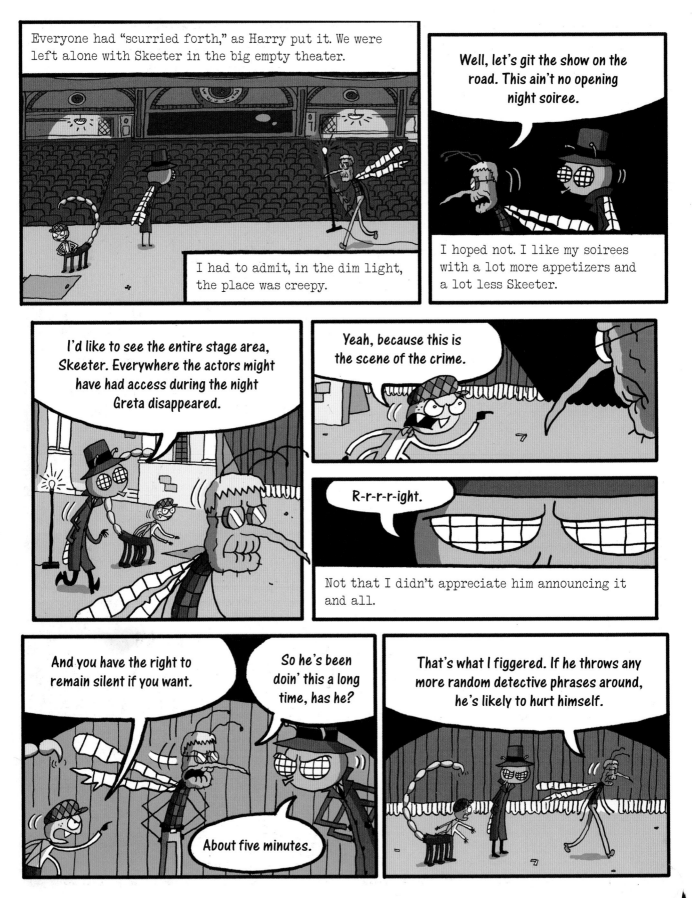

Everyone had "scurried forth," as Harry put it. We were left alone with Skeeter in the big empty theater.

I had to admit, in the dim light, the place was creepy.

Well, let's git the show on the road. This ain't no opening night soiree.

I hoped not. I like my soirees with a lot more appetizers and a lot less Skeeter.

I'd like to see the entire stage area, Skeeter. Everywhere the actors might have had access during the night Greta disappeared.

Yeah, because this is the scene of the crime.

R-r-r-r-ight.

Not that I didn't appreciate him announcing it and all.

And you have the right to remain silent if you want.

So he's been doin' this a long time, has he?

About five minutes.

That's what I figgered. If he throws any more random detective phrases around, he's likely to hurt himself.

44

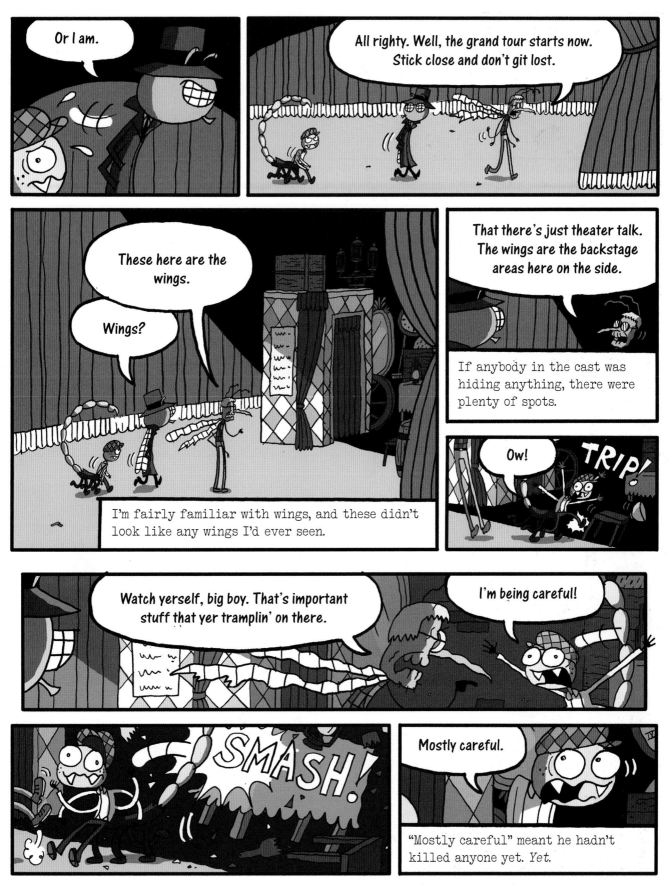

Or I am.
All righty. Well, the grand tour starts now. Stick close and don't git lost.
These here are the wings.
Wings?
I'm fairly familiar with wings, and these didn't look like any wings I'd ever seen.
That there's just theater talk. The wings are the backstage areas here on the side.
If anybody in the cast was hiding anything, there were plenty of spots.
Ow!
TRIP!
Watch yerself, big boy. That's important stuff that yer tramplin' on there.
I'm being careful!
SMASH!
Mostly careful.
"Mostly careful" meant he hadn't killed anyone yet. *Yet.*

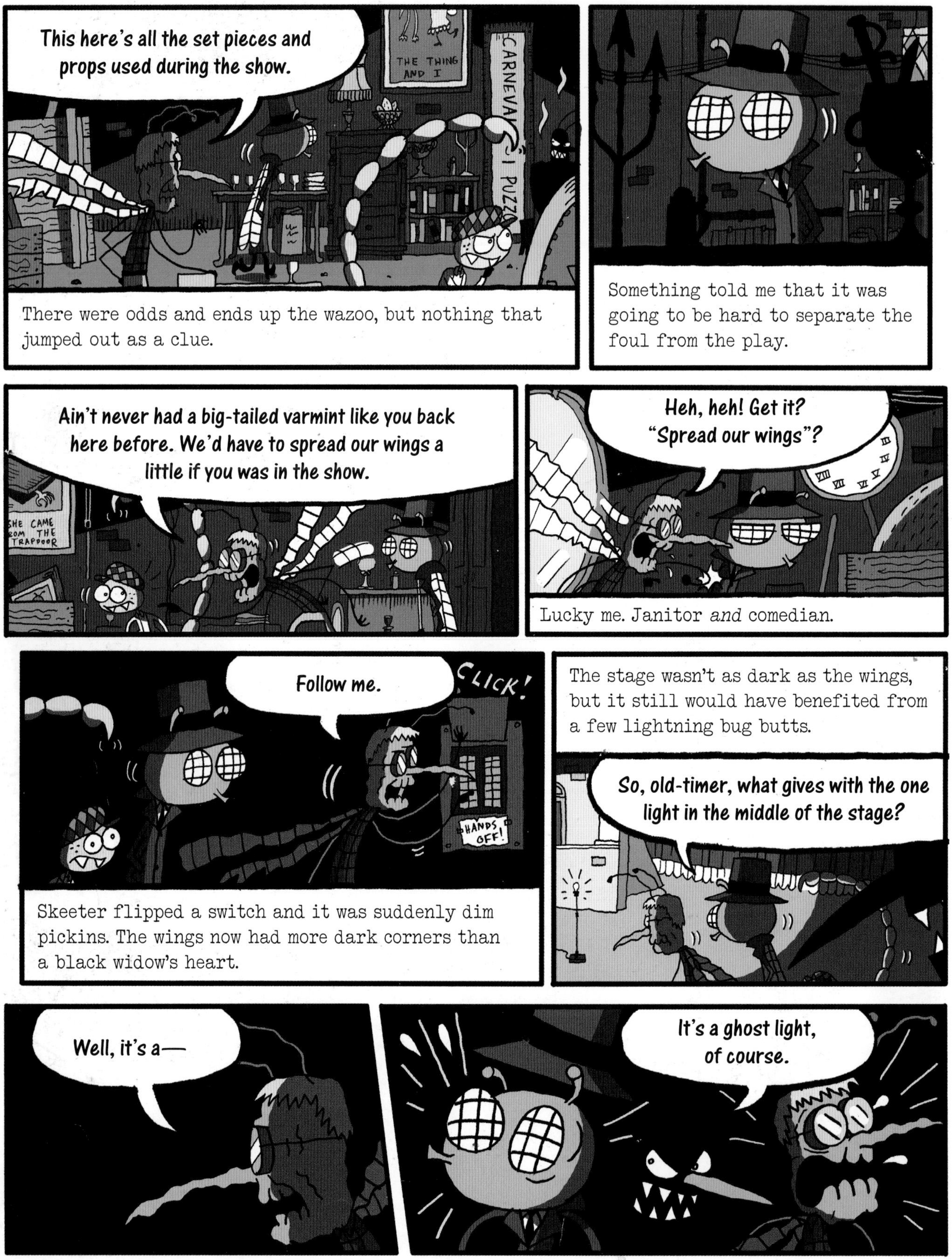
This here's all the set pieces and props used during the show.
THE THING AND I
CARNEVA
There were odds and ends up the wazoo, but nothing that jumped out as a clue.
Something told me that it was going to be hard to separate the foul from the play.
Ain't never had a big-tailed varmint like you back here before. We'd have to spread our wings a little if you was in the show.
SHE CAME FROM THE TRAPDOOR
Heh, heh! Get it? "Spread our wings"?
Lucky me. Janitor *and* comedian.
Follow me.
CLICK!
HANDS OFF!
Skeeter flipped a switch and it was suddenly dim pickins. The wings now had more dark corners than a black widow's heart.
The stage wasn't as dark as the wings, but it still would have benefited from a few lightning bug butts.
So, old-timer, what gives with the one light in the middle of the stage?
Well, it's a—
It's a ghost light, of course.

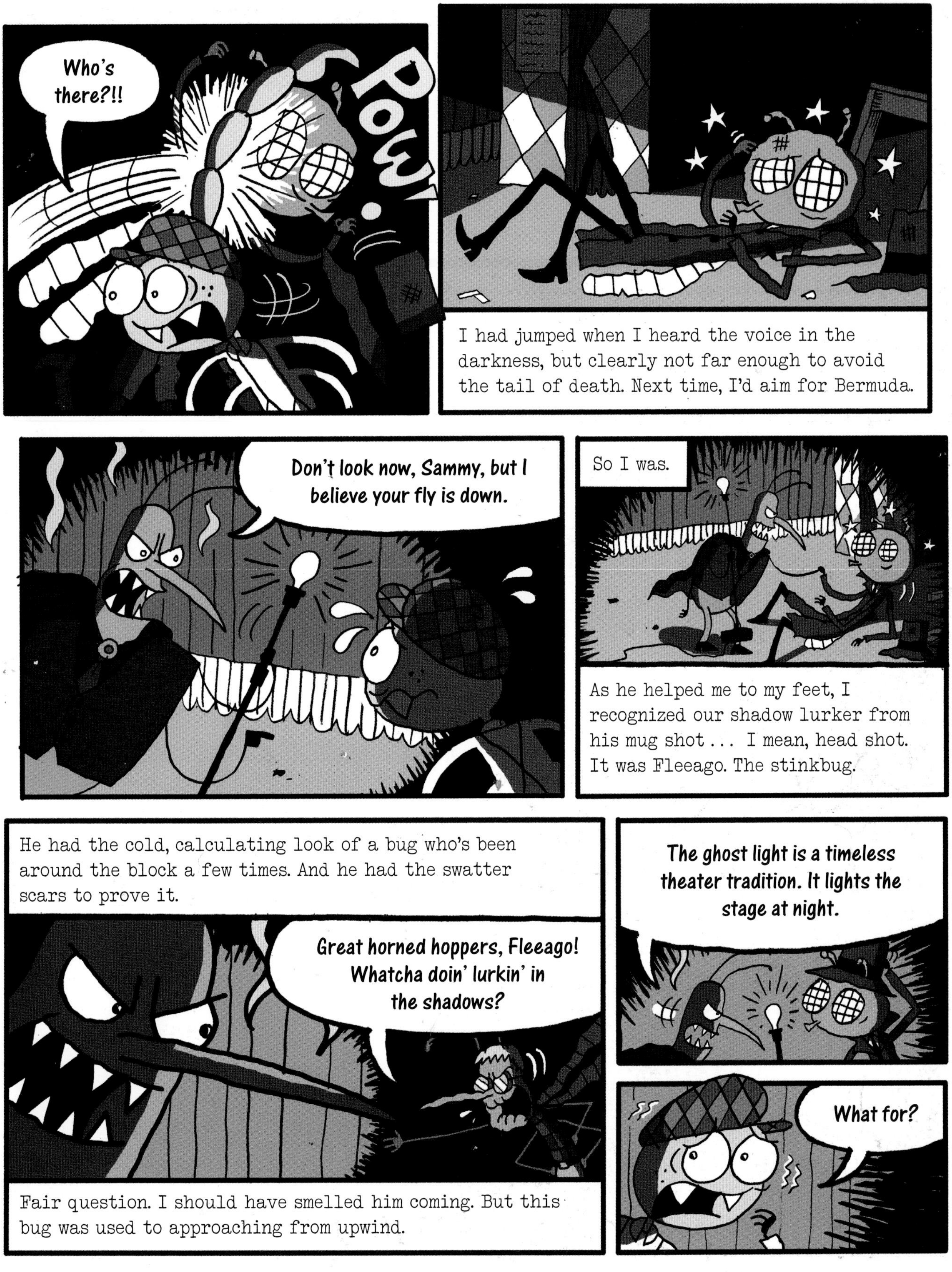
Who's there?!!
POW!
I had jumped when I heard the voice in the darkness, but clearly not far enough to avoid the tail of death. Next time, I'd aim for Bermuda.
Don't look now, Sammy, but I believe your fly is down.
So I was.
As he helped me to my feet, I recognized our shadow lurker from his mug shot . . . I mean, head shot. It was Fleeago. The stinkbug.
He had the cold, calculating look of a bug who's been around the block a few times. And he had the swatter scars to prove it.
Great horned hoppers, Fleeago! Whatcha doin' lurkin' in the shadows?
Fair question. I should have smelled him coming. But this bug was used to approaching from upwind.
The ghost light is a timeless theater tradition. It lights the stage at night.
What for?

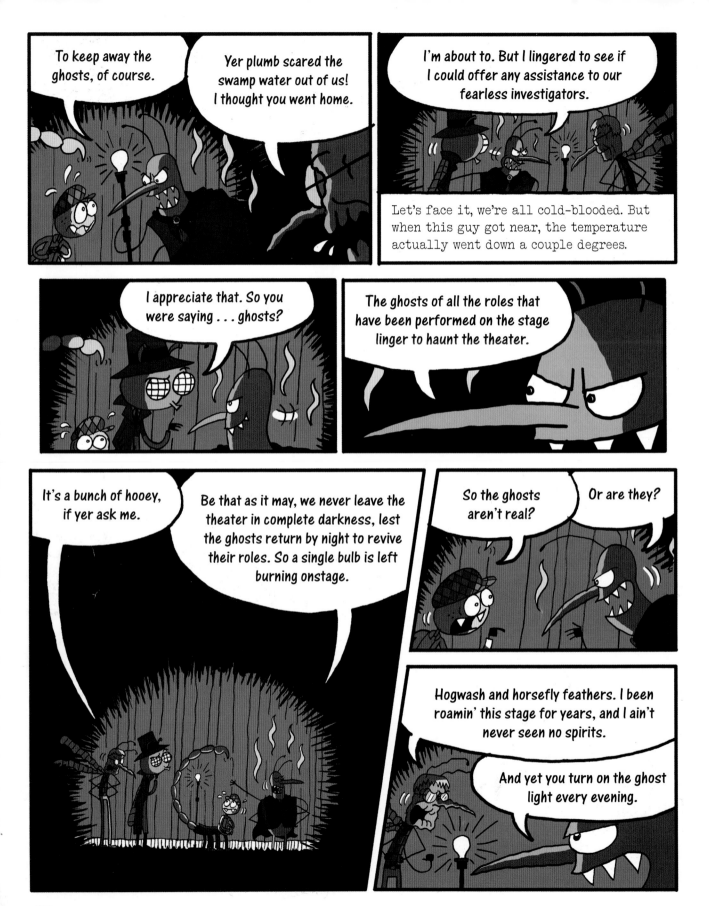

48

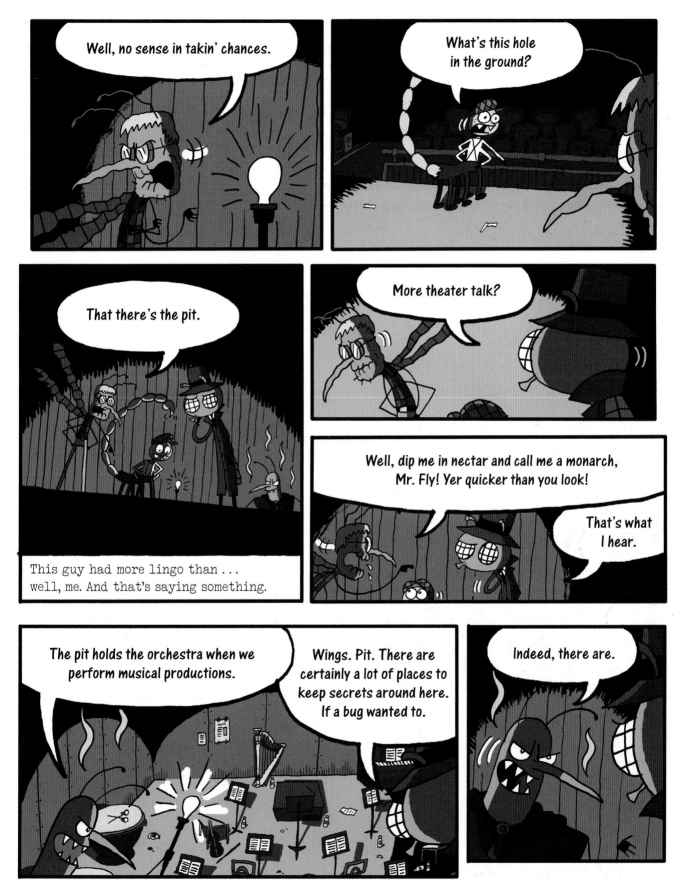

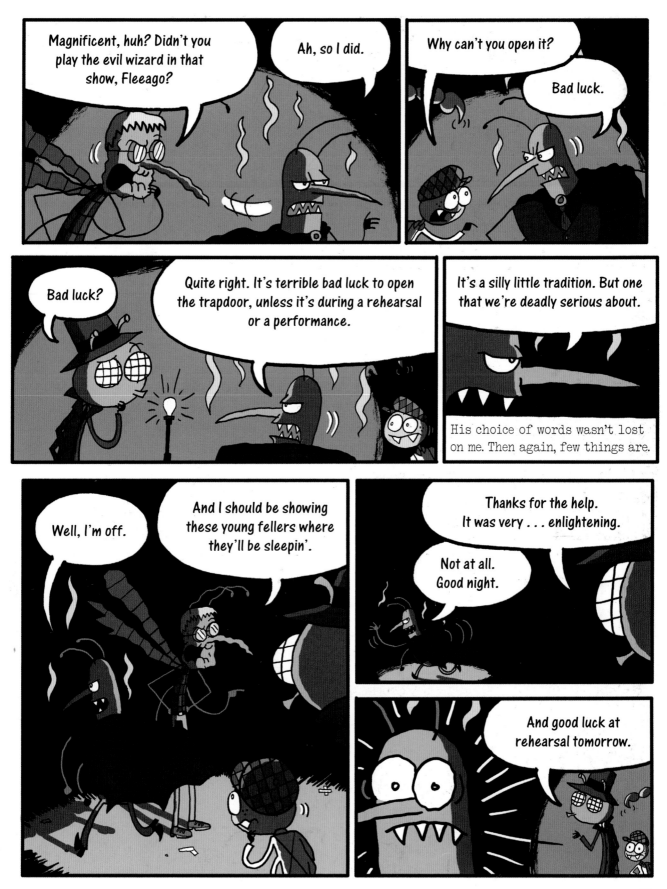

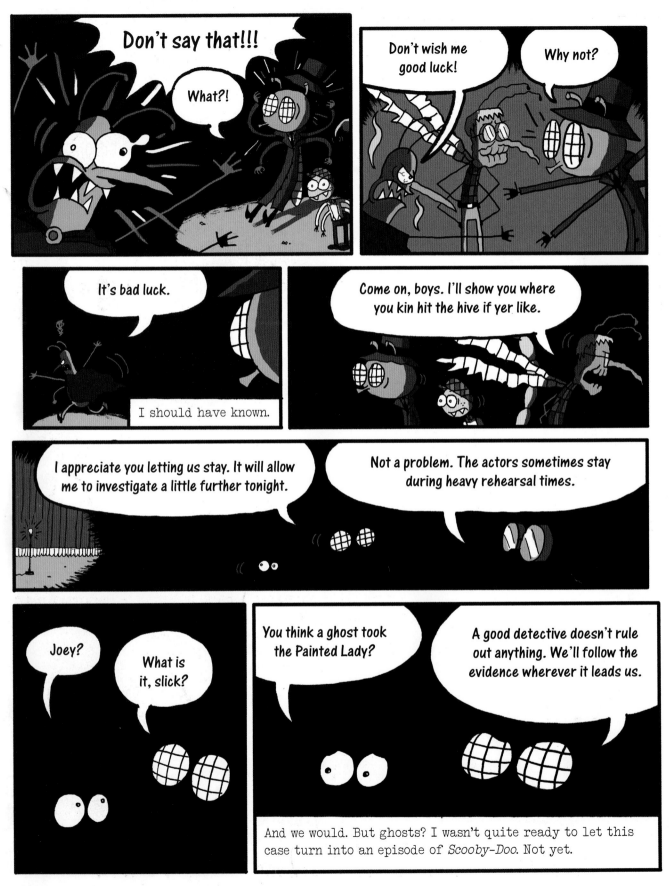

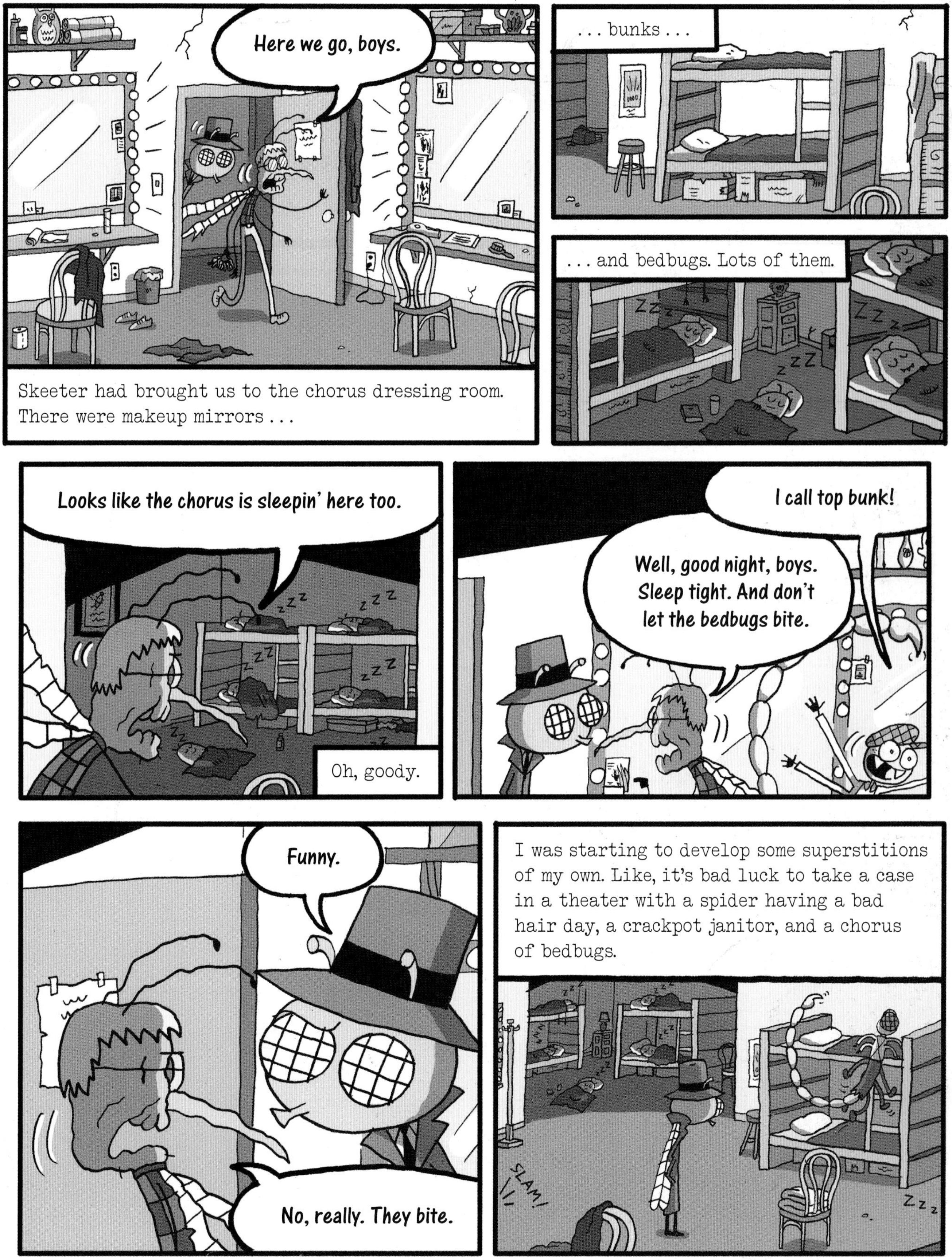
Here we go, boys.
Skeeter had brought us to the chorus dressing room. There were makeup mirrors . . .
. . . bunks . . .
. . . and bedbugs. Lots of them.
Looks like the chorus is sleepin' here too.
Oh, goody.
I call top bunk!
Well, good night, boys. Sleep tight. And don't let the bedbugs bite.
Funny.
No, really. They bite.
I was starting to develop some superstitions of my own. Like, it's bad luck to take a case in a theater with a spider having a bad hair day, a crackpot janitor, and a chorus of bedbugs.
SLAM!

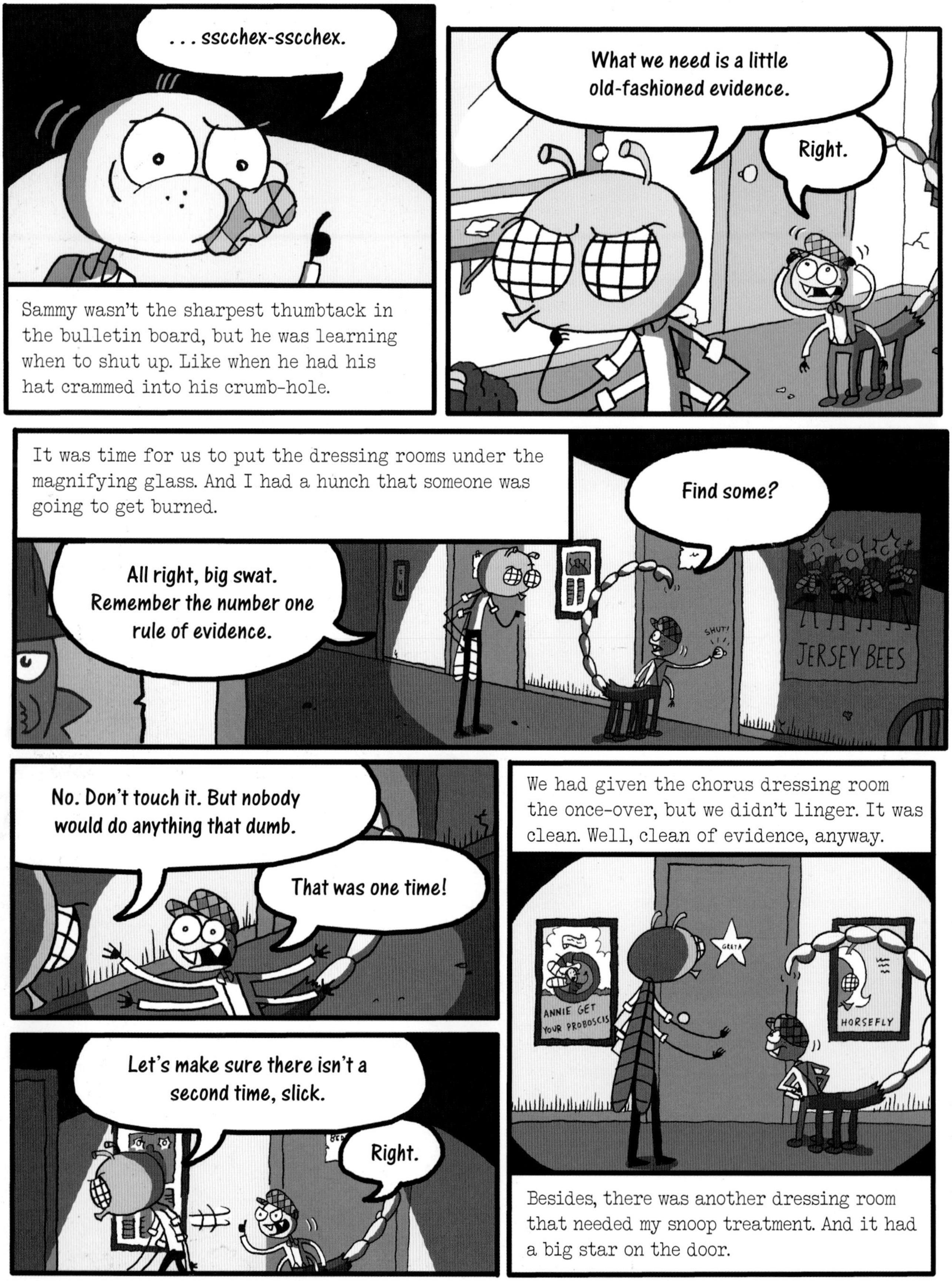
. . . sscchex-sscchex.
Sammy wasn't the sharpest thumbtack in the bulletin board, but he was learning when to shut up. Like when he had his hat crammed into his crumb-hole.
What we need is a little old-fashioned evidence.
Right.
It was time for us to put the dressing rooms under the magnifying glass. And I had a hunch that someone was going to get burned.
Find some?
All right, big swat. Remember the number one rule of evidence.
SHUT!
JERSEY BEES
No. Don't touch it. But nobody would do anything that dumb.
That was one time!
Let's make sure there isn't a second time, slick.
Right.
We had given the chorus dressing room the once-over, but we didn't linger. It was clean. Well, clean of evidence, anyway.
ANNIE GET YOUR PROBOSCIS
GRETA
HORSEFLY
Besides, there was another dressing room that needed my snoop treatment. And it had a big star on the door.

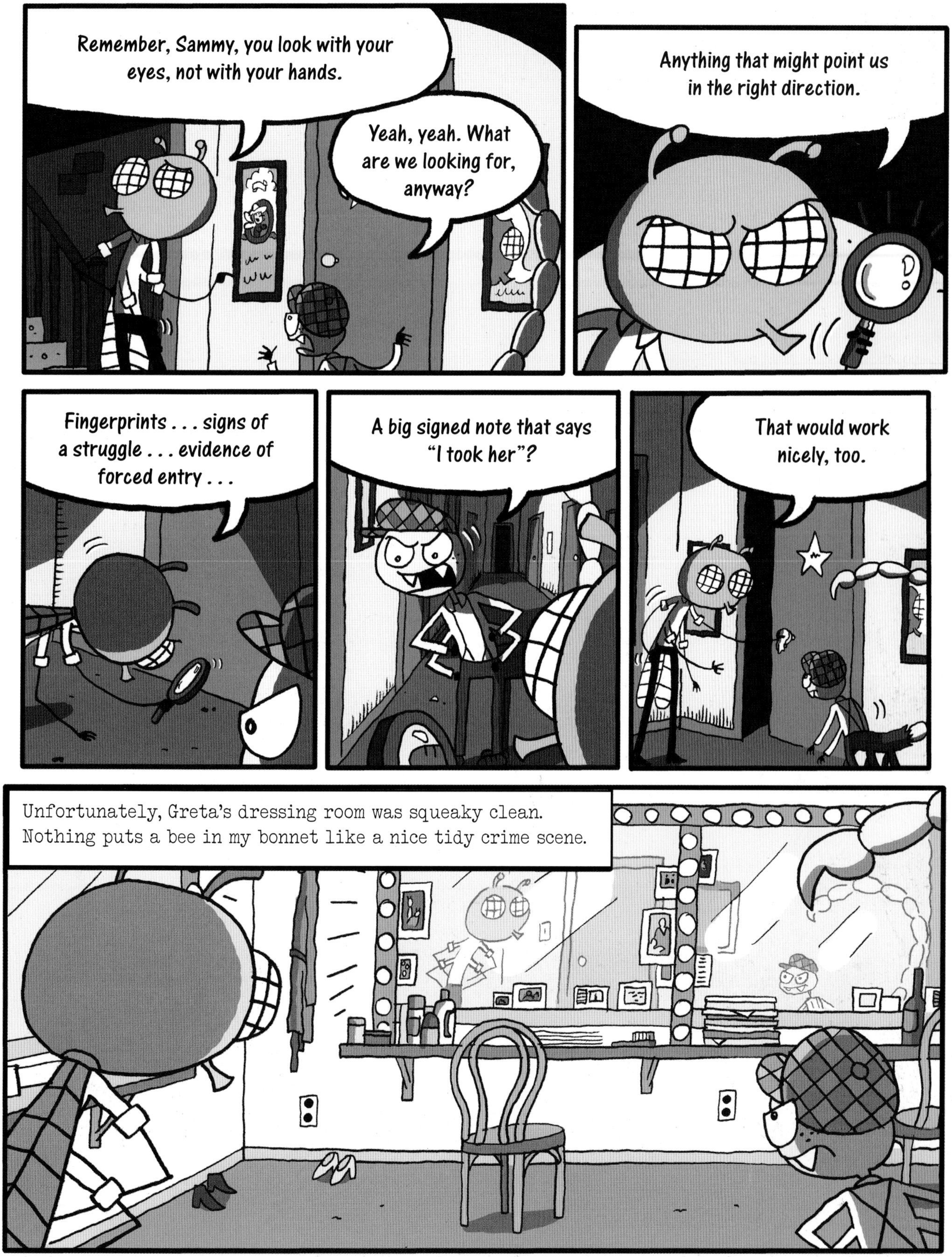
Remember, Sammy, you look with your eyes, not with your hands.
Yeah, yeah. What are we looking for, anyway?
Anything that might point us in the right direction.
Fingerprints . . . signs of a struggle . . . evidence of forced entry . . .
A big signed note that says "I took her"?
That would work nicely, too.
Unfortunately, Greta's dressing room was squeaky clean. Nothing puts a bee in my bonnet like a nice tidy crime scene.

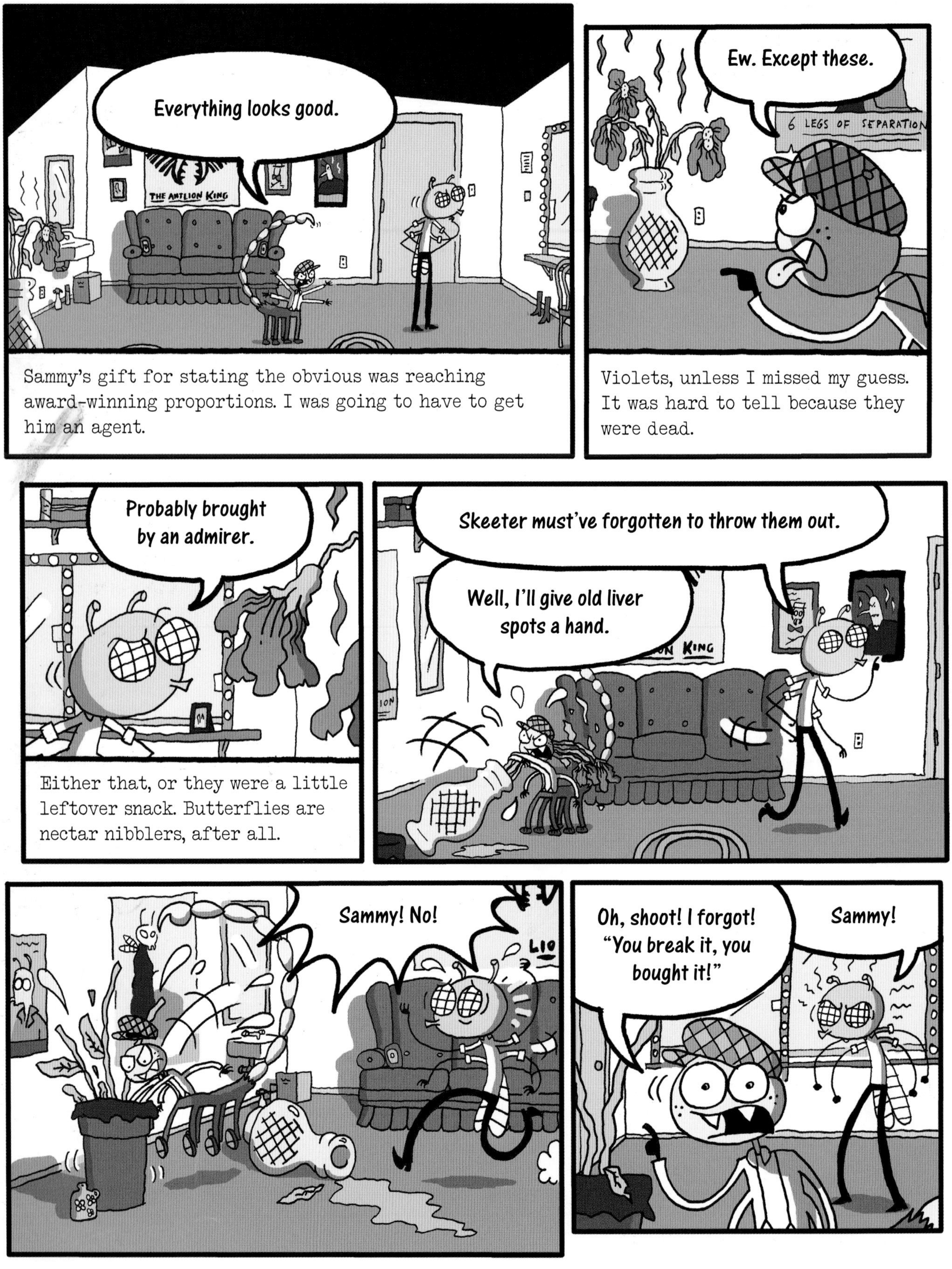
THE ANTLION KING
Everything looks good.
Sammy's gift for stating the obvious was reaching award-winning proportions. I was going to have to get him an agent.
Ew. Except these.
6 LEGS OF SEPARATION
Violets, unless I missed my guess. It was hard to tell because they were dead.
Probably brought by an admirer.
Either that, or they were a little leftover snack. Butterflies are nectar nibblers, after all.
Skeeter must've forgotten to throw them out.
Well, I'll give old liver spots a hand.
Sammy! No!
Oh, shoot! I forgot! "You break it, you bought it!"
Sammy!

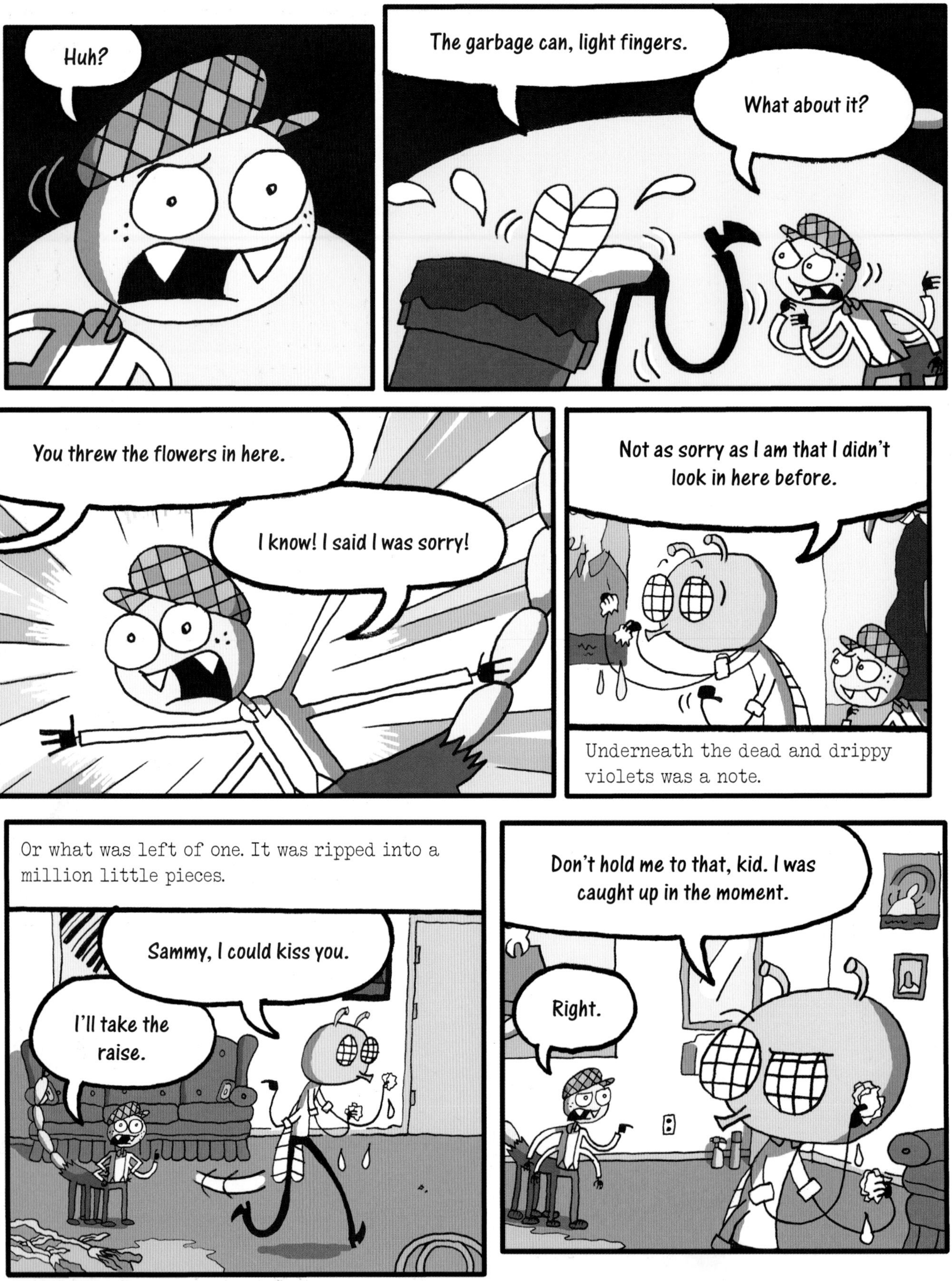
Huh?
The garbage can, light fingers.
What about it?
You threw the flowers in here.
I know! I said I was sorry!
Not as sorry as I am that I didn't look in here before.
Underneath the dead and drippy violets was a note.
Or what was left of one. It was ripped into a million little pieces.
Sammy, I could kiss you.
I'll take the raise.
Don't hold me to that, kid. I was caught up in the moment.
Right.

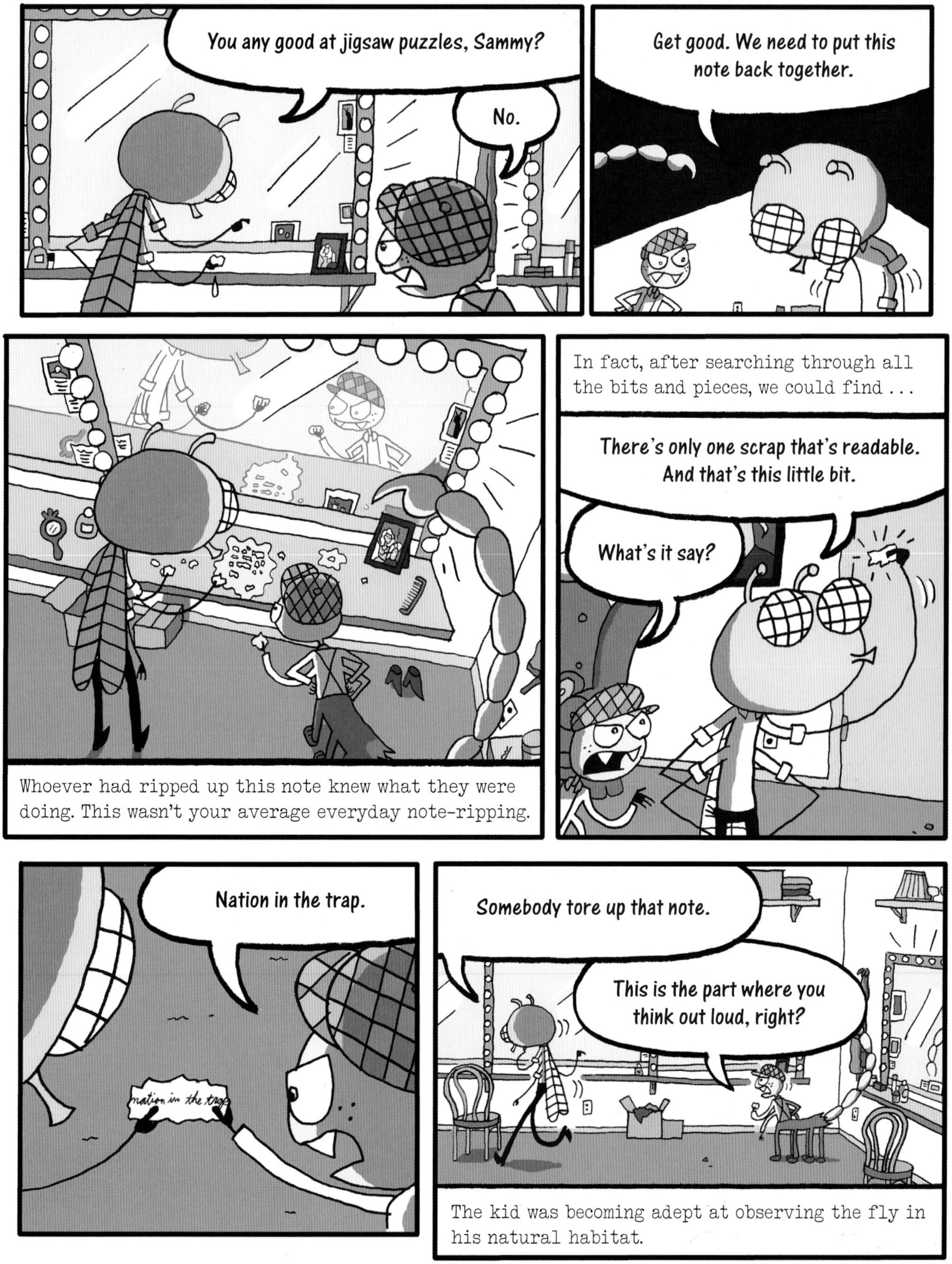
You any good at jigsaw puzzles, Sammy?
No.
Get good. We need to put this note back together.
Whoever had ripped up this note knew what they were doing. This wasn't your average everyday note-ripping.
In fact, after searching through all the bits and pieces, we could find . . .
There's only one scrap that's readable. And that's this little bit.
What's it say?
Nation in the trap.
Somebody tore up that note.
This is the part where you think out loud, right?
The kid was becoming adept at observing the fly in his natural habitat.

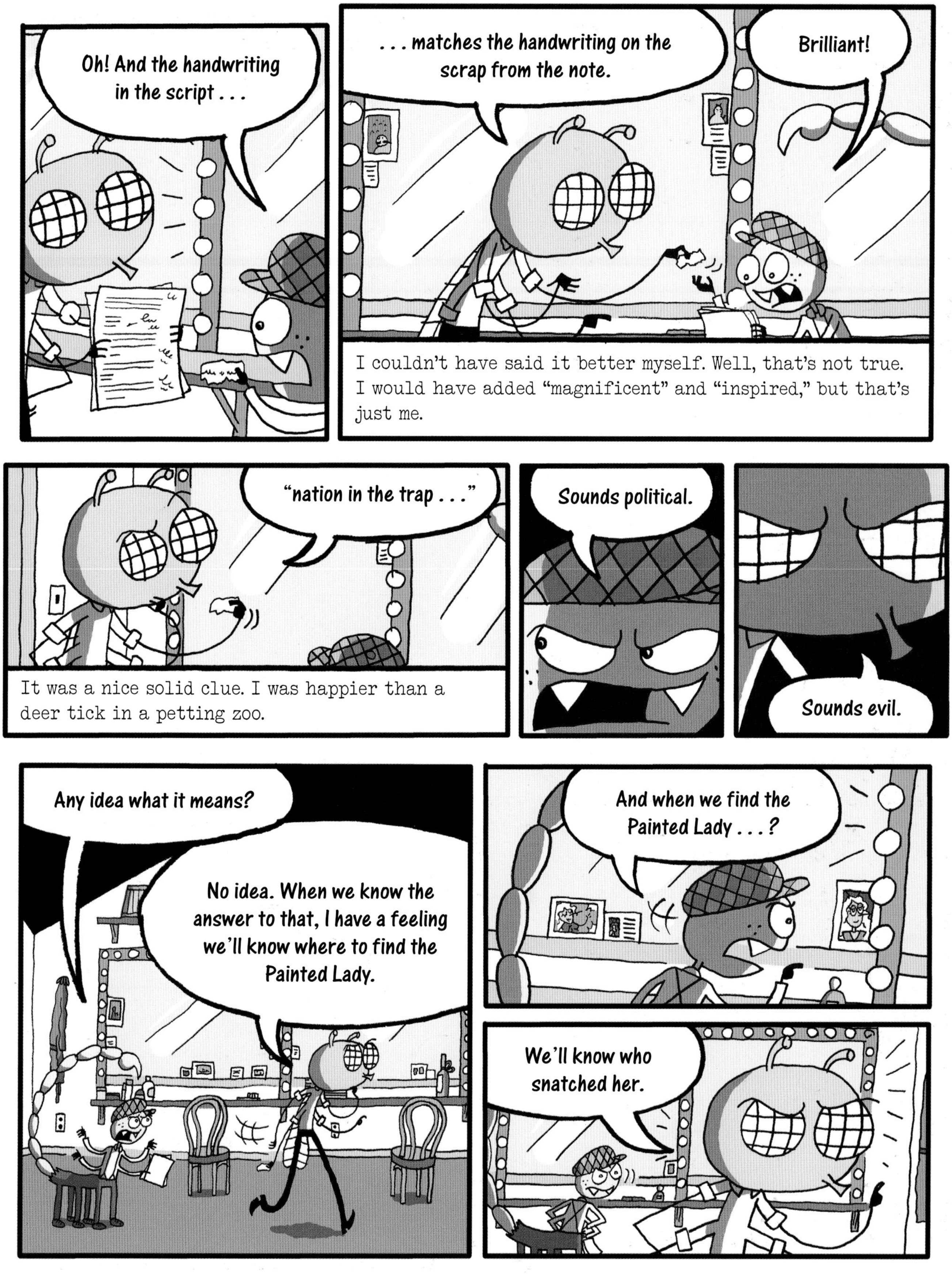
Oh! And the handwriting in the script . . .
. . . matches the handwriting on the scrap from the note.
Brilliant!
I couldn't have said it better myself. Well, that's not true. I would have added "magnificent" and "inspired," but that's just me.
"nation in the trap . . ."
It was a nice solid clue. I was happier than a deer tick in a petting zoo.
Sounds political.
Sounds evil.
Any idea what it means?
No idea. When we know the answer to that, I have a feeling we'll know where to find the Painted Lady.
And when we find the Painted Lady . . . ?
We'll know who snatched her.

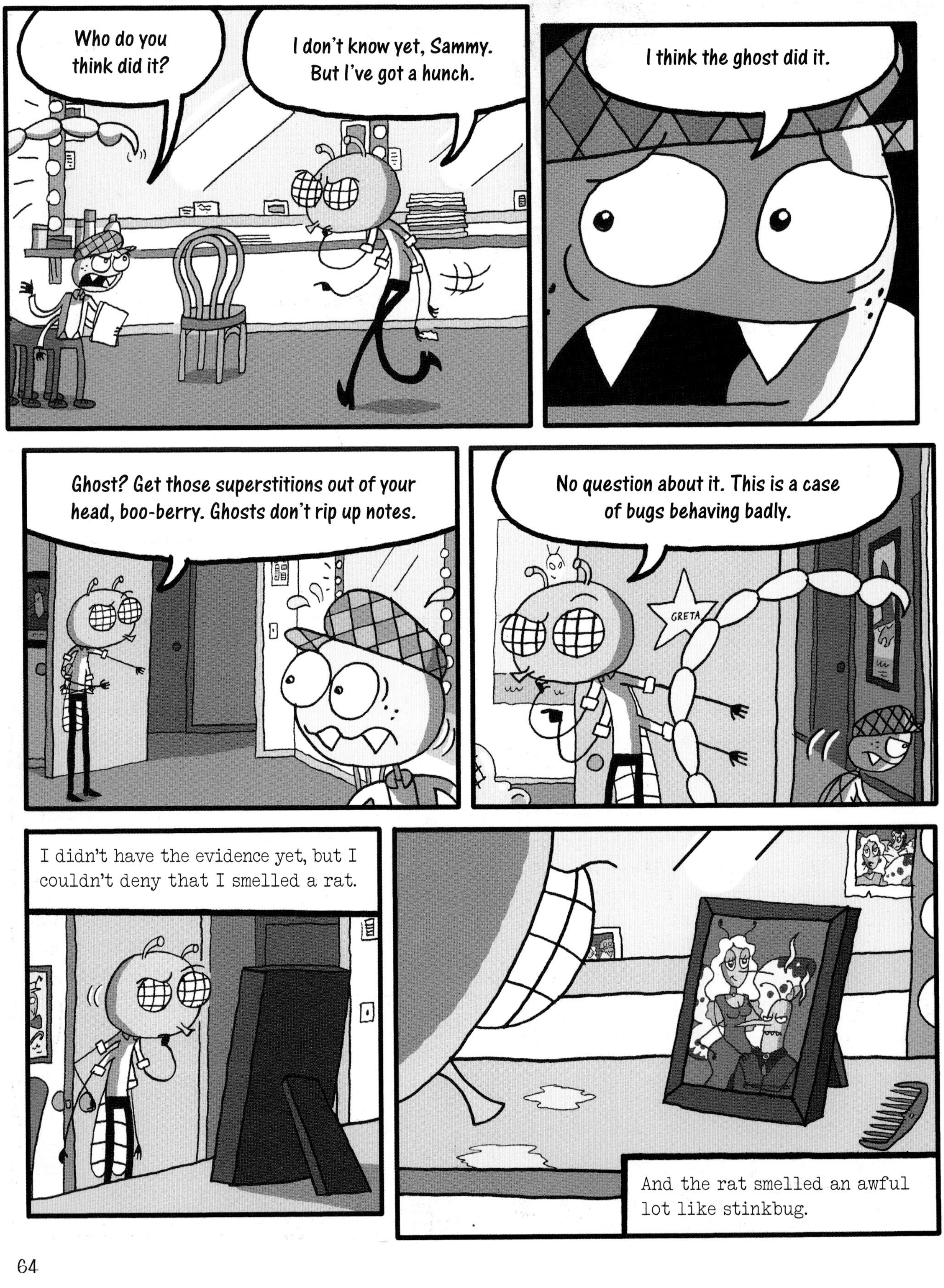

Who do you think did it?
I don't know yet, Sammy. But I've got a hunch.
I think the ghost did it.
Ghost? Get those superstitions out of your head, boo-berry. Ghosts don't rip up notes.
No question about it. This is a case of bugs behaving badly.
GRETA
I didn't have the evidence yet, but I couldn't deny that I smelled a rat.
And the rat smelled an awful lot like stinkbug.

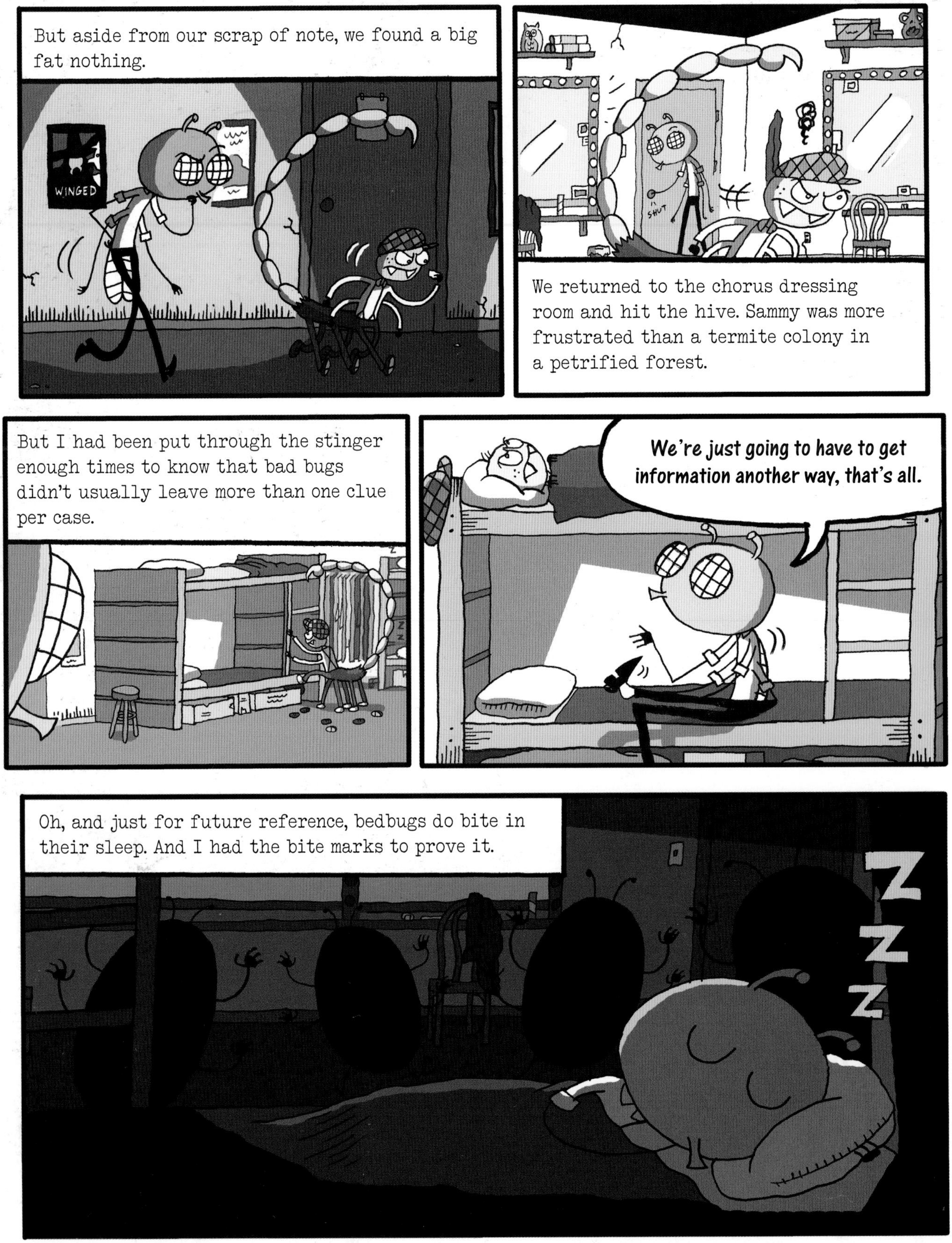

But aside from our scrap of note, we found a big fat nothing.
WINGED
SHUT
We returned to the chorus dressing room and hit the hive. Sammy was more frustrated than a termite colony in a petrified forest.
But I had been put through the stinger enough times to know that bad bugs didn't usually leave more than one clue per case.
We're just going to have to get information another way, that's all.
Oh, and just for future reference, bedbugs do bite in their sleep. And I had the bite marks to prove it.
Z Z Z

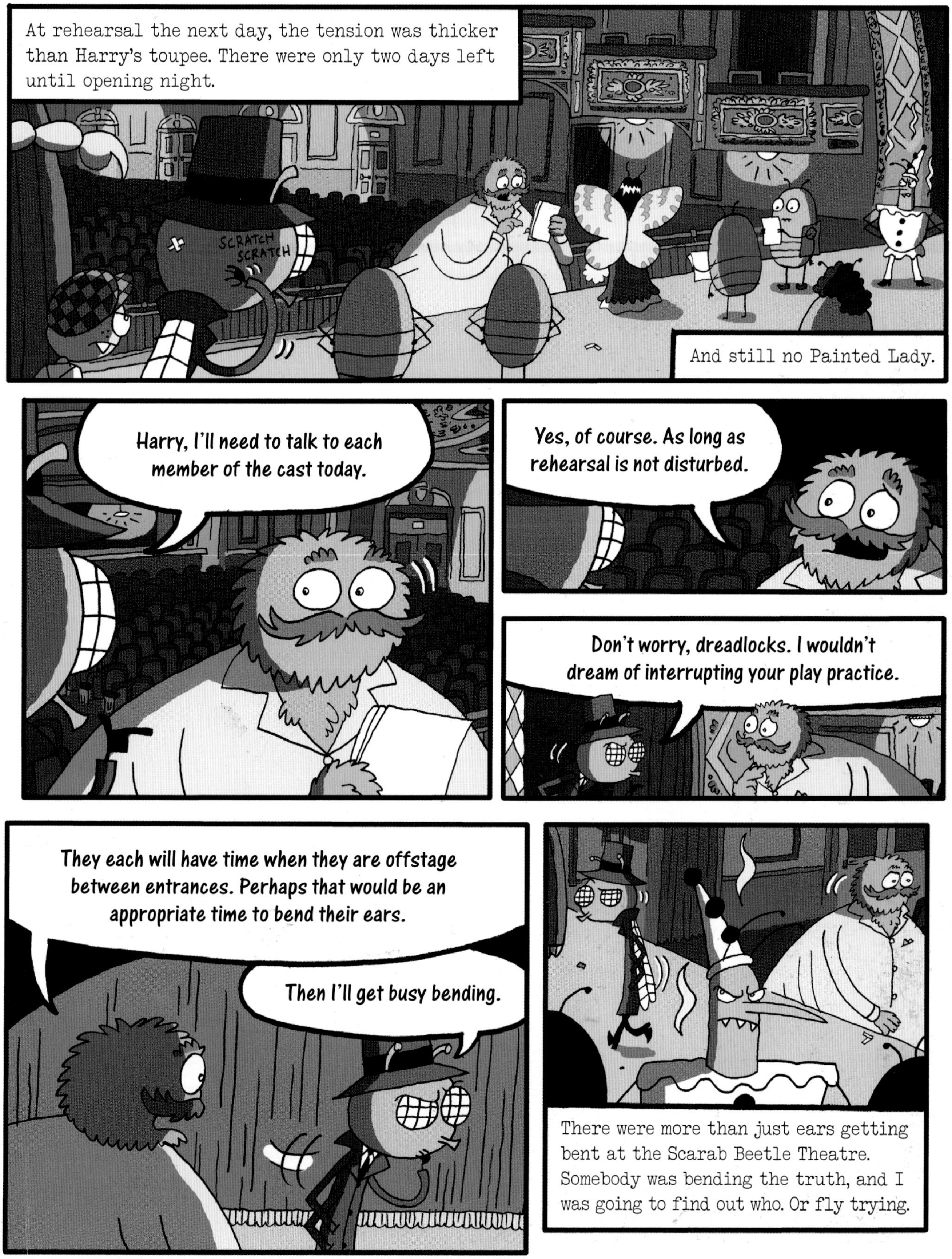
At rehearsal the next day, the tension was thicker than Harry's toupee. There were only two days left until opening night.
SCRATCH SCRATCH
And still no Painted Lady.
Harry, I'll need to talk to each member of the cast today.
Yes, of course. As long as rehearsal is not disturbed.
Don't worry, dreadlocks. I wouldn't dream of interrupting your play practice.
They each will have time when they are offstage between entrances. Perhaps that would be an appropriate time to bend their ears.
Then I'll get busy bending.
There were more than just ears getting bent at the Scarab Beetle Theatre. Somebody was bending the truth, and I was going to find out who. Or fly trying.

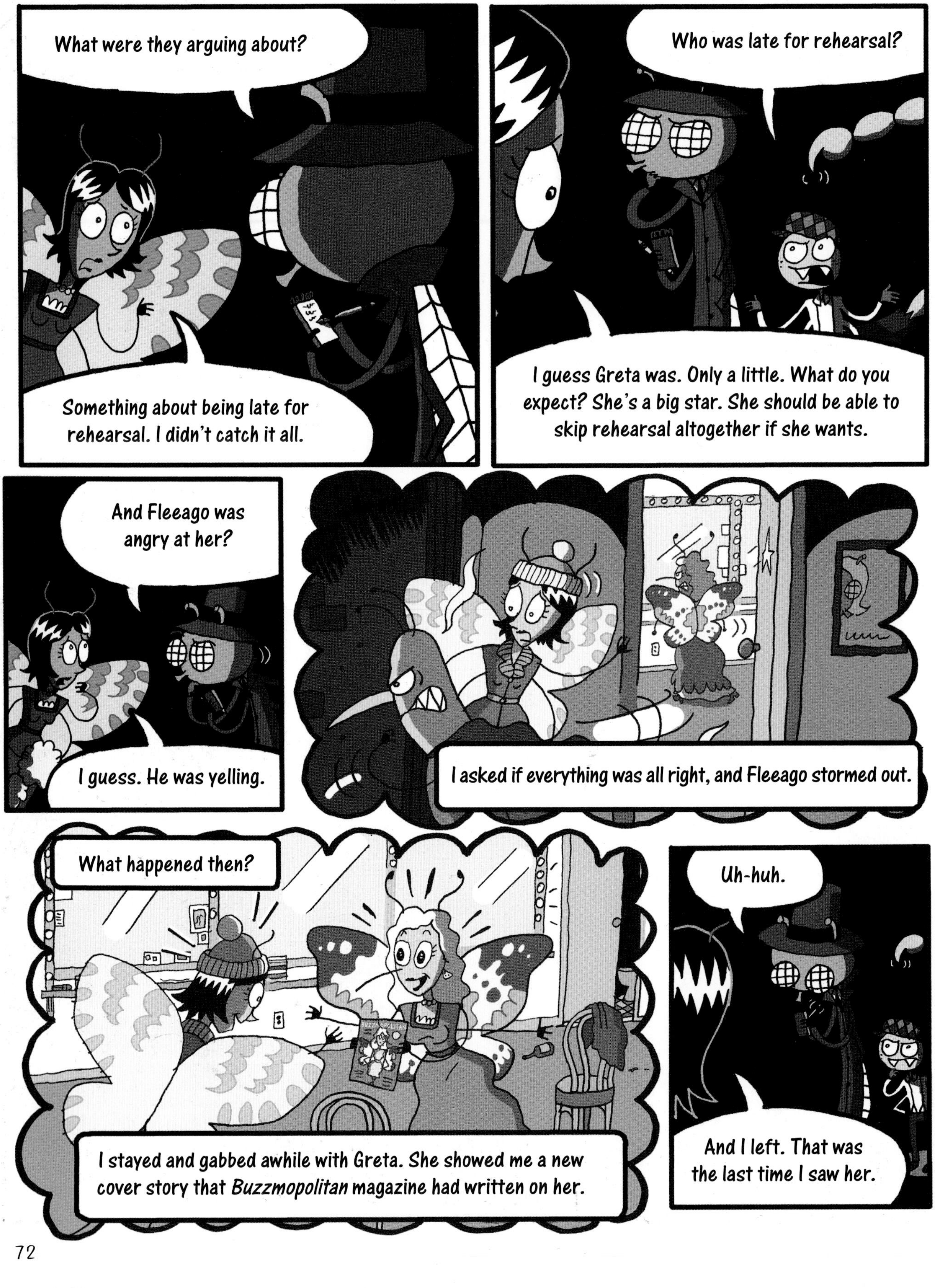
What were they arguing about?
Something about being late for rehearsal. I didn't catch it all.
Who was late for rehearsal?
I guess Greta was. Only a little. What do you expect? She's a big star. She should be able to skip rehearsal altogether if she wants.
And Fleeago was angry at her?
I guess. He was yelling.
I asked if everything was all right, and Fleeago stormed out.
What happened then?
I stayed and gabbed awhile with Greta. She showed me a new cover story that *Buzzmopolitan* magazine had written on her.
Uh-huh.
And I left. That was the last time I saw her.

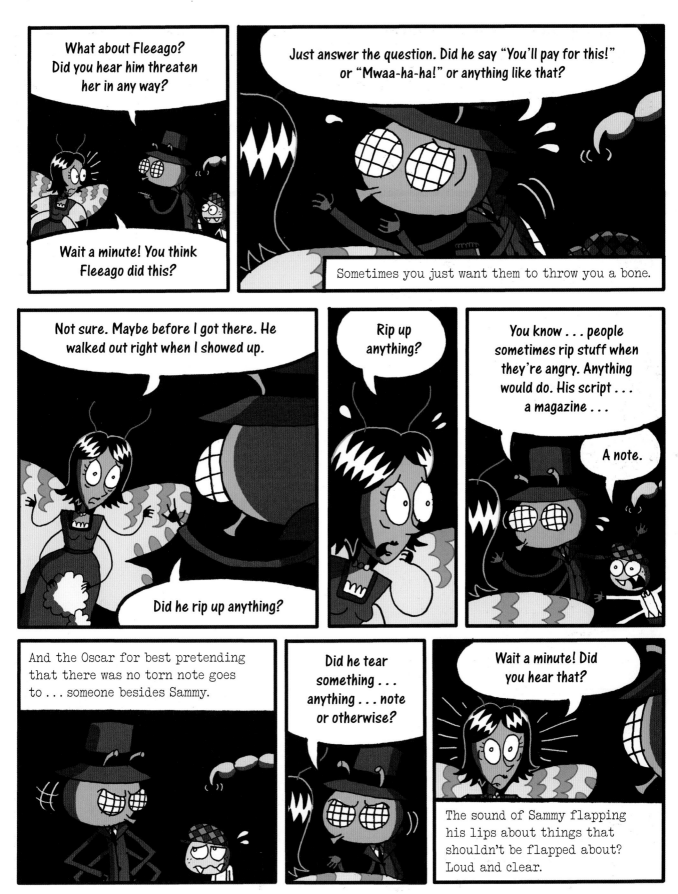

Oh my gosh! I've got to go!

She bolted like she'd been bull's-eyed by a bumblebee. Either I had hit on a sensitive subject, or little miss Trixie was late for a bus.

Not so fast, sister!

I was right on her tail. If I had a dime for every time a witness tried to give me the slip mid-interview, I'd be ... well, I'd be crushed under the weight of all those dimes.

Joey.

Not now, lover boy.

What gives, pixie stick?

Verily I say unto thee, fair sir, wouldst that I could reveal my true nature!

Well, I would . . . wouldst . . . like that a lot.

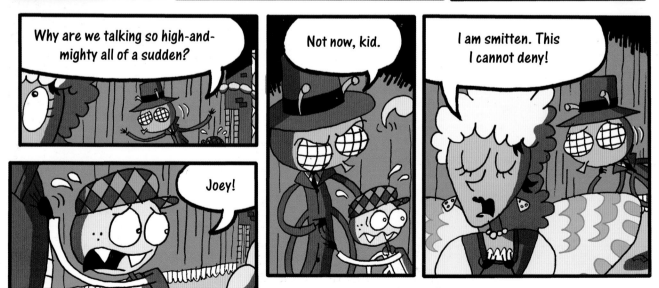

Why are we talking so high-and-mighty all of a sudden?

Joey!

Not now, kid.

I am smitten. This I cannot deny!

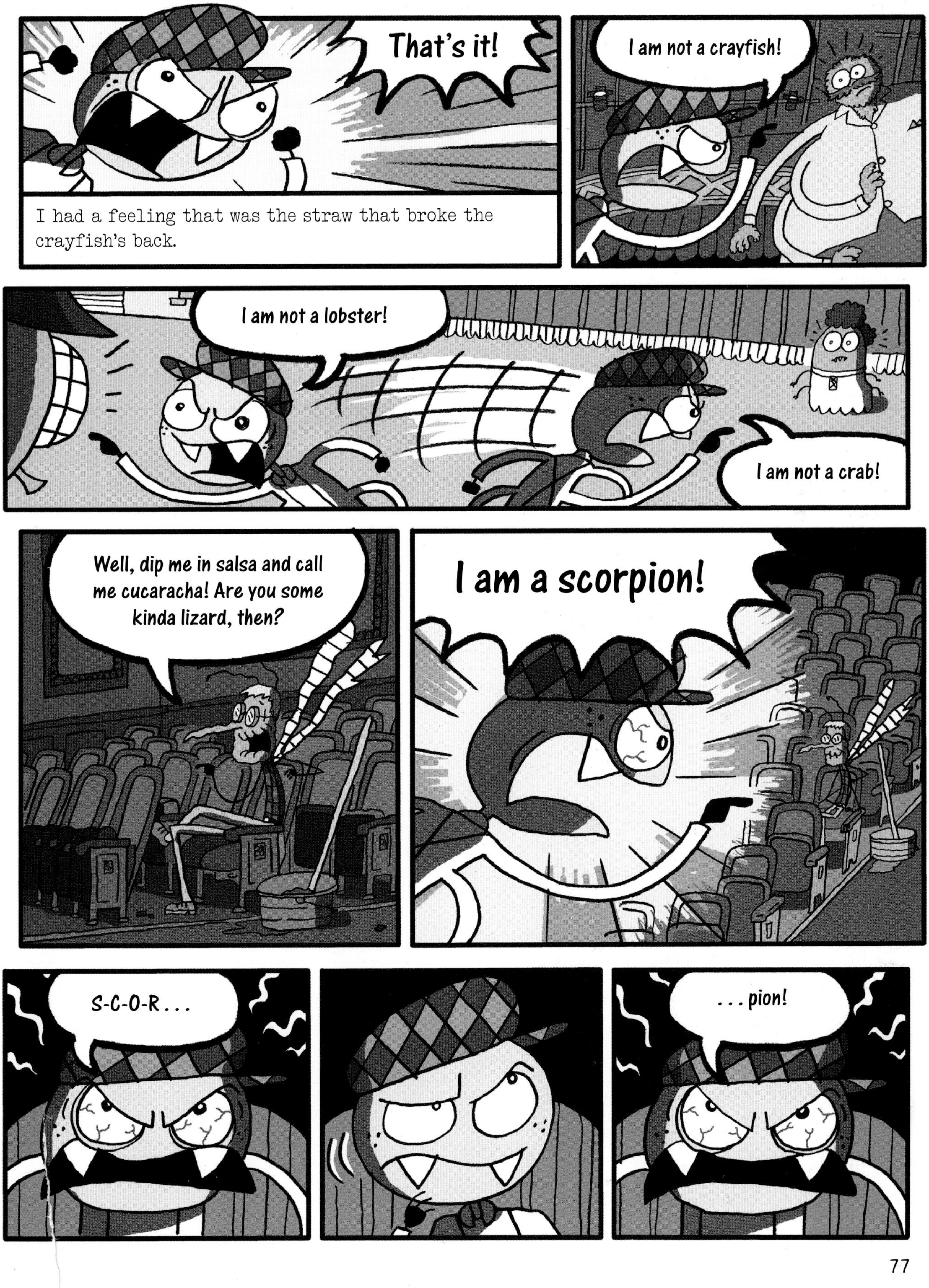
That's it!
I had a feeling that was the straw that broke the crayfish's back.
I am not a crayfish!
I am not a lobster!
I am not a crab!
Well, dip me in salsa and call me cucaracha! Are you some kinda lizard, then?
I am a scorpion!
S-C-O-R . . .
. . . pion!

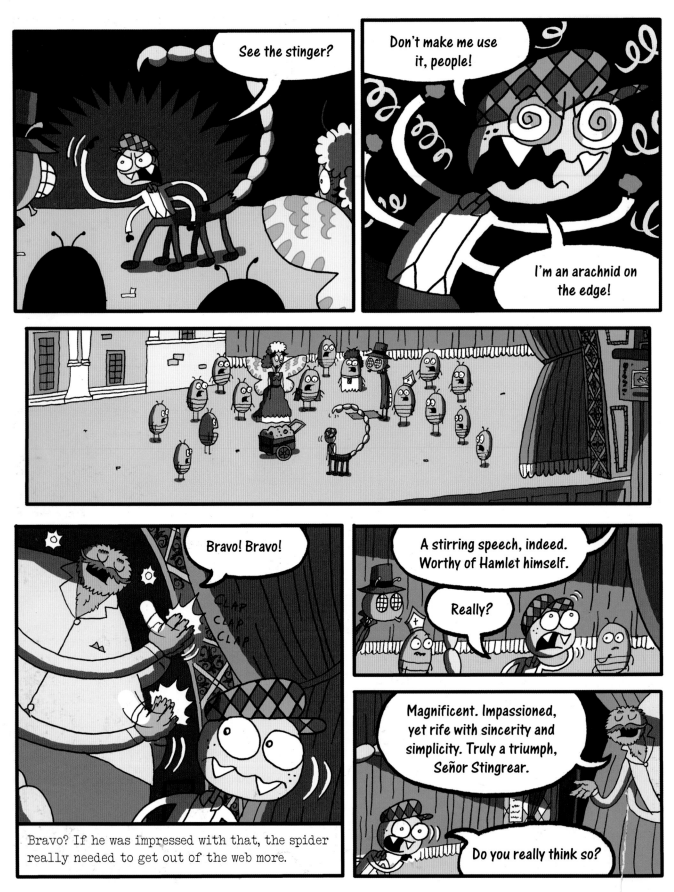

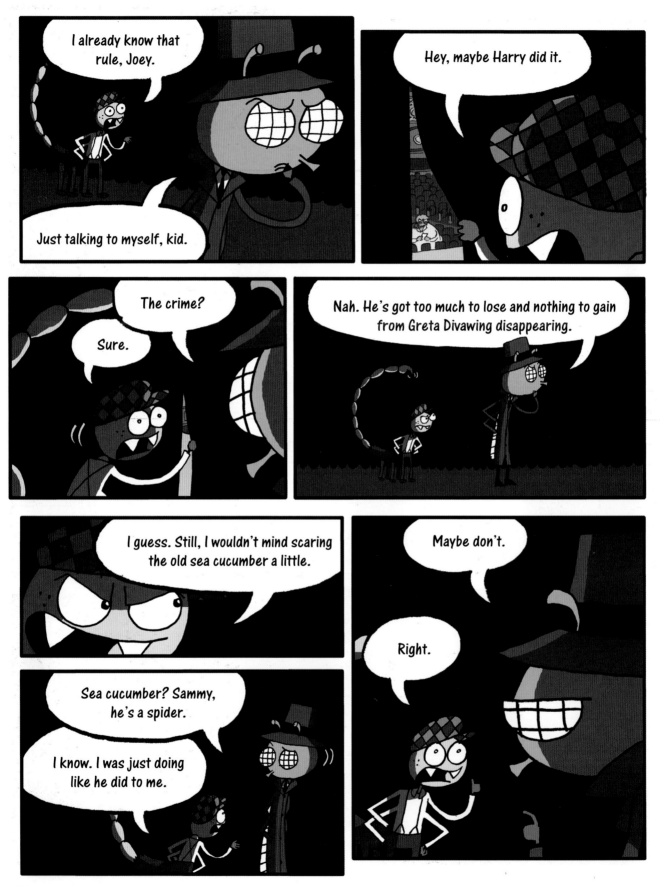

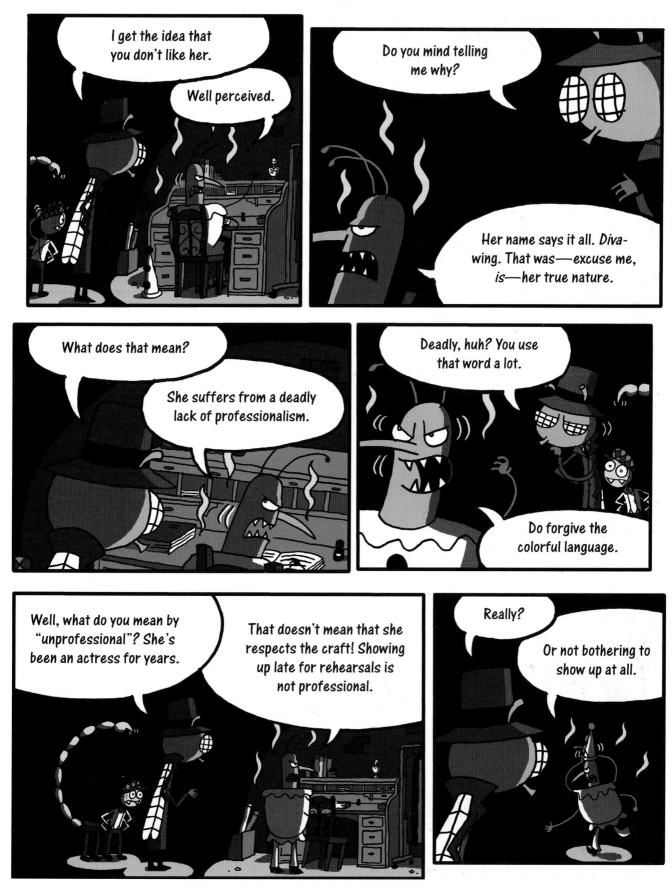

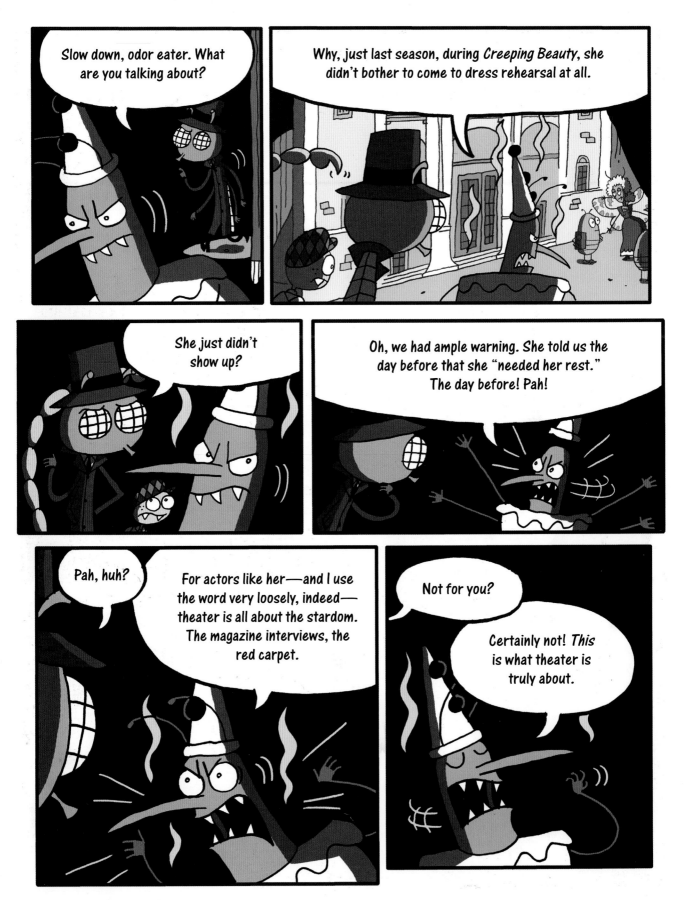

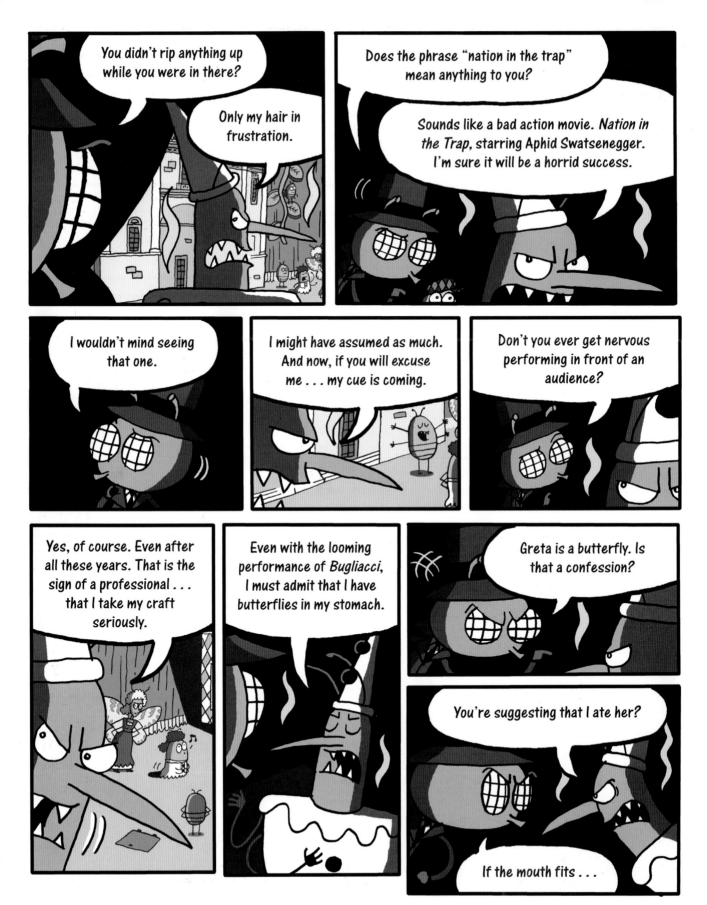

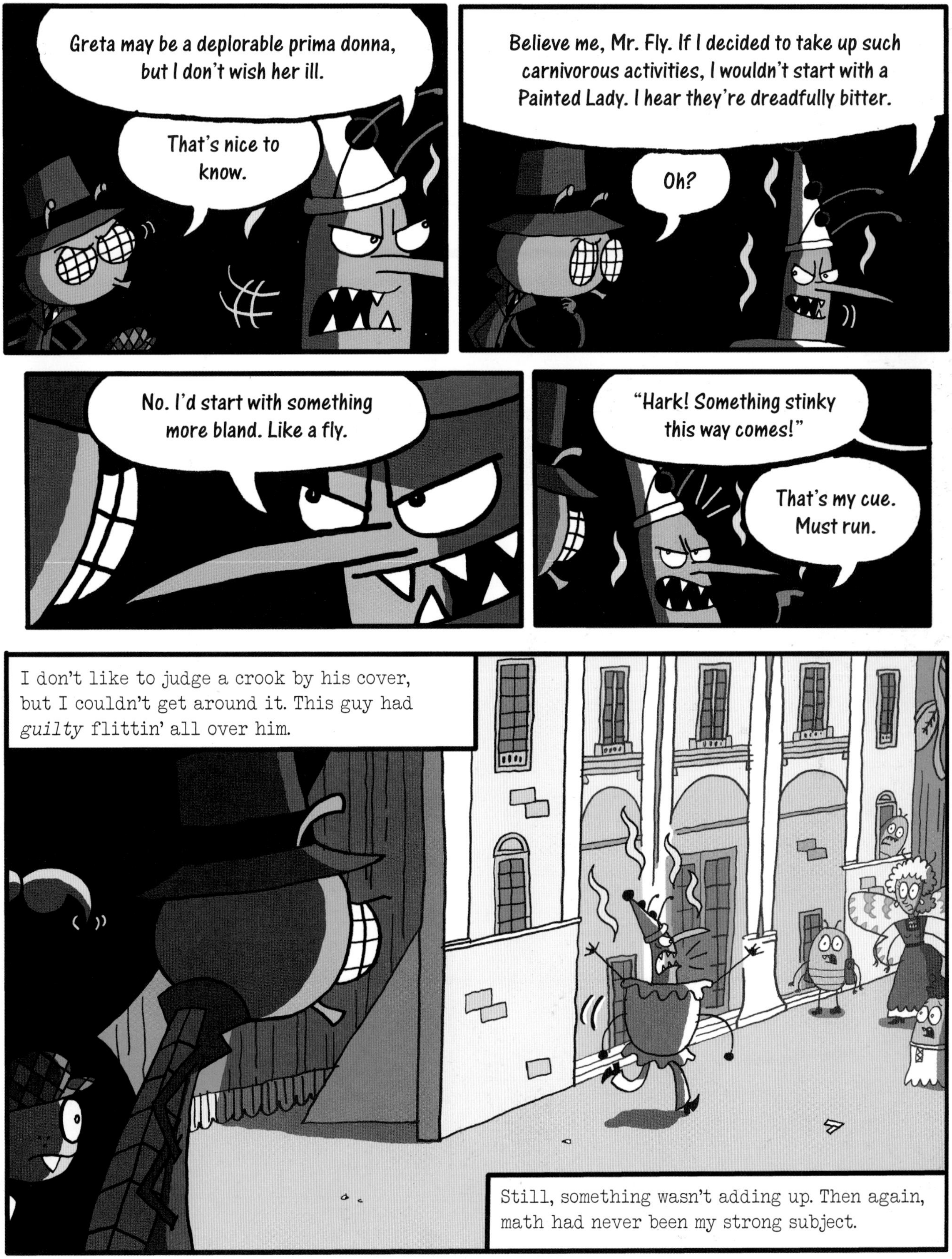
Greta may be a deplorable prima donna, but I don't wish her ill.
That's nice to know.
Believe me, Mr. Fly. If I decided to take up such carnivorous activities, I wouldn't start with a Painted Lady. I hear they're dreadfully bitter.
Oh?
No. I'd start with something more bland. Like a fly.
"Hark! Something stinky this way comes!"
That's my cue. Must run.
I don't like to judge a crook by his cover, but I couldn't get around it. This guy had *guilty* flittin' all over him.
Still, something wasn't adding up. Then again, math had never been my strong subject.

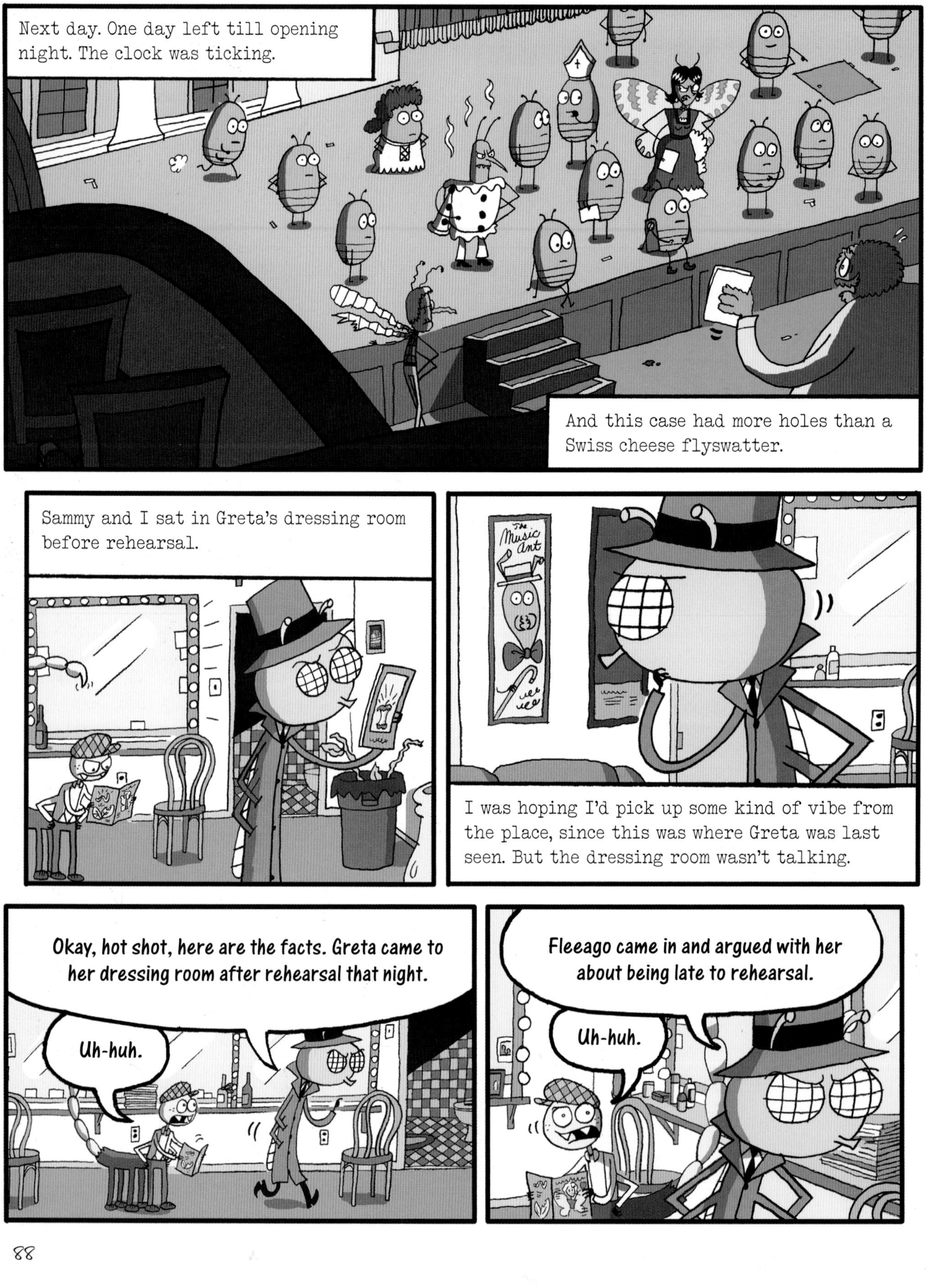
Next day. One day left till opening night. The clock was ticking.
And this case had more holes than a Swiss cheese flyswatter.
Sammy and I sat in Greta's dressing room before rehearsal.
The Music Ant
I was hoping I'd pick up some kind of vibe from the place, since this was where Greta was last seen. But the dressing room wasn't talking.
Okay, hot shot, here are the facts. Greta came to her dressing room after rehearsal that night.
Uh-huh.
Fleeago came in and argued with her about being late to rehearsal.
Uh-huh.

Do you have any word on Greta yet?

We're zeroing in on the culprit, Harry.

Emphasis on "zero."

I was hoping a closer inspection of Greta's dressing room would turn up a new clue, but so far it's been pretty uncooperative.

I see.

As I sat to rest my weary wings, I flipped through the small pile of magazines I had noticed before.

That's when I noticed that these were far from casual reading material.

"Up Close and Personal with the Painted Lady."

BUZZMOPOLITAN

SUMMER FASHION

RATE HIS ANTENNA

THE PAINTED LADY

THORAX POLL

MARRY A DRONE BEE

LOSE TEN MILLIGRAMS IN ONE WEEK

BEHIND THE WINGS WITH THE

The newest issue of *Buzzmopolitan* sat at the top of the pile. "Behind the Wings with the Painted Lady."

GUE

UP CLOSE AND PERSONAL WITH THE PAINTED LADY

MOLTING SEASON PREPARATIONS

BEAUTY SECRETS FROM THE PAINTED LADY

DIVAWING

WORK OUT ALL 3 SEGMENTS AT ONCE!

"Beauty Secrets from the Painted Lady."

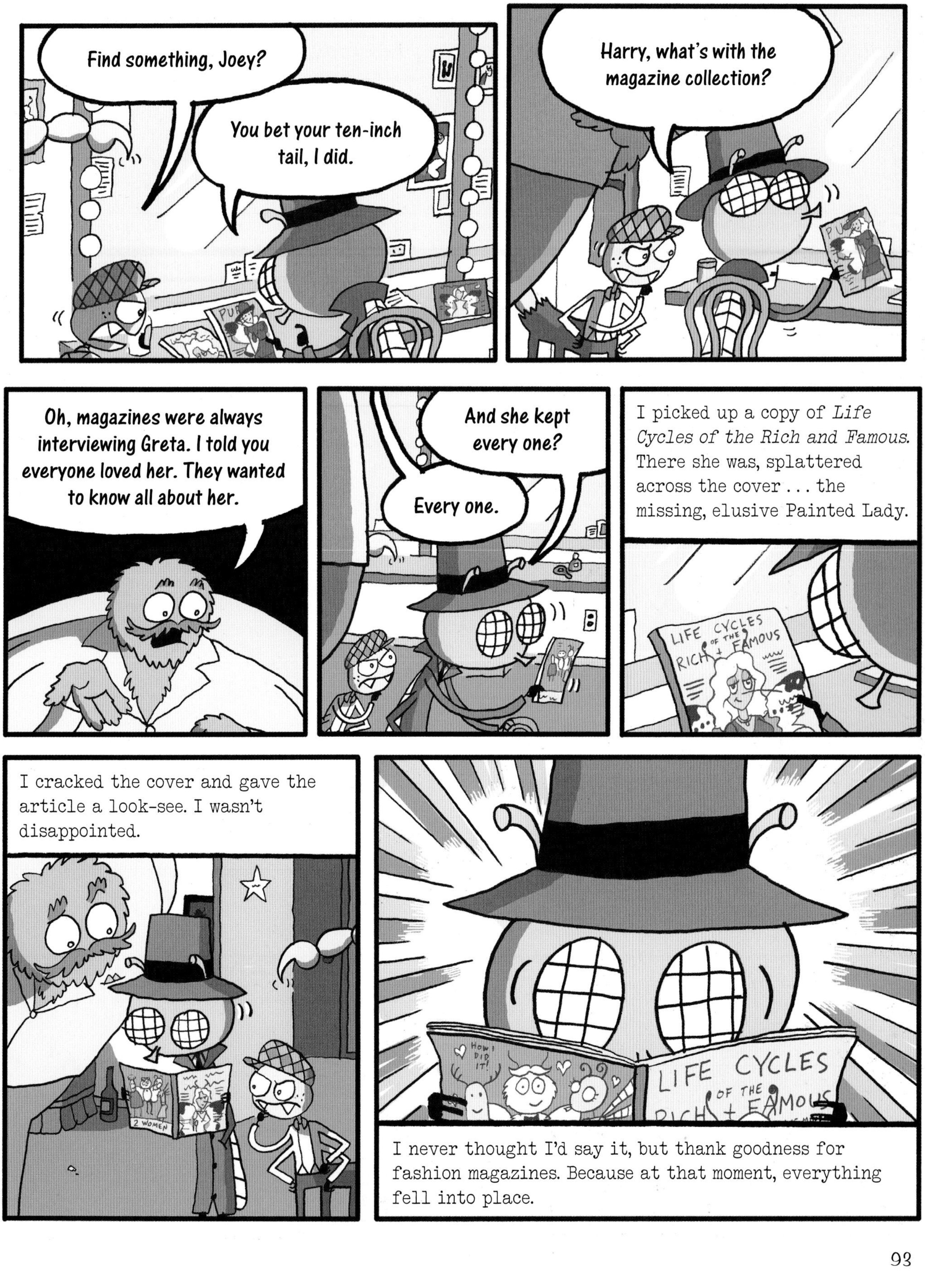

Find something, Joey?
You bet your ten-inch tail, I did.
Harry, what's with the magazine collection?
Oh, magazines were always interviewing Greta. I told you everyone loved her. They wanted to know all about her.
And she kept every one?
Every one.
I picked up a copy of *Life Cycles of the Rich and Famous.* There she was, splattered across the cover . . . the missing, elusive Painted Lady.
LIFE CYCLES OF THE RICH + FAMOUS
I cracked the cover and gave the article a look-see. I wasn't disappointed.
2 WOMEN
HOW I DID IT!
LIFE CYCLES OF THE RICH + FAMOUS
I never thought I'd say it, but thank goodness for fashion magazines. Because at that moment, everything fell into place.

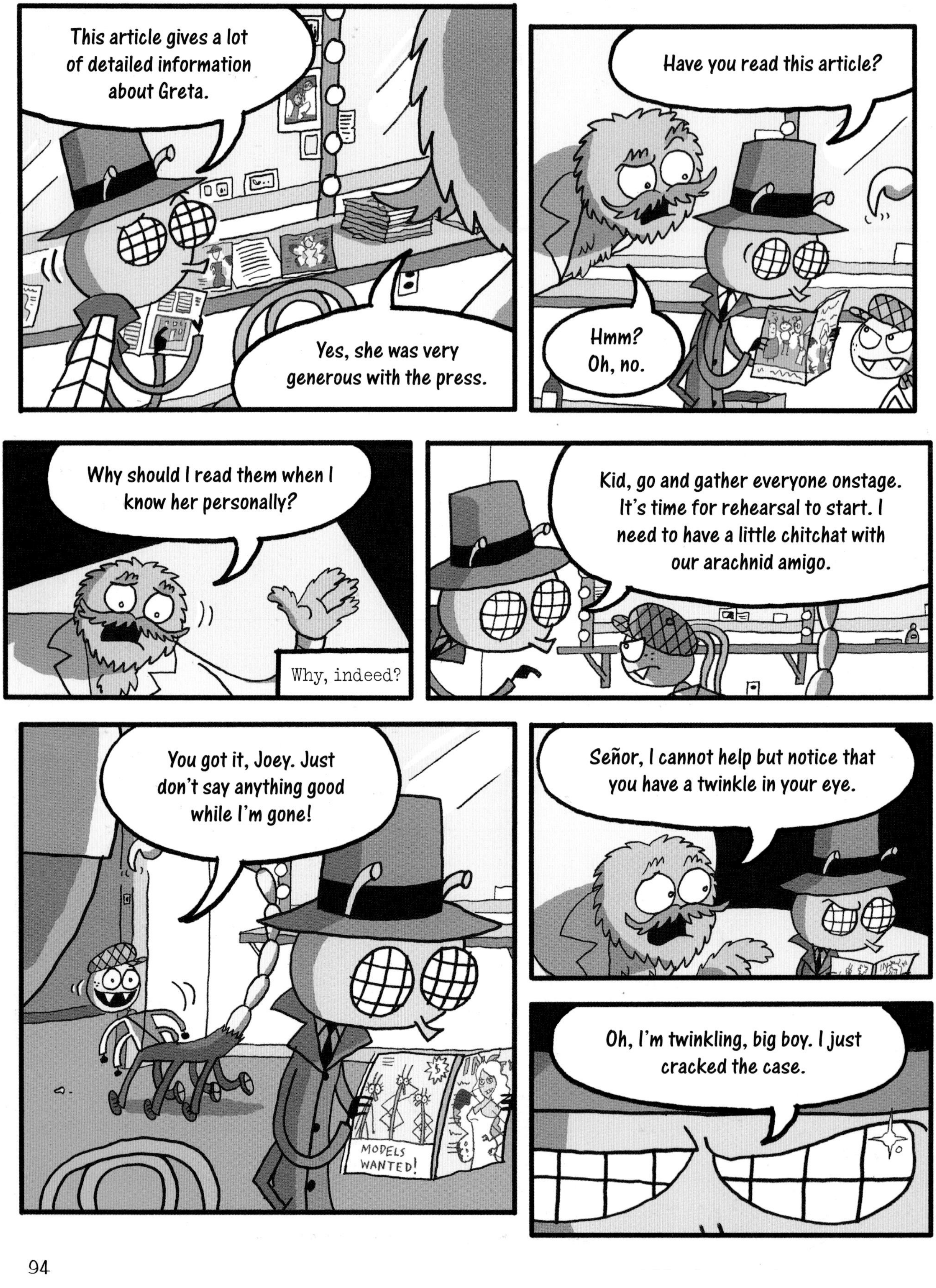
This article gives a lot of detailed information about Greta.
Yes, she was very generous with the press.
Have you read this article?
Hmm? Oh, no.
Why should I read them when I know her personally?
Why, indeed?
Kid, go and gather everyone onstage. It's time for rehearsal to start. I need to have a little chitchat with our arachnid amigo.
You got it, Joey. Just don't say anything good while I'm gone!
MODELS WANTED!
Señor, I cannot help but notice that you have a twinkle in your eye.
Oh, I'm twinkling, big boy. I just cracked the case.

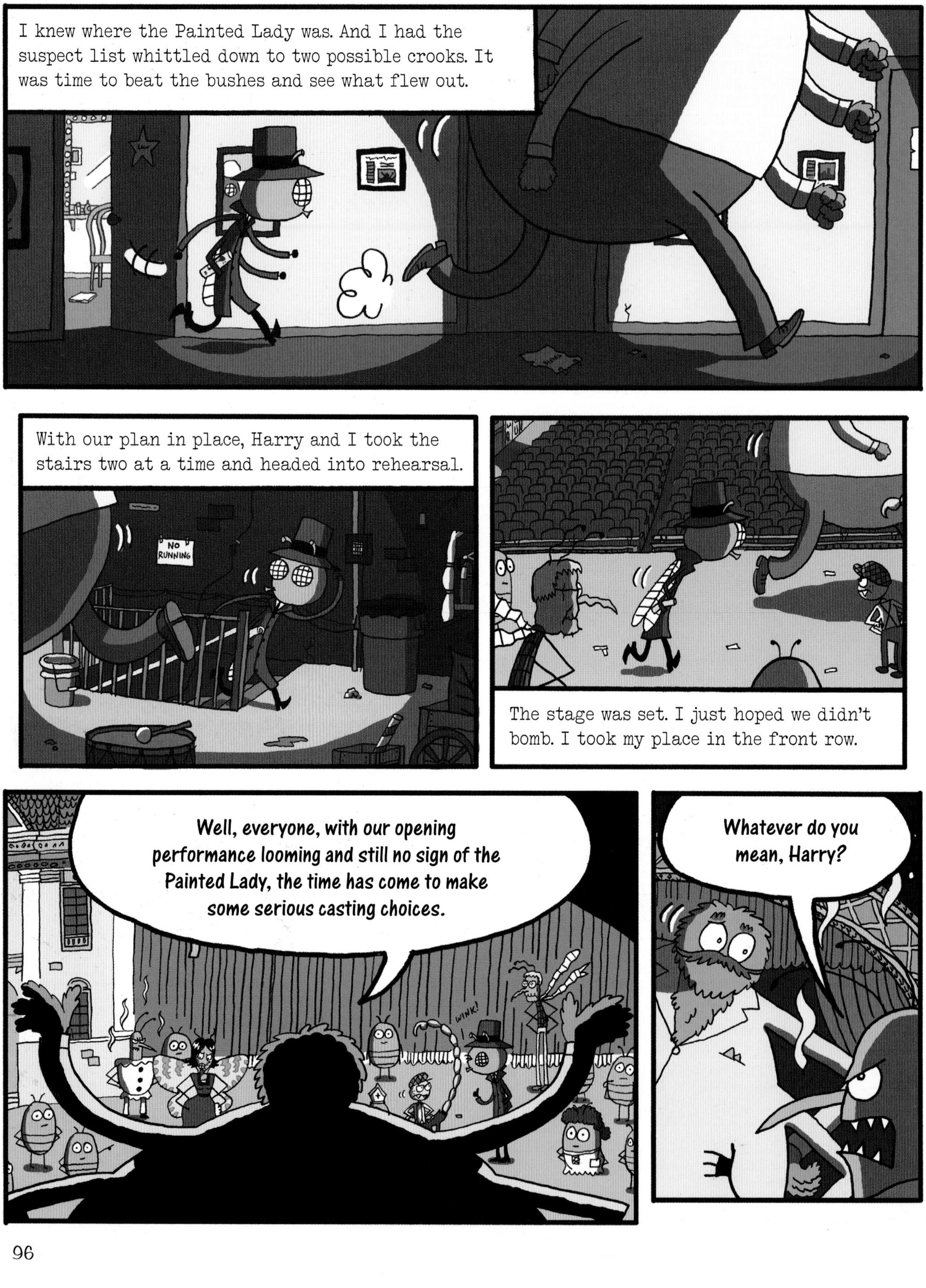
I knew where the Painted Lady was. And I had the suspect list whittled down to two possible crooks. It was time to beat the bushes and see what flew out.
With our plan in place, Harry and I took the stairs two at a time and headed into rehearsal.
NO RUNNING
The stage was set. I just hoped we didn't bomb. I took my place in the front row.
Well, everyone, with our opening performance looming and still no sign of the Painted Lady, the time has come to make some serious casting choices.
WINK!
Whatever do you mean, Harry?

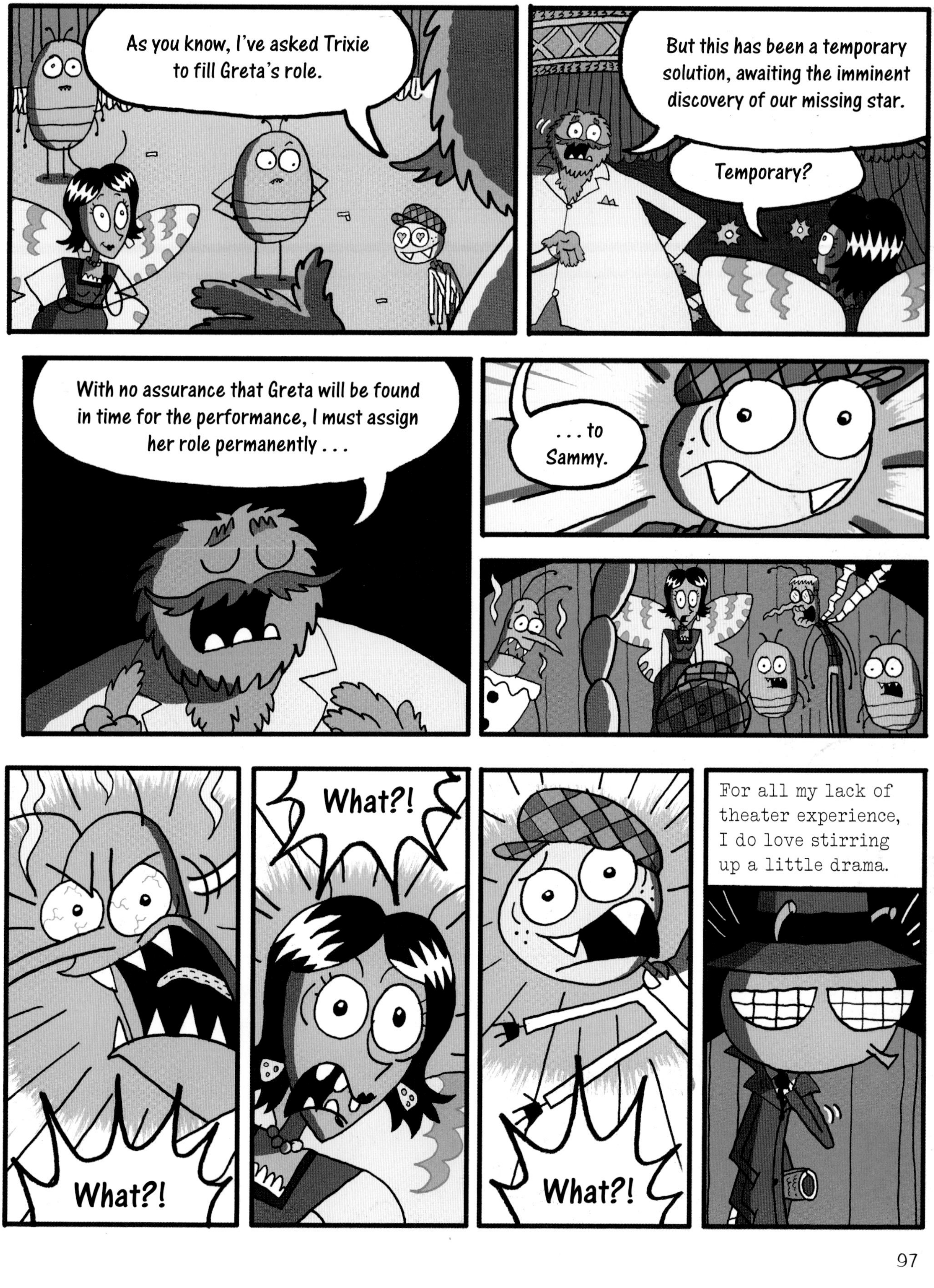
As you know, I've asked Trixie to fill Greta's role.
But this has been a temporary solution, awaiting the imminent discovery of our missing star.
Temporary?
With no assurance that Greta will be found in time for the performance, I must assign her role permanently . . .
. . . to Sammy.
What?!
What?!
What?!
For all my lack of theater experience, I do love stirring up a little drama.

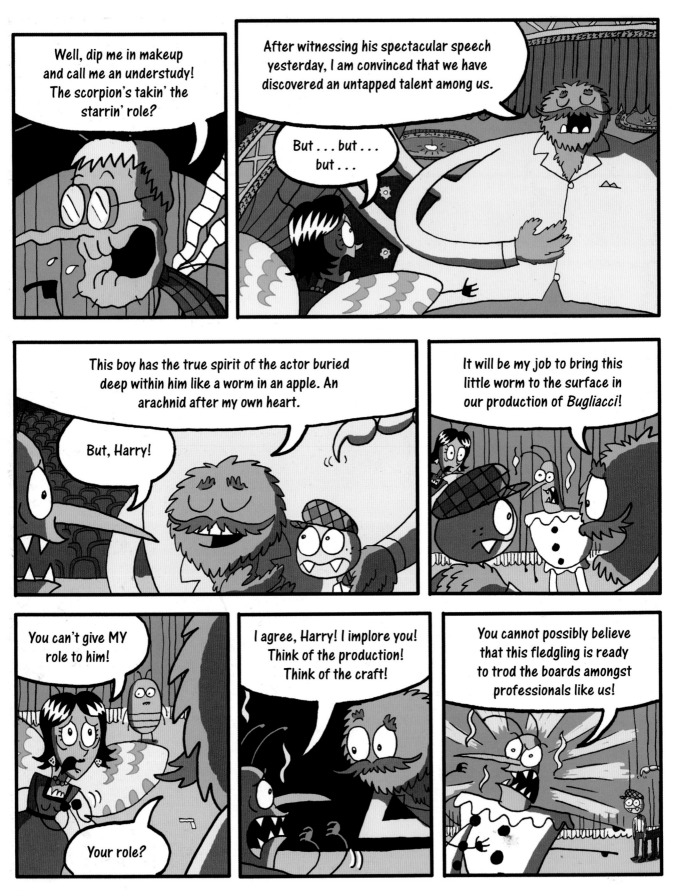

The hook was baited. And my two main suspects had gulped it down hook, line, and oversized stinger.

Fleeago was clearly unhappy. The guy looked like he had a bad smell stuck in his nose. Which was ironic, given his species.

And Trixie was fuming. The girl was hotter under the collar than fire-ant fajitas with extra salsa.

I hated putting Sammy on the end of the hook like this. Funny thing about fishing ... it never works out too well for the bait.

All right, Harry. I'm in. I won't let you down.

But he seemed to be warming to the idea.

That's my boy!

Skeeter, get young Sammy a script.

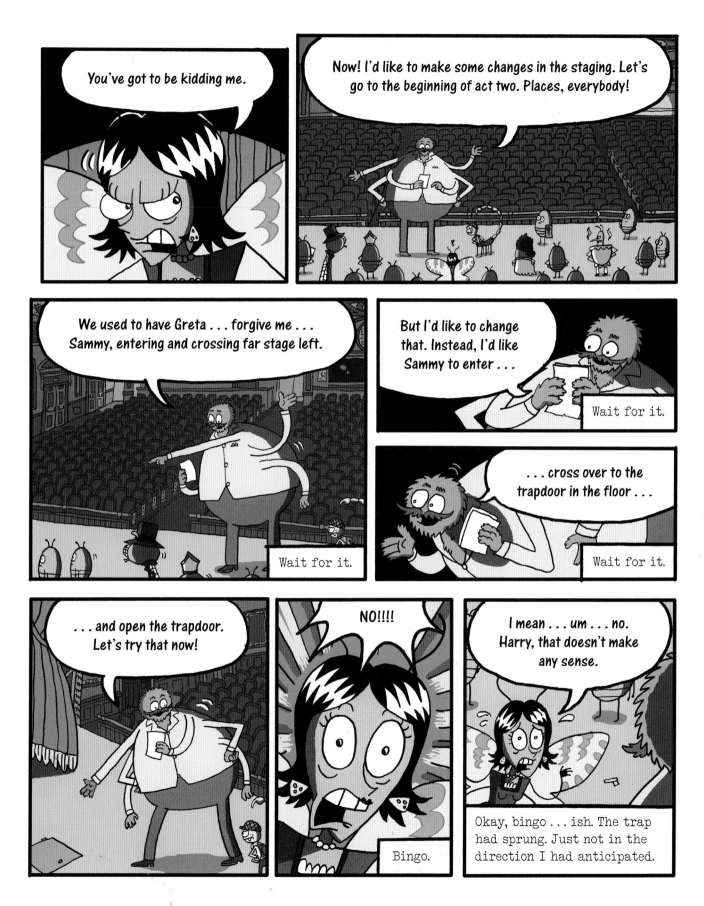

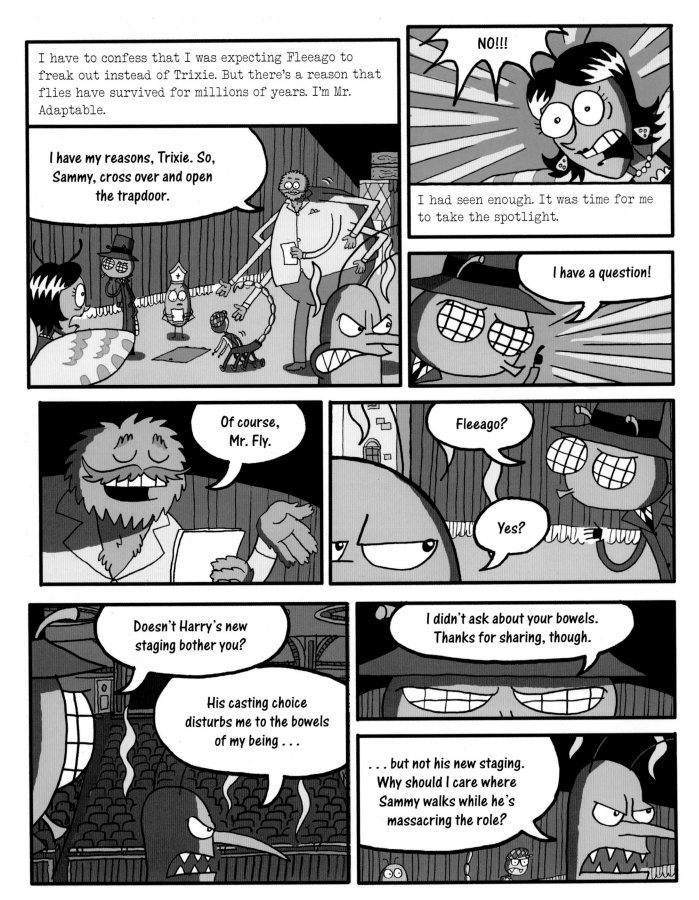

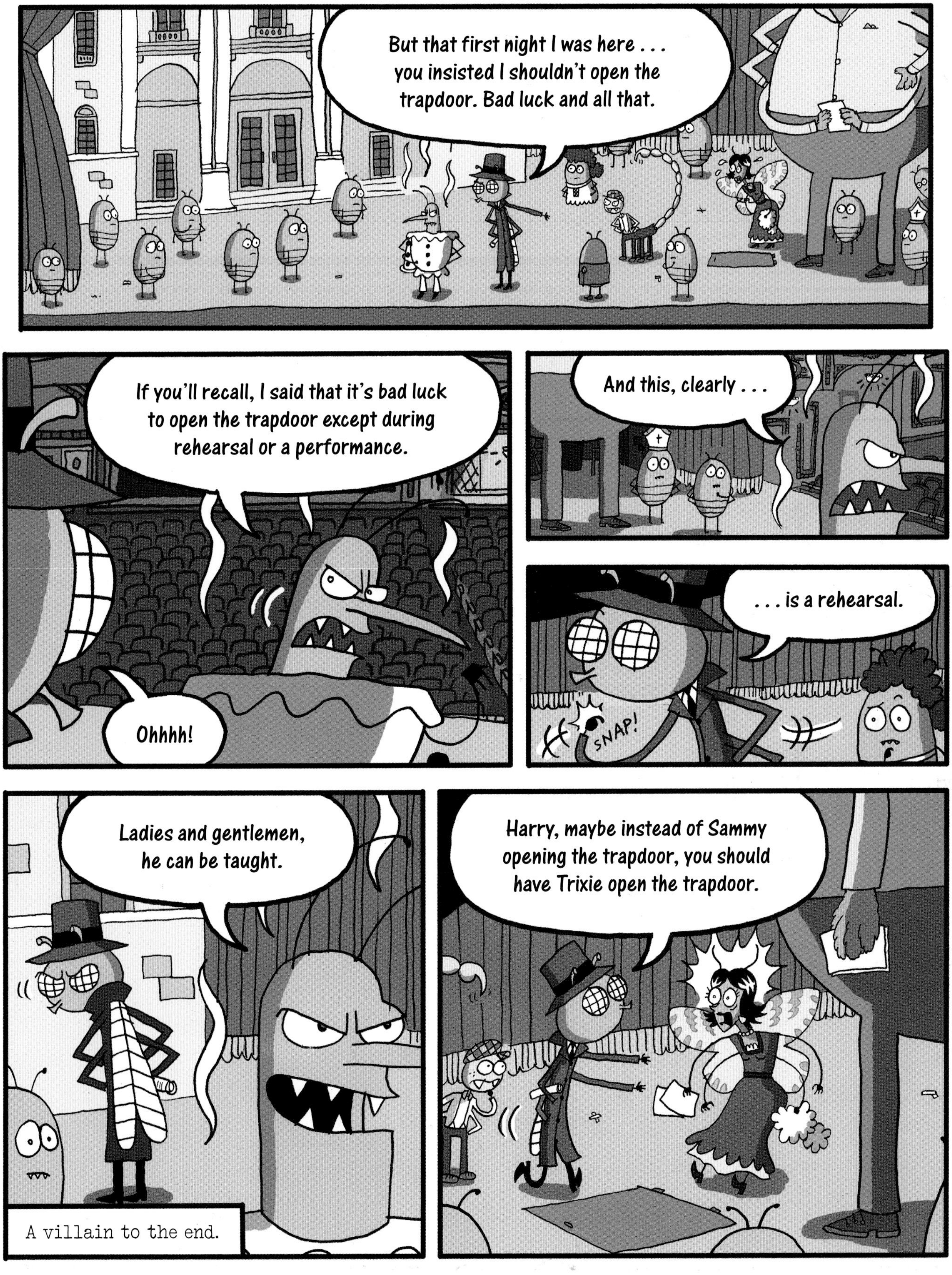
But that first night I was here . . . you insisted I shouldn't open the trapdoor. Bad luck and all that.
If you'll recall, I said that it's bad luck to open the trapdoor except during rehearsal or a performance.
Ohhhh!
And this, clearly . . .
. . . is a rehearsal.
SNAP!
Ladies and gentlemen, he can be taught.
A villain to the end.
Harry, maybe instead of Sammy opening the trapdoor, you should have Trixie open the trapdoor.

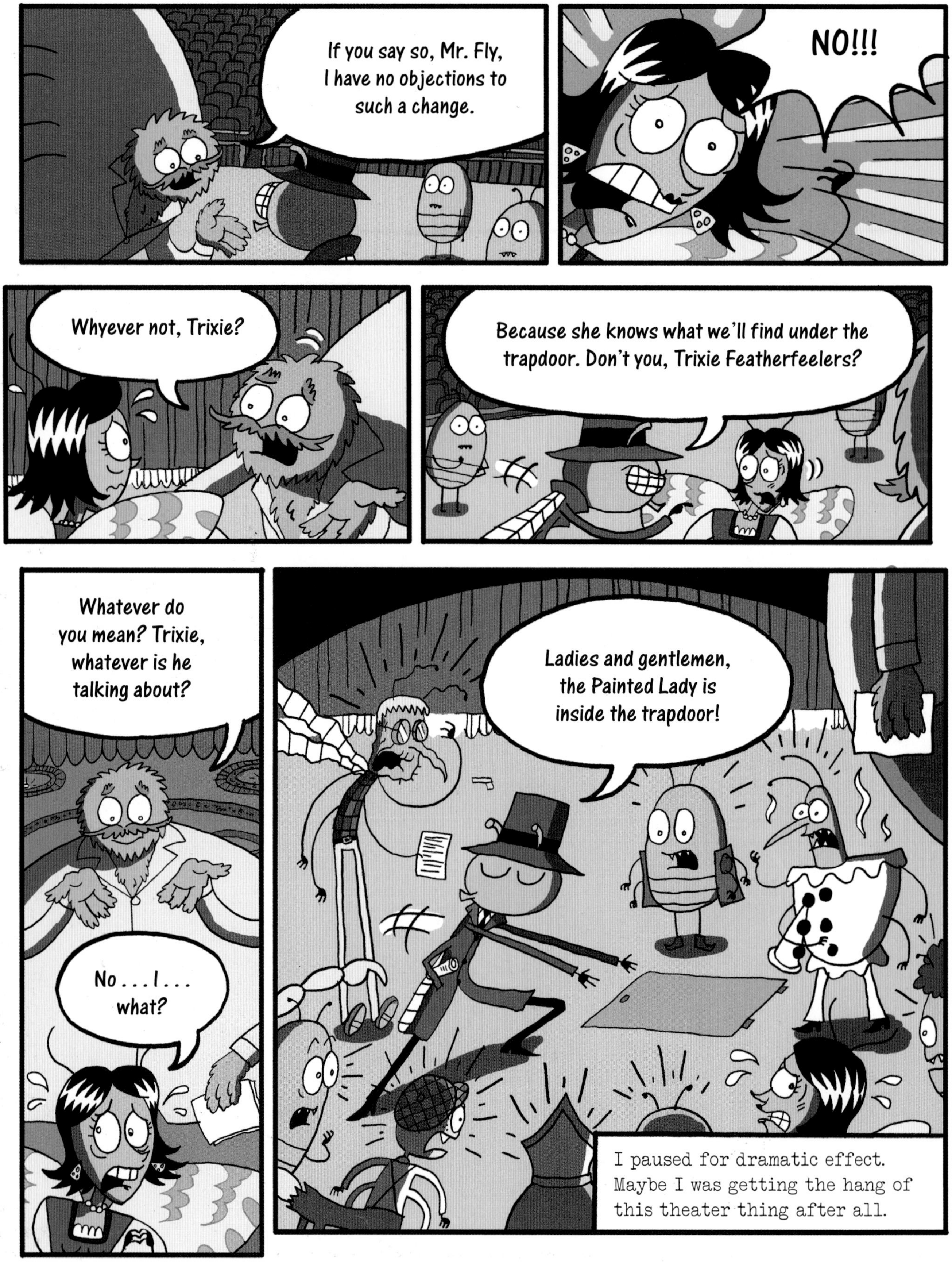
If you say so, Mr. Fly, I have no objections to such a change.
NO!!!
Whyever not, Trixie?
Because she knows what we'll find under the trapdoor. Don't you, Trixie Featherfeelers?
Whatever do you mean? Trixie, whatever is he talking about?
No . . . I . . . what?
Ladies and gentlemen, the Painted Lady is inside the trapdoor!
I paused for dramatic effect. Maybe I was getting the hang of this theater thing after all.

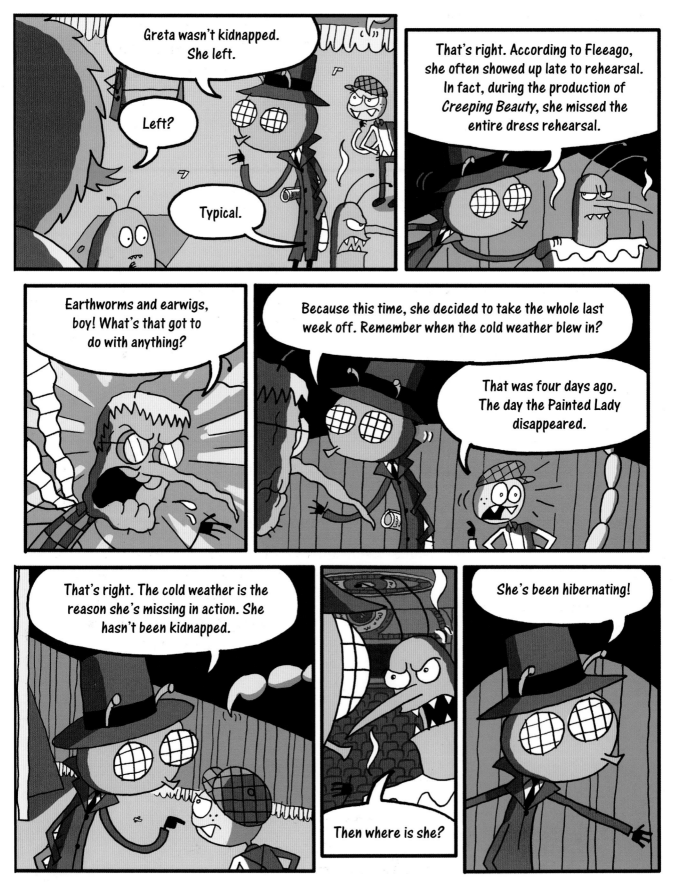

Right under our very feet?

That's right.

Without telling anyone? I'll kill her!

This guy really needed a monocle or some other villain accessory to go with that attitude of his.

Hold on a second, Dr. Evil. Laying down on the job may not be nice, but she did tell someone. In fact, she told everyone.

Didn't she, Trixie?

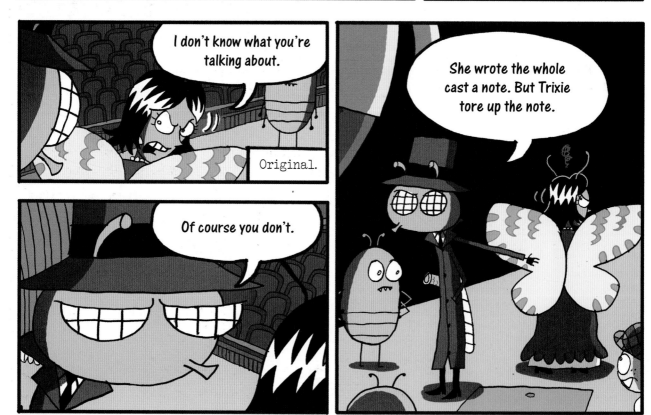

I don't know what you're talking about.

Original.

Of course you don't.

She wrote the whole cast a note. But Trixie tore up the note.

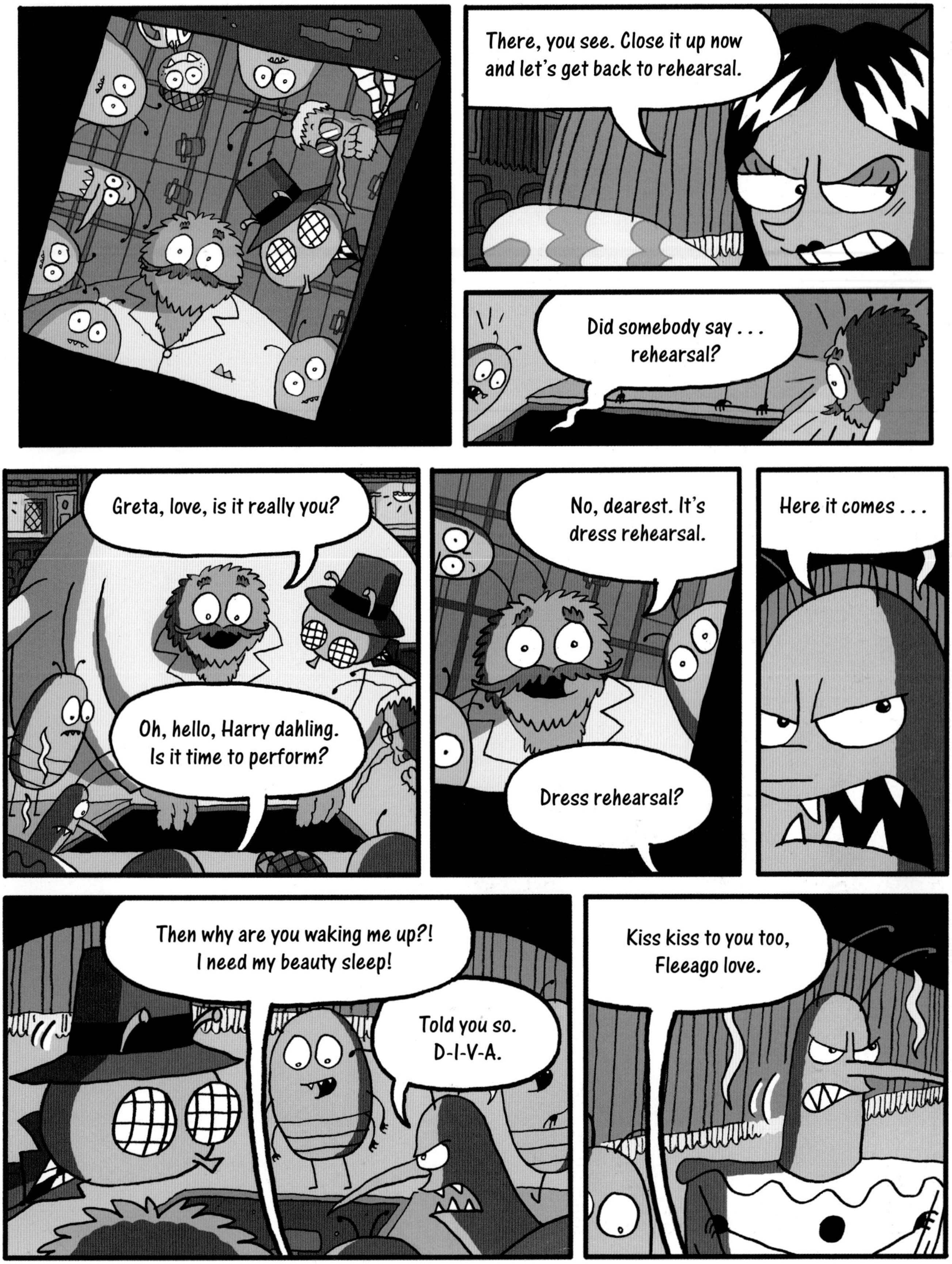
There, you see. Close it up now and let's get back to rehearsal.
Did somebody say . . . rehearsal?
Greta, love, is it really you?
Oh, hello, Harry dahling. Is it time to perform?
No, dearest. It's dress rehearsal.
Dress rehearsal?
Here it comes . . .
Then why are you waking me up?! I need my beauty sleep!
Told you so. D-I-V-A.
Kiss kiss to you too, Fleeago love.

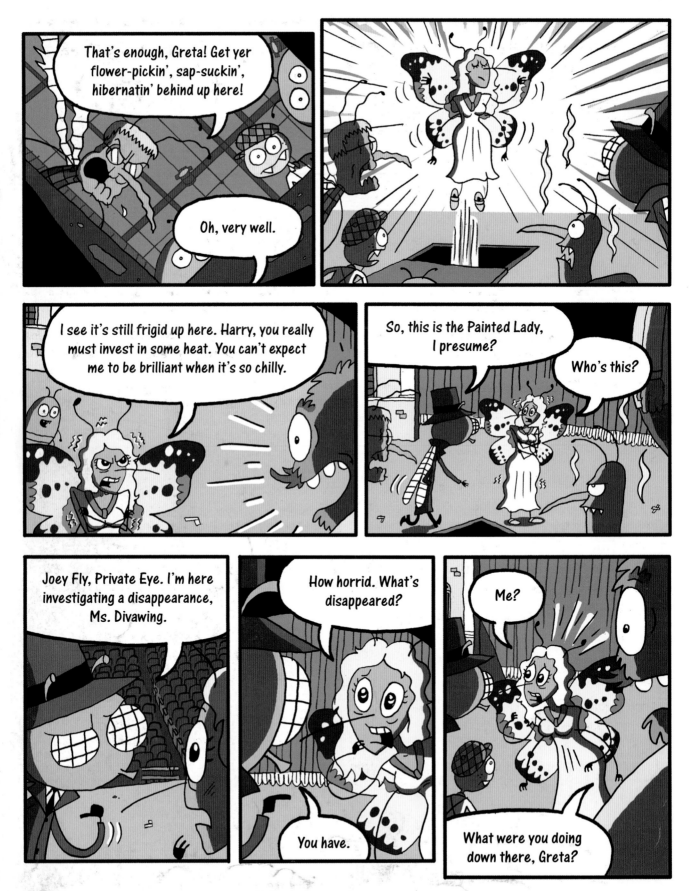

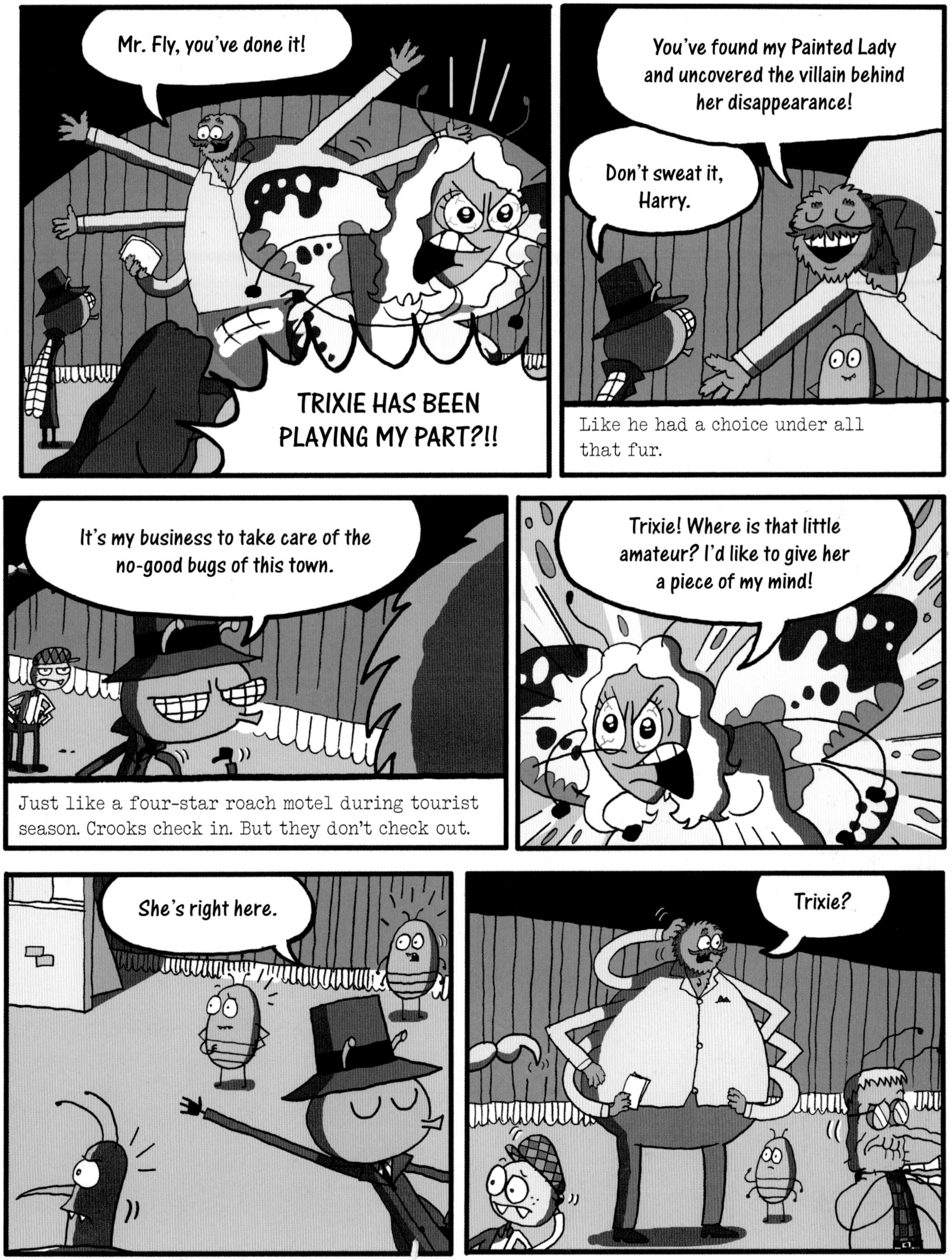
Mr. Fly, you've done it!
TRIXIE HAS BEEN PLAYING MY PART?!!
You've found my Painted Lady and uncovered the villain behind her disappearance!
Don't sweat it, Harry.
Like he had a choice under all that fur.
It's my business to take care of the no-good bugs of this town.
Just like a four-star roach motel during tourist season. Crooks check in. But they don't check out.
Trixie! Where is that little amateur? I'd like to give her a piece of my mind!
She's right here.
Trixie?

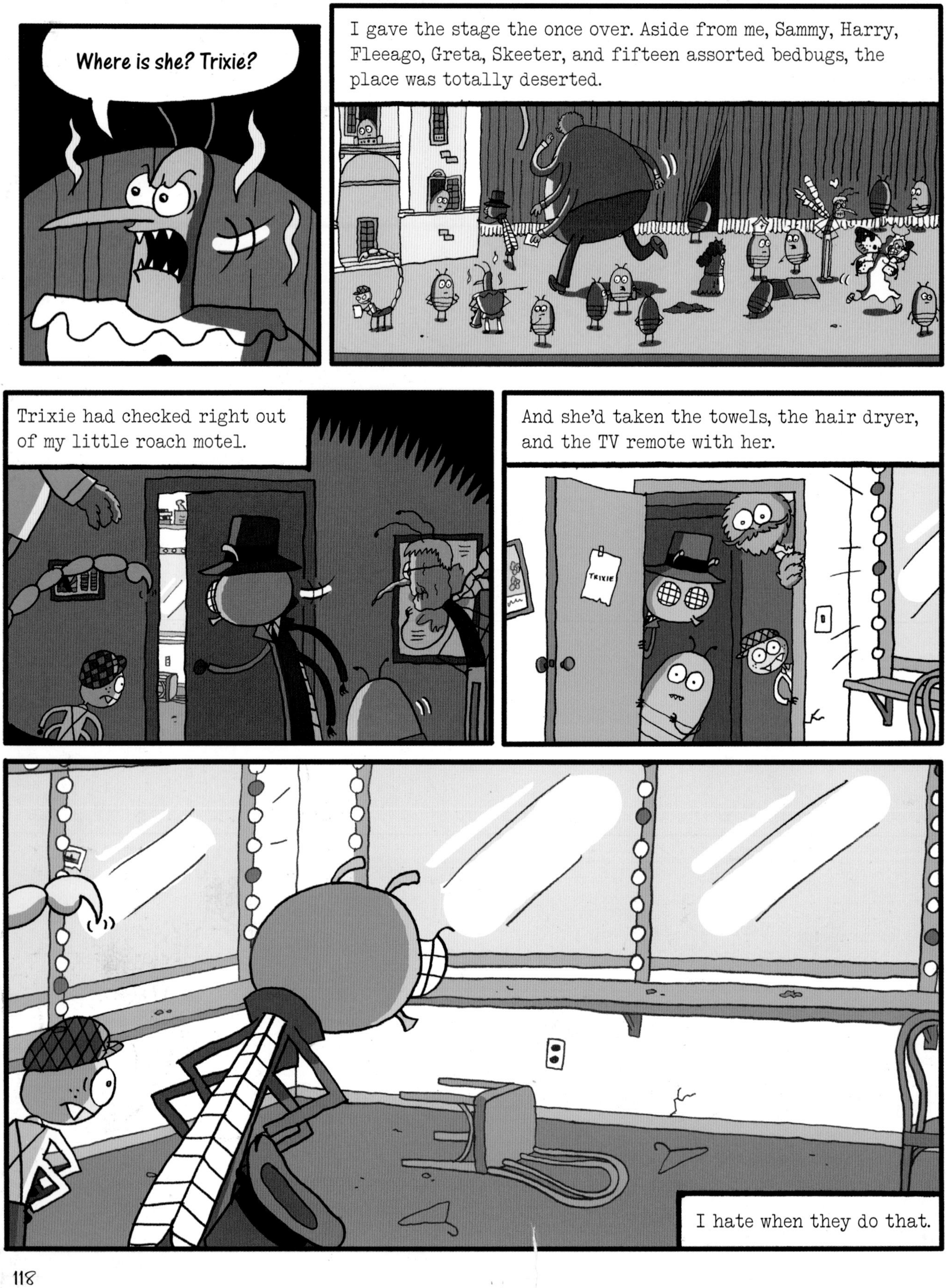
Where is she? Trixie?
I gave the stage the once over. Aside from me, Sammy, Harry, Fleeago, Greta, Skeeter, and fifteen assorted bedbugs, the place was totally deserted.
Trixie had checked right out of my little roach motel.
And she'd taken the towels, the hair dryer, and the TV remote with her.
TRIXIE
I hate when they do that.

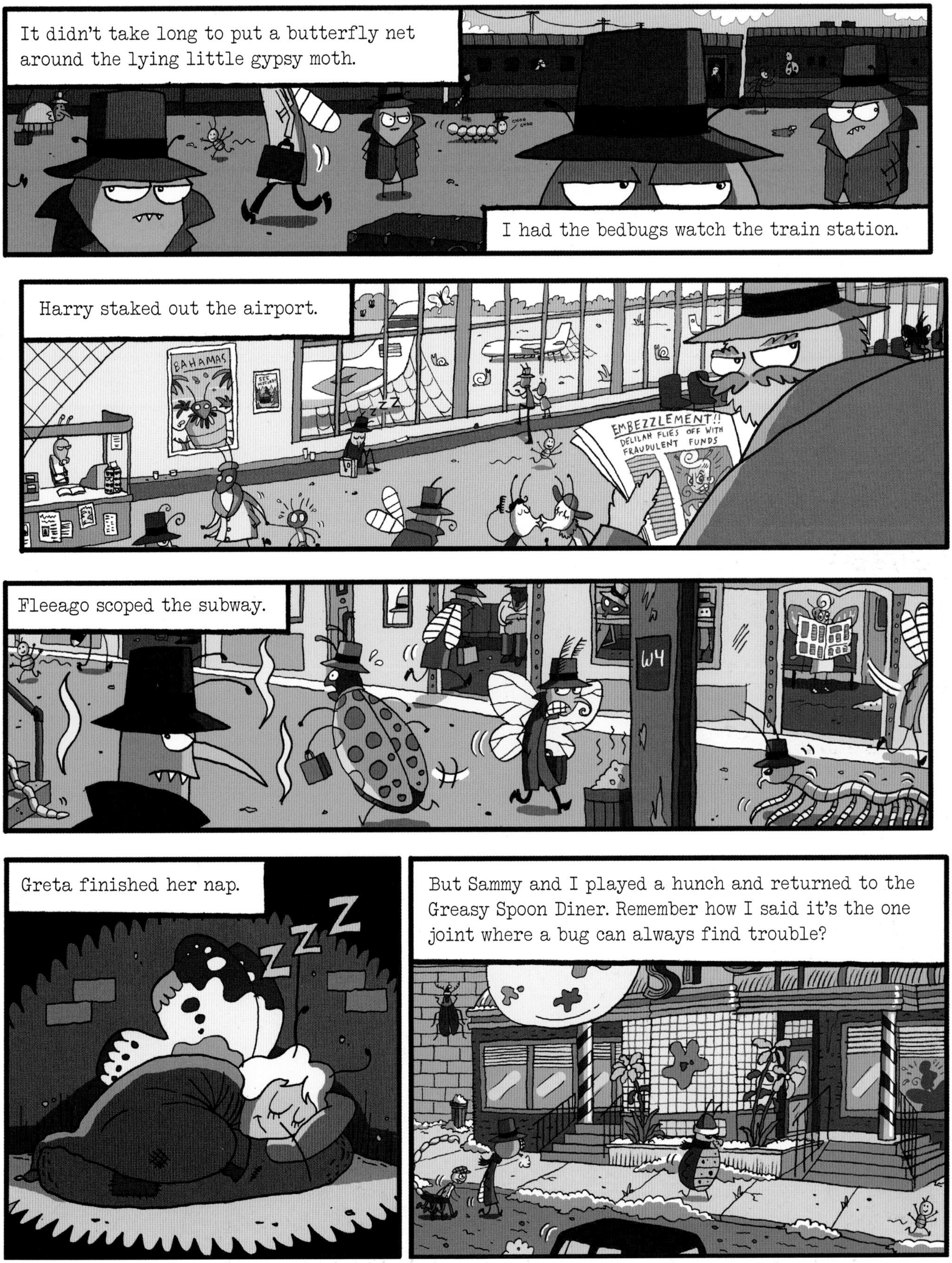

It didn't take long to put a butterfly net around the lying little gypsy moth.
I had the bedbugs watch the train station.
Harry staked out the airport.
BAHAMAS
EMBEZZLEMENT!!
DELILAH FLIES OFF WITH FRAUDULENT FUNDS
Fleeago scoped the subway.
W4
Greta finished her nap.
But Sammy and I played a hunch and returned to the Greasy Spoon Diner. Remember how I said it's the one joint where a bug can always find trouble?

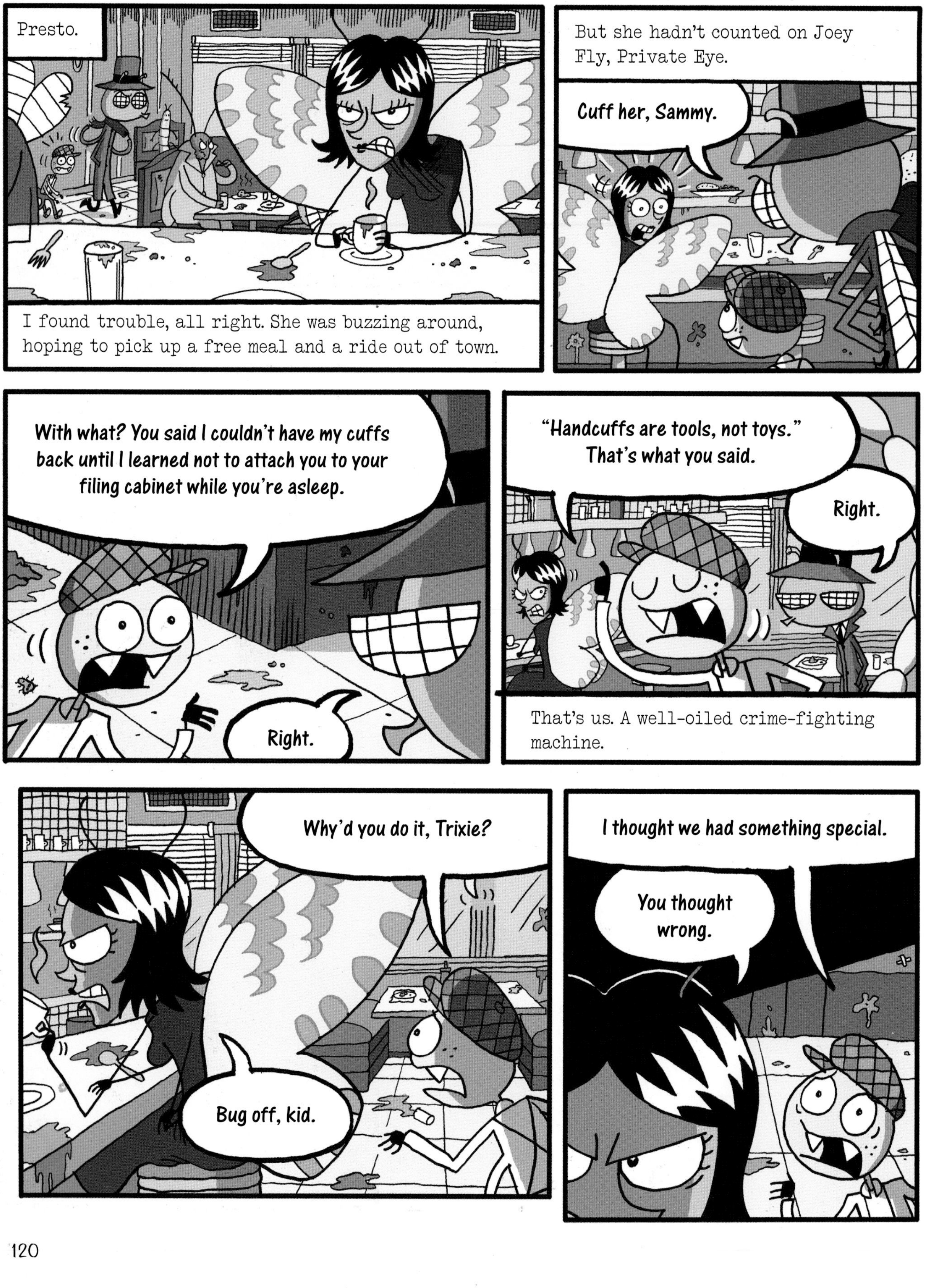
Presto.
I found trouble, all right. She was buzzing around, hoping to pick up a free meal and a ride out of town.
But she hadn't counted on Joey Fly, Private Eye.
Cuff her, Sammy.
With what? You said I couldn't have my cuffs back until I learned not to attach you to your filing cabinet while you're asleep.
Right.
"Handcuffs are tools, not toys." That's what you said.
Right.
That's us. A well-oiled crime-fighting machine.
Why'd you do it, Trixie?
Bug off, kid.
I thought we had something special.
You thought wrong.

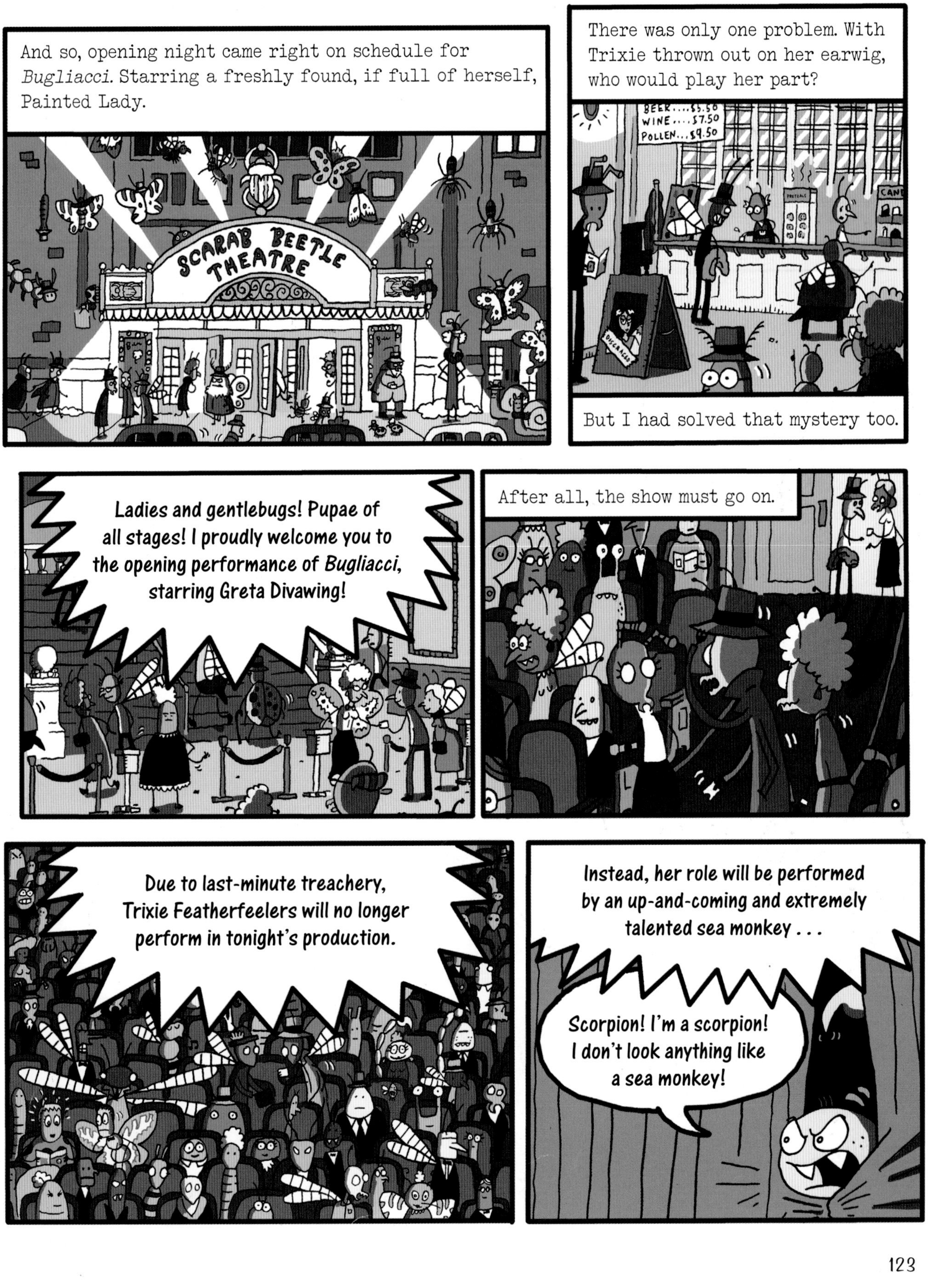
And so, opening night came right on schedule for *Bugliacci*. Starring a freshly found, if full of herself, Painted Lady.
SCARAB BEETLE THEATRE
There was only one problem. With Trixie thrown out on her earwig, who would play her part?
BEER....$5.50
WINE....$7.50
POLLEN...$9.50
But I had solved that mystery too.
Ladies and gentlebugs! Pupae of all stages! I proudly welcome you to the opening performance of *Bugliacci*, starring Greta Divawing!
After all, the show must go on.
Due to last-minute treachery, Trixie Featherfeelers will no longer perform in tonight's production.
Instead, her role will be performed by an up-and-coming and extremely talented sea monkey . . .
Scorpion! I'm a scorpion! I don't look anything like a sea monkey!

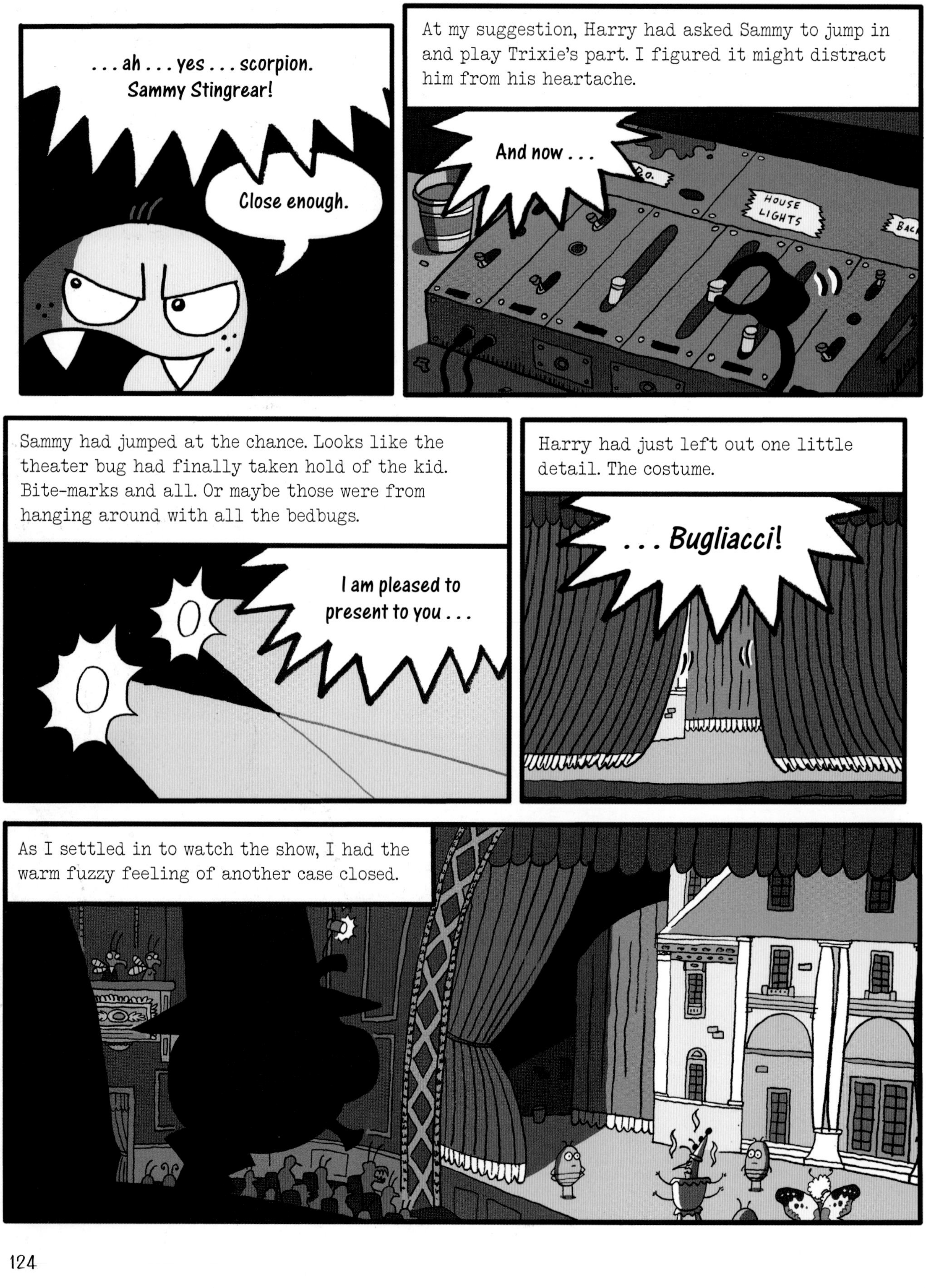

. . . ah . . . yes . . . scorpion. Sammy Stingrear!
Close enough.
At my suggestion, Harry had asked Sammy to jump in and play Trixie's part. I figured it might distract him from his heartache.
And now . . .
HOUSE LIGHTS
Sammy had jumped at the chance. Looks like the theater bug had finally taken hold of the kid. Bite-marks and all. Or maybe those were from hanging around with all the bedbugs.
I am pleased to present to you . . .
Harry had just left out one little detail. The costume.
. . . Bugliacci!
As I settled in to watch the show, I had the warm fuzzy feeling of another case closed.

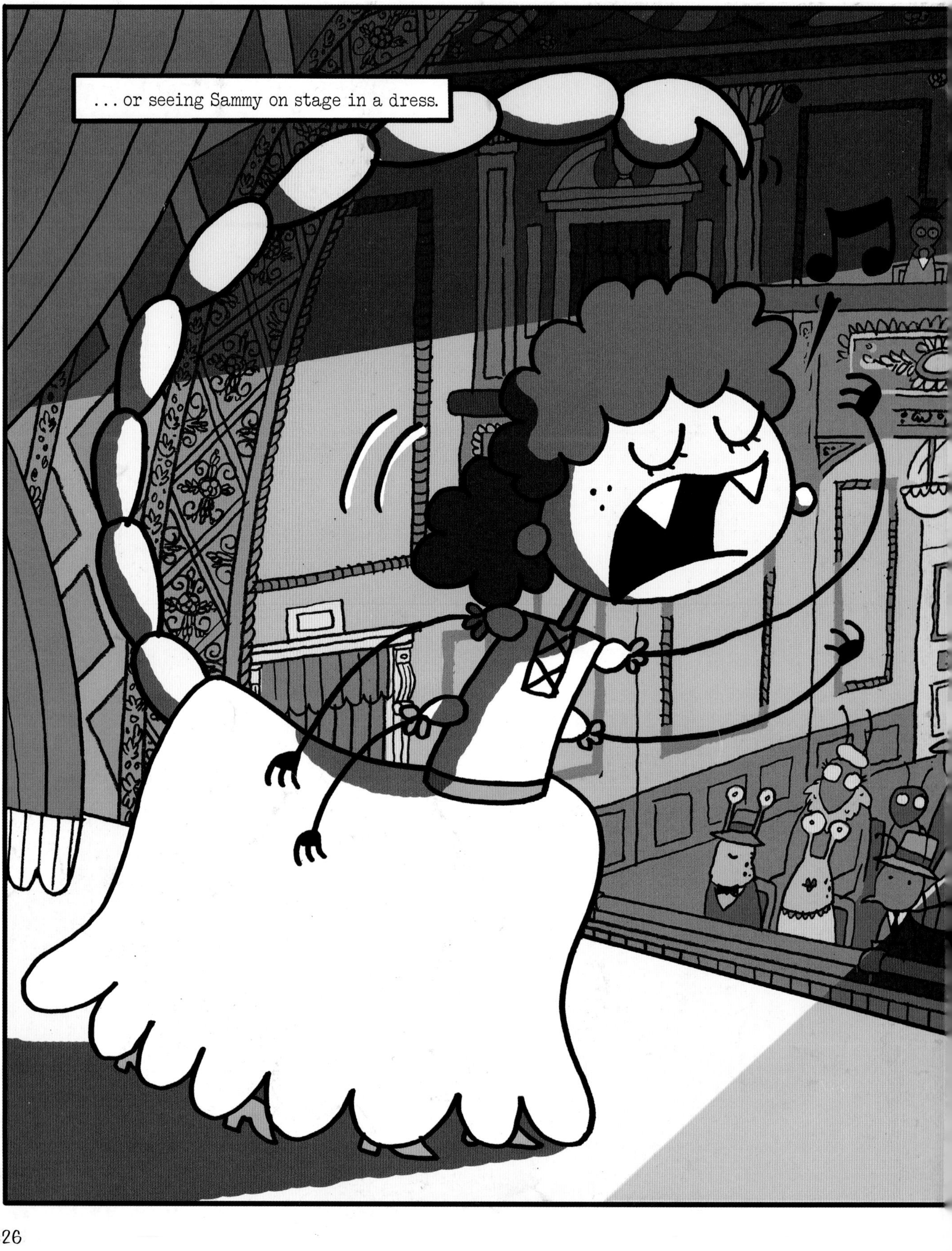

. . . or seeing Sammy on stage in a dress.

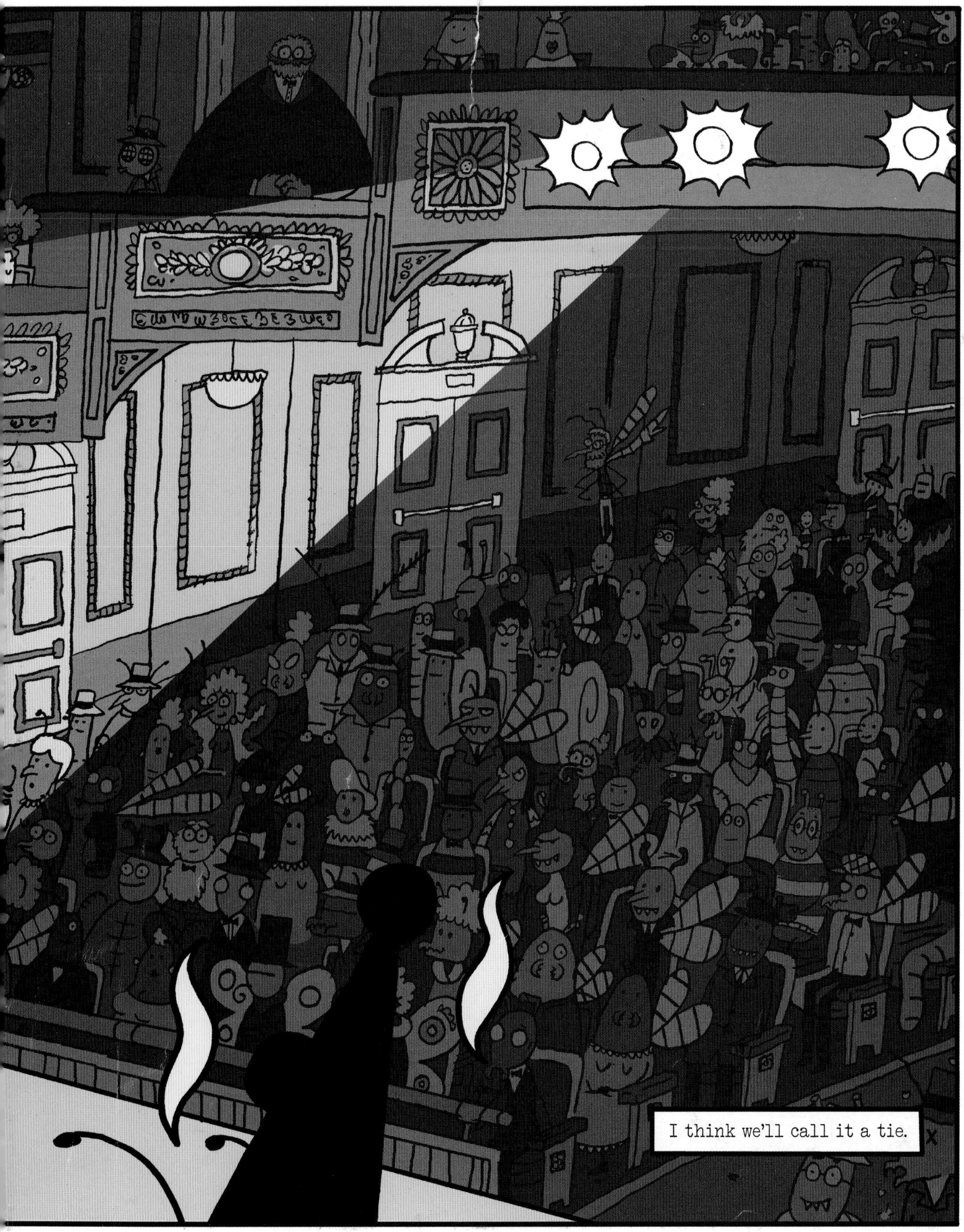
I think we'll call it a tie.

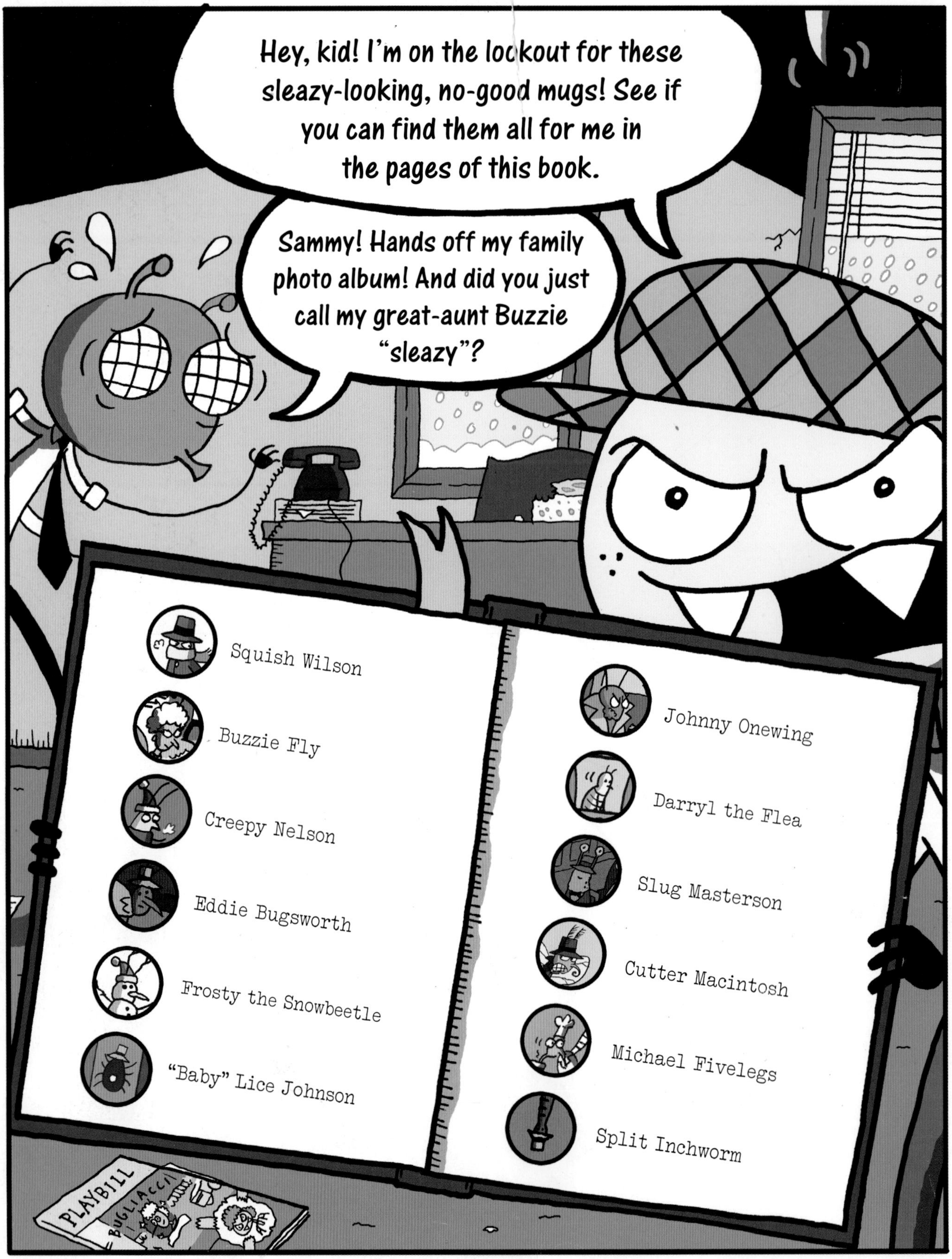
Hey, kid! I'm on the lookout for these sleazy-looking, no-good mugs! See if you can find them all for me in the pages of this book.
Sammy! Hands off my family photo album! And did you just call my great-aunt Buzzie "sleazy"?
Squish Wilson
Buzzie Fly
Creepy Nelson
Eddie Bugsworth
Frosty the Snowbeetle
"Baby" Lice Johnson
Johnny Onewing
Darryl the Flea
Slug Masterson
Cutter Macintosh
Michael Fivelegs
Split Inchworm
PLAYBILL
BUGLIACCI

Answers are on the copyright page.